I0766953

# The Tacomancer and the Cursed Blood Knife

**A Briar Egibi Novel, Volume 1**

Christina Dickinson

Published by Christina Dickinson, 2021.

THE TACOMANCER AND THE CURSED BLOOD KNIFE

**First edition. October 25, 2021.**

Copyright © 2021 Christina Dickinson.

ISBN: 978-1952009082

Written by Christina Dickinson.

# Also by Christina Dickinson

**A Briar Egibi Novel**
The Tacomancer and the Cursed Blood Knife

**Ashes of the Past Saga**
Waking the Burning Valley
Dropping the Keystone

**Standalone**
Strange Stars and Stranger Songs

Watch for more at https://christinadickinsonwrites.com.

To Ria, Ama, and Jill

We've been sisters longer than I can remember. Might've
come together thousands of years ago or last Tuesday...
Who knows.

In Memory of Papouli

A man of great hugs and the best brisket.

In Memory of Amulet, Mad Cat, and Scythe

Best kitties.

Also, to everyone that's ever made a taco, burrito, or nachos.
Or makes hot sauce. Or eats hot sauce. Or is hot sauce.

WHEN HAGEN AWOKE AND found himself imprisoned, he was aware that his fate rested on the sacrificial altar at the top of the gods' house. The rains hadn't come yet this season, which meant the gods were displeased. Being a warrior from the thwarted invasion meant his blood would be spilled to appease the gods. He remembered his warrior brothers falling around him to the thick, wooden shafts hurled by enemy atlatls. His tribesmen never would have attempted the raid in a good season, but their families were getting desperate.

Food and drink befitting an offering arrived. It wouldn't do to present the gods with a starving wretch. They might do worse than withhold the rains. Hagen ate and drank, savoring his final meal. If his sacrifice here would bring the rains, his family would also benefit. There was no point in trying to deny his captors a choice bounty.

When they came for him, Hagen didn't fight to get free. Willing blood was always more acceptable to the gods. Self immolation was best, but only from a noble lineage. Hagen was no nobleman that the gods would find his hands worthy to touch their drink. He tripped his way up the stairs of the pyramid, barking his shins on the rough stone. Already, his blood was being taken by the gods. He'd been a good warrior for his tribe. He was young and handsome. The gods were eager to drink from him. Hagen hoped he would be enough to slake their thirst.

Turning his eyes toward the greedy rays of the sun, Hagen whispered his own prayers. He wanted to help break the dryness. His younger brothers and cousins might have to follow him to war, and then to the gods, should his blood not sate the thirst holding the rains at bay.

This was the way of things. Hagen was a believer, and he was willing.

He was willing up until the moment he caught sight of the knife the priest was holding. The priest's eyes shined with madness, and the knife held a curious glint. Something in Hagen cried out in protest that the knife itself would consume him. It would leave nothing for the gods and their thirst would go unquenched. For the first time since his guards had collected him from his cell, Hagen tried to fight their grip. The man on Hagen's left was sweating from more than just the heat. A touch of fear lingered in the man's eyes as he kept hold of his prisoner.

Hagen turned his gaze to the man on his right. This guard also knew there was something amiss. Something about the way the obsidian glinted with cool malice in the jungle heat was wrong... *Evil.* All three men could feel it.

Turning his eyes to the sun once more, Hagen continued to pray to the gods that they would accept him. He hoped they would take his blood before the knife drank it away and made his sacrifice meaningless.

The priest approached and brought the knife up under Hagen's throat with a hiss. Birds went silent and the entire world seemed to pause. There was a sensation across Hagen's throat like the priest had drawn his finger over the tight skin, and for one shining moment, Hagen believed he'd been spared. Then he felt the wetness trickling down his bare chest. Pain beyond anything he'd ever experienced filled his entire consciousness. Darkness overtook the sun as Hagen's prayers faded into nothing.

# Present
# Day

# 1

IT HAD BEEN A LONG time coming, but it was finally here—Moving Day! Or rather, it would be Moving Day tomorrow. But I was finally, officially, packed.

I heaved the last of the boxes onto the pile sitting in front of my bedroom. Not that it had been *my* room for very long. It had been Aunt Shay's room when she was alive. A lot of memories in this room. I used to sneak in here and hide in her giant walk-in closet when I was a kid. I was sure that if I hid well enough, she'd let slip some sort of adult secret that I wasn't allowed to know yet. Like maybe my parents had actually survived the tornado that had taken them, and they were spies living in Paraguay or something. The pain in my chest grew when I looked and saw it as a bare room full of boxes. It was time to get out of this house. My aunt died in a car accident almost two years ago, and Wichita, Kansas lost what little charm it still held for me. It hadn't had much to start with.

Most of the boxes were labelled *Books* but there were a few that held kitchen utensils and clothes. What was left of the furniture I was including with the house. It was hard enough to convince people to buy a house in Kansas, let alone one without beds, and I didn't mind the idea of purchasing a turnkey place or buying new furniture. The boxes and other items I intended to keep would spend some time in a storage facility while I searched for a new place. Then they'd get shipped to my new address as soon as I contacted the moving company.

I sold Aunt Shay's coffee shop, Sit-a-Spell Coffee, to the business manager, Debra Downs, for a reasonable rate a month or so ago. Debra deserved to own the business. She'd been working there since I was a teenager. Everyone knew and liked Debra. They still acted like I was the new girl, even after I'd inherited the business. Between what I'd gotten for the coffee shop and what I was getting for the house, I could live comfortably for several months before I would need to find work, even with the cost of a new house and new furnishings. Assuming I didn't go nuts and buy myself a palace or something. Maybe...

No. No palaces.

Way to be a bummer, me.

With the world wide open, I was heading south. Past Oklahoma, past Texas, and past the southern border of the United States. I was twenty-eight and I'd never been anywhere but Wichita. Tropical waters and jungle ruins were calling my name. It was time to do some exploring. I was going to start with Belize.

Belize had always held a certain fascination for me. My dad had grown up there. My Aunt Shay was born there. Grandpa and Grandma Egibi had immigrated there from London. About the time my dad was twelve and my aunt was two, they packed up again and moved to Kansas. Why Kansas? I'm not sure. That wasn't a question I ever got to ask them. They died when I was still a toddler.

Before I drifted too far into my daydreams about aqua seas, I needed to find lunch. It was nearing three o'clock as my stomach rumbled a protest at being ignored for so long.

I tugged my fingers through the dark brown ringlets that had escaped from my long braid and ducked into the bathroom to check my appearance. I had a smudge of something on my otherwise beach sand-bland face, so I gave my cheeks and nose a quick scrub. My cheekbones were barely visible and my face was more of an oval than a heart. I was pretty happy with my nose, though. It's a cute nose. Kinda stubby and it tilts up, but cute. My denim blue eyes have always seemed too large for my face, but a lot of people seem to compliment them. I got Bette Davis comparisons a lot as I was growing up, even though I thought they were closer to something out of a nineties anime. While I toweled my face dry, I inspected my multicolored striped shorts and charcoal tank top in the mirror. They were pretty dusty but nothing that would revolt the neighbors, so I slipped my shoes on and walked out the door.

I'd already sold my old, comfortable sedan to a dealership, so until I got to the airport tomorrow, I was in a big blue SUV rental. It lurked like a monster in my driveway, waiting to roar to life with a twist of its key. I felt too tall every time I sat in the driver's seat. Tall and large. I was looking forward to leaving this monster behind.

As though it were trying to dampen my mood, the sky was a ceiling of sullen grey clouds. The Aunt Shay-sized hole in my heart throbbed as I drove past her coffee shop. Sometimes it felt like I could still hear Aunt Shay laughing with her regulars when I saw the place. On a whim, I pulled into one of the parking spaces in front of the building. It only seemed right that I dropped in to say goodbye one last time.

Debra hadn't changed much of the shop after purchasing it. The countertops were dark granite, the walls were red brick, the floor was blue stained concrete, and there were red chairs surrounding round, wooden tables. A big glass case held the cakes, cookies, and pies baked in the back of the shop. Three or four patrons sat as far away from each other as their tables would allow. Not unusual for this time of day. Most of the friendly sorts would come in during the early morning, or they mixed in with the evening crowd. People that came in to get their coffee fix midday tended to be a bit surlier. The old green chalkboard menu had been replaced with a black one, but that was the only thing that looked even slightly different.

"Briar, hun! What brings you in here?" Debra's voice boomed through the shop. It wasn't that Debra tried to be loud. She just was. Everything about the woman was loud: her overly orange hair; her extremely freckled, moonlight pale skin; her bright blue eyeshadow and red lipstick; her five foot eleven inch barrel frame; and her penchant for wearing neon colors. Today, she'd donned a highlighter yellow, short sleeved blouse under her black and umber apron.

"Stopped packing to grab lunch at Taco Rancho, and I thought I might drop in to say goodbye," I answered with a shrug, hooking my thumbs into the pockets of my shorts. I wasn't really sure why I'd stopped in but, with my bloodline, such urges were normally worth pursuing.

Not even Debra knew about our heritage. Aunt Shay and I were the last in a long line of witches. Witches, not Wiccans. Wicca is a religion with one of its core beliefs being to "Harm none." My witchiness isn't a matter of belief. I was born with certain powers and abilities. It isn't glamorous. No wands, no flying broomsticks, no secret magical school... Growing up as a witch while reading Harry Potter books had been something of a disappointment. Mostly, my powers consisted of following small hunches, having a gift for divination, knowing people's names without being told and being able to tell when people were lying. Some spells. Minor cantrips, mostly. Anytime I tried to do something larger, it tended to go wrong. My favorite part of my heritage was that I never lost my keys. So the question today was: what had called me into the coffee shop on my last day in town?

"Well, I'm glad you decided to stop in," Debra said. "I found something in the back the other day, and I'd been meaning to call you about it. Shay left a box in a file drawer. I don't know how we both managed to overlook it for so long."

I had an inkling as to how it had stayed hidden, whatever it held. My aunt's gifts had run in that direction. When Shay Egibi had wanted a thing to stay hidden, it had stayed hidden. My aunt's power probably just wore off over time without her energy there to renew it.

Following Debra into the back office, I nodded to the two baristas manning the counter. One of the original baristas had retired shortly after I sold the shop, and then I also had to be replaced. These must have been the new employees, because I didn't recognize them. Their names were Erin and Tom, and I knew that without looking at their name tags.

Once we were in the back office, Debra pulled a tattered old box off the top of her filing cabinet. The box had started life as a receptacle for copy paper, but it had seen some hard use: torn corners, rubbed off labels, and squished sides. It was held together with grungy rubber bands. In black marker, the top lid had the words "For Briar!"scrawled in Aunt Shay's distinctive, loopy cursive.

"I decided not to open it, since it was clearly meant for you, hun," Debra sighed. "But Lord knows, I been more than a touch curious about what's been waiting for you all this time."

Tingles ran up my arms as I reached out to touch this relic from my aunt's life. This was my last day in Kansas, and somehow Aunt Shay had found a way to say goodbye from beyond the grave. Had my aunt anticipated Debra's presence when she'd hidden this box for me? Had she known that the crash was coming? Neither seemed likely. Maybe this was some bygone birthday gift even Aunt Shay had forgotten was lurking under the shadows in her office. Being magically inclined didn't mean that we were above being absent minded.

Years of caution warred with curiosity. Here, in the office that had belonged to my aunt, me, and now Debra, I felt safe. Even if Aunt Shay had left something that betrayed the family secret, what would it matter by tomorrow? I had a plane ticket and the rest of my things were being picked up in a few hours. At worst, Debra would probably kick me out of the shop.

I tugged one rubber band free and held my breath. *Here goes nothing*, I thought. Untangling the box from the second rubber band was a bit more difficult. The band got caught on the ripped box lid and snapped apart, falling onto the table. While such things could be portentous, I got the feeling this one was due to normal wear and tear. In any case, it hadn't caught my fingers.

Debra sucked air in through her teeth as the box lid came away. Both of us leaned in to see what had been awaiting discovery for two years.

A pair of bracelets. Not even expensive bracelets. They were the woven parachute cord bracelets that had been popular for a brief burst a few years before Aunt Shay had gotten into her accident. There wasn't a note, but there was a card that had information on how to get a new bracelet if one of them ever got unwound due to use.

"Huh," Debra said. "Can't say that's what I expected."

"Yeah..." I agreed. "That... isn't even close to what I would've guessed."

"Well, hun, I hope you ain't disappointed, now. Your aunt, she was a sweet thing, and probably bought those way back when, hopin' you'd like 'em." Debra laid a heavy, comforting hand on my shoulder.

It would've been easy to turn my back on the package, drive down the road and forget the whole thing, but my intuition was screaming at me not to make that mistake. I had been pulled into Sit-a-Spell Coffee for a reason, and this was it. These were important.

"Who knows?" I tried to smile at the older woman as I reached down and picked up the bracelets. "Maybe they'll come in handy to hang some hammocks or something?"

"I know you're going on this big adventure, and all..." Debra said, her eyes starting to well up. "...but, don't forget us, hun!"

That was all the warning I got before being enveloped in one of the biggest hugs I'd ever received. I didn't realize I was going to miss Debra until that moment. Returning the hug, I made some promises about calling once in a while and sending postcards. I even told her I'd invite her down once I found a place, though I was pretty sure that would be more than a little awkward for both of us.

Once I was back in my car, I snapped both bracelets around one wrist and continued on my way to Taco Rancho.

TACO RANCHO WAS BASICALLY deserted at this time of day. Housed in what had been built as a franchise location for some larger fast food chain, it now specialized in street tacos and guacamole. Frozen margaritas were on tap at all times, which had been a definite plus during my college years.

Sharp drops of frigid water were beginning their assault on the ground as I jumped out of the Beast and jogged toward the automatic doors. I hoped the rain would let up before the moving guys arrived at my house.

Rick took my order without much interest. My number was called, and I retrieved my food. Grabbing a few packets of hot sauce and filling my drink cup with Sprite and some limes, I looked longingly at the frozen margarita slush as it swirled in its machine. There would be time for margaritas when I got down to the Caribbean.

Rick started scrubbing the drink station as soon as I was done with it. It seemed more like he was trying to look busy than he actually thought I'd made a mess, but it was still annoying. I tried to be grateful he was keeping himself distracted as I placed my first taco on a napkin and let my eyes unfocus.

Aunt Shay had attempted to teach me how to read tea leaves starting when I was only six years old. For some reason, it never seemed to work for me. Where she saw portents and webs of fate, I saw mushy blobs of junk. For years, she'd plied me with every kind of tea imaginable. We both were about to give up on my divination abilities. I'd never cared much for the flavor of tea anyway. When I was thirteen, she took me to get tacos and I discovered the previously absent webs of fate lurking within my hot sauce. After that, Aunt Shay had started calling me a tacomancer.

The trick was not to pay attention to the packet while the drips were falling. It was important not to try and nudge the patterns, otherwise you'd see a future you wanted rather than actual portents. After I squeezed the packet as empty as I could, I scanned the results on my taco.

*"New beginnings,"* *no surprise there,* I thought as I licked the spicy, smokey remnants of sauce off my thumb. *"Encounters with stranger(s?)"* *also not much of a stretch.* *"Danger!"*

I stared at the bit that read "Danger," trying to imagine what the sauce could possibly be warning me about. My eyes slipped from the taco to the bracelets that hung around my wrist. What the hell was waiting for me in the Caribbean?

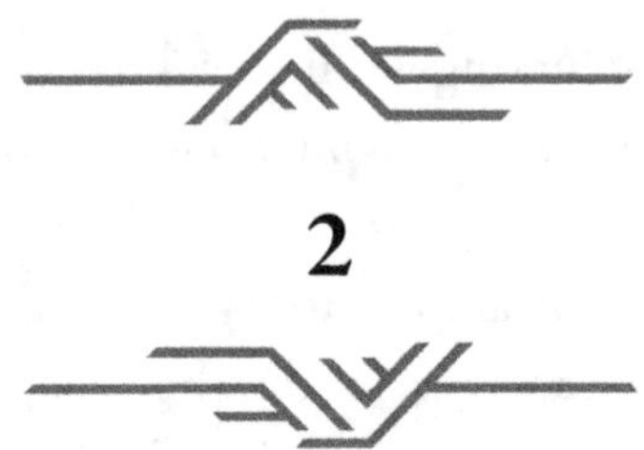

## 2

ON THE PLANE, I HAD intended to sleep or read to pass the time, but I was too excited to actually do either. With the sun glinting off of the azure ocean, my only thoughts were about the new life I was about to embark on. This was my chance to really see what I could make of myself! No safety nets. No family waiting in the wings to bail me out. No back up plan.

Excited?

Yes.

Elated?

Yes.

Scared?

*Terrified.*

I watched the plane drift over the specs of green dotting the ocean and tried to identify land masses based on the maps I'd poured over for weeks. Cozumel and the Yucatan Peninsula were gorgeous from the air. I was pretty sure I could see Tulum, but it might also have been my imagination.

My original plan was to move to the U.S. Virgin Islands or Puerto Rico because they didn't require me to get a visa or a passport, but something about Belize called to me. I *needed* to go there. Whether I was putting down roots, or simply visiting before moving on, I wasn't entirely sure. It was similar to the tugging that had drawn me into Sit-a-Spell Coffee, only stronger. I'd checked out a vacation rental online as a place to set up for at least the next month while I tried to figure out my next step.

The pressure on my ears suddenly increased and the ground began growing as the captain announced we were making our approach. Unsure of what to expect, I gripped the arms of my seat and hoped I'd gotten it fully upright, despite never adjusting it. I was too excited for logic to matter. There was a rush of sound as the roar of the engines caught up with the plane. Waiting for the plane to coast to a stop, I thought I'd never been so impatient in my life. All I wanted to do was jump up, grab my carry-on and sprint into the jungle.

*Odd*, I thought as that sunk in. *I've been practically salivating over pictures of the beach.*

It seemed that now that I'd made it to Belize, the compulsion drawing me down here was recalibrating. I was getting closer to where I needed to go, but I had to be smart about it. Rushing into a foreign country with foreign dangers was a good way to get myself killed. If I hadn't been in such a hurry to leave Kansas behind, I could have done some scrying and gotten things rolling; I could have found a tour that got me closer to where I needed to go or rented a house that was a bit farther off the beach. Not that it mattered what I could've done. What mattered was what I did now.

As I gathered my carry-on luggage from the plane's overhead compartment, I felt another twinge of something. It wasn't like the pull inland that I was experiencing, but it was definitely another tug. I flashed on that last stop at Taco Rancho and the patterns in the sauce that told me about encounters with strangers. At the time, I'd thought that was obvious. New country, new people. Now I was wondering if that portent hadn't been referring to a specific stranger, or maybe even a group of strangers. The passengers at the front of the cabin began to move forward and the people standing behind me seemed to surge toward the door. My thoughts about scrying, ethereal tugs on my spirit, and possible encounters all took a backseat. First, I needed to stay on my feet in a wave of impatient tourists and other travelers.

Heat landed on my entire body like a physical weight the moment I stepped out of the plane's air-conditioned protection. The terminal was a short walk away, across unsheltered pavement, and the sun was making sure that people knew they'd entered its domain. If not for the crisp, briny breeze carried in from the shore, I would've been very tempted to turn around and fly back then and there. I knew the urge was spurred on by my fear of the unknown, so I squelched my inner protests and made my way toward the shade.

In less time than I'd feared, but more than I'd hoped, I was through customs and in a taxi riding toward my rented house.

I'd thrown my bags into the trunk and climbed into the backseat with a "Buenos dias," to be polite, because I'd read online that it was good manners to acknowledge your drivers. I almost forgot to give my address because I was so nervous about my first interaction with someone that wasn't a customs agent.

"This your first time to Belize?" the woman, Elena Tillett, driving the cab asked from the front seat. She had warm, terra-cotta skin, a strong, wiry build, broad swimmers' shoulders and a thick Belizean accent. Her sable hair was swept up in a bun on the top of her head that brushed against the roof of the car every time she turned her head, while her yellow and black striped nails fought with the scenery for my attention as they rested against the charcoal steering wheel.

"Yep. First time anywhere, really," I told her.

"Well, you made a prime choice comin' to Belize, then," she grinned broadly at me through the mirror. "Everyone wants to come to Belize. Once you come here, you always come back. Looks like you be headin' to San Pedro, so I'm gonna be droppin' you at the water taxi and they gonna have to take you up to the island."

I'd known that, but I'd forgotten in between the plane landing and making it through customs. That was going to take me even farther away from whatever was drawing me toward the interior jungles of the mainland.

She drove us through several neighborhoods, honking every time we passed someone walking down the road. According to my research, this was a signal her taxi still had free seats. I was glad I'd read some blogs about Belize before coming because otherwise I wouldn't have known what to think when she pulled over and another person climbed into the taxi with me. He nodded to the driver and said, "Good afternoon."

The new passenger, Yuri Knowles, was interesting to me for a number of reasons. His accent had struck me as British, nice and deep, filling me with some delicious chills at the base of my neck. I would've guessed he was roughly my age, give or take about five years, and he was *hot*. With tawny beige skin, killer dimples, slightly unkempt, crimpy hair and his professor-style glasses framing to his hooded, amber-brown eyes, it was all I could do not to blush when he smiled at me. He wasn't terribly tall, maybe 5'9". His Hawaiian shirt hung open, showing the white tank top beneath, and his cargo shorts didn't exactly hide the fact that he wasn't Mr. Workout. Not that he was flabby. He was toned, but he didn't look like he was about to star in a superhero movie. Maybe not for everyone, but he was definitely ticking my boxes. But what made him the most interesting to me was the fact that the moment he entered the taxi, one of those tugging sensations that had started when the plane touched down stopped tugging.

*Of course I'd be dressed for travel when this guy gets into my cab.*

I tried to pretend I wasn't hyper aware that I was wearing some old, brown, over-stretched exercise leggings, an aged white sports bra and an ancient heather-grey university t-shirt that I'd tried to cut into a tank top after watching an online tutorial. It was an outfit that I generally reserved for lazy afternoon housework.

He handed Elena a slip of paper. "Can you take me here?"

Elena squinted at the scrawled address. Even from my seat behind her, I could tell that was some impressive chicken scratch. "Are you kidding with this? I can't even read this! Just tell me where you want to go."

"I'm terribly sorry," Yuri said, rubbing the back of his neck. "It's the address of a friend I met recently at a pub, and he didn't actually tell me... He only scribbled it on a paper napkin."

*Lie!* my internal senses bristled.

Not for the first time, I wished I got more information from my inherited powers. What part was he lying about? Was the person not his friend? Was it an old acquaintance or a total stranger? Was it not a man's address, but a woman's? Or possibly the address wasn't written on a bar napkin... Something Yuri said wasn't true and that's all I knew for certain. At least I could tell when sales people were trying to rip me off.

"You are wasting my time and that of my passenger," Elena said. "Give me a destination or get out."

"May I have my address back, please?" Yuri asked. "I don't want to be a bother."

"Wait..." I said. "May I give it a shot?"

Both Elena and Yuri paused. Elena's broad nostrils were flaring with aggravation, but two fares was still a better deal for her in the long run. She handed me the paper scrap. I'd never tried this before, but I'd gotten the idea when Yuri had lied about the origin of the address. Under the guise of trying to make out the letters, I let my lie sensor loose. *ABCD—truth, u—truth, n—false, r? truth, abcdefg—truth, e—truth, a? false, o—truth, n—truth.*

"It looks like Durgeon Avenue?" *Truth* rang through my senses confirming my guess before Elena could.

"Why didn't you say you're goin' near the university?"

"I'm sorry, I really didn't know..."

"You're lucky it's on the way to where she's going," Elena grumbled. "Lucky she's here at all..."

"Thank you for that," Yuri said, leaning in close enough that I could feel his breath slide over my shoulder as he spoke. A torrent of flutters swept through me, like a whirlwind of butterflies seeking to escape my insides. His next words stopped my inner butterflies cold. "My name is Curtis Johanson."

It flowed out of him so naturally that if I hadn't possessed supernatural senses, I might have believed him. He'd lied twice since he'd entered my cab. Still, he was tied into my future somehow. And he was really freaking cute.

"Briar Egibi," I said. "It's nice to meet you... Curtis."

I didn't mean to hesitate that long. Yuri schooled his expression in a hurry, but I could tell he'd noticed the significant pause. We only endured a few moments of awkward silence before Elena turned on the radio and began pointing out things that she thought I should come back to later, once I'd settled in on the island. "Belize City is special. San Pedro is mostly for tourists. You'll want to spend more time down here, I promise you."

After a bit, Yuri leaned in and spoke to me in a hushed tone that wouldn't carry to the front seat. "I'd love to know how you managed to decipher this address. I've been staring at it for two days hoping to make it out. I took a chance on it being something a local would know."

"Fresh eyes and a lot of time working in a coffee shop," I told him with a shrug. If he had anything similar to my inner voice, he either had a hell of a poker face or I'd been able to mix in the right amount of truth. More than likely he didn't have my abilities. I knew other witch families had to exist, but I'd never met anybody like me. It would be nice to know for sure I wasn't alone.

"I should thank you properly," Yuri said. This time he was speaking loud enough for Elena to hear. Maybe it was to reassure our driver of his intentions, or maybe it was to reassure me that he wasn't trying to be sneaky and lure me to some dark alley. "How about we meet for a drink once you're unpacked? Tonight? seven o'clock? There's a beach bar on the island of San Pedro called the Coconut Cabana."

Nothing he said felt false. "Sure, I'd like that."

"Good," he said. "I get the feeling we should get to know each other better."

ELENA ACTUALLY GOT out of her cab and helped me get my ticket for the water taxi. I didn't think this was normal cab service, which was confirmed for me when she spoke up. "I heard that man make a date with you. You should be careful, gyal. Can never be too careful when the bally knows you're alone."

"I'll be careful. Is this beach bar he mentioned a public place?"

"It is... But why is he making a date with you on San Pedro? We didn't tell him where you were goin.'"

"Maybe he happens to be staying there, too." I shrugged and smiled, trying to project an air of confidence that I'd never really possessed. "Thank you, for introducing me to the city and for looking out for me. I appreciate it. A lot. If it'd make you feel better, you could always come to the Coconut Cabana about seven o'clock. Make sure I'm not in over my head?"

"Now you're inviting other people on your date? Is this an American thing?" Elena looked at me like I was completely insane.

"No," I said. "It's a friends thing. I could use a friend down here."

Elena's expression still said I was the most bizarre person she'd ever encountered, but a smile was also starting to tug at the corner of her mouth. "Okay, yes. I'll be your friend. My name is Elena Tillet. But I cannot go to San Pedro tonight because the last water taxi run is much too early for your date. I'd have to stay the night."

"Briar Egibi," I said as we clasped hands. "I still need to get a phone set up down here, but I guess we can exchange email for now?"

"Or PMs," Elena suggested.

"Or that," I agreed.

# 3

ONCE ELENA AND I HAD exchanged information, she told me that she would send reinforcements to the Coconut Cabana to keep an eye on her American friend. Then, she jumped back in her cab to hunt for more fares. I had service on my phone, but I didn't relish the idea of making a lot of calls and texts at international rates while I was settling in. My vacation rental had free Wi-Fi. I just had to get there.

I bought my ticket for the water taxi and was shown onto a large white, green and yellow pontoon with passenger space on the bottom level. There was a second level which looked like it was reserved for the boat pilot or captain and maybe a crewmate or two. A member of the crew told me to secure my luggage in an area under the seats, next to the life vest. If I felt even the slightest bit sea sick, I was told to wave for a vomit bag. He offered to leave one with me, just in case. I took it. I didn't want to risk needing one only to have them not get to me in time.

I'm not sure how long my first trip by water taxi actually lasted, but I loved every minute of it. I wished the sides of the vessel had been open so I could feel more of the wind whipping through my hair. If I were moving to Belize permanently, maybe I'd look into getting my own boat.

Another taxi ride, much less eventful than the first, found me standing in front of my sanctuary for the next month. It was a bright pink beach front condo complex. My rental was on the bottom floor with a patio right over the sand. Two wooden deck chairs were set up adjacent to a small table in the shade under the upper floor's balcony. A small set of stairs, all of four steps, led me off the beach into the shade. Before I wrestled my bags into the unit, I climbed up to lean against the patio railing. It was glorious to breathe in the sun and sea. This was so far from the Kansas home that I'd grown up in that it could've been another planet. Waves lulled my brain with their sleepy harmony while I lost myself trying to count all the different colors of blue.

*Aunt Shay would've loved this,* I thought with a pang of sorrow. The bracelets I'd acquired the day before sent a surge of reassuring warmth through me. She would've been proud of me for making this journey. Maybe it was my imagination, but my new bracelets felt warmer for a moment. Almost like a comforting hand squeezing my wrist.

After what may have been anything between two minutes to half an hour, I opened my screenshot with the Wi-Fi password and got connected. I tapped out a quick message to Debra to let her know I'd landed safely and made a friend. With that accomplished, I located the promised lockbox hanging on the back of one of the railing posts and input the code for that. As it opened I let out a little, "Da da du Duuuh!" like I was in a Zelda game. It amused me. I amuse me. Finally, I opened the door to my new home. For the next month, anyway.

A burst of chilled air rewarded me for finding a place with air conditioning. As gorgeous as it was outside, I wasn't used to the tropical levels of humidity. White tile and white walls would normally have been stark and unwelcoming, but here it seemed breezy. An entire kitchen of polished orange-red wooden cabinets and counters with matching bar stools on my right contrasted against a large aqua sofa and two wooden chairs with aqua cushions on my left. Canvases with rich landscapes of lagoons and sunsets hung next to window frames of the same orange-red wood as the kitchen. The windows were partially masked with sheer white curtains that still allowed in a lot of natural light. There was a small television. It was all but lost, hidden in the front corner between the welcoming windows. In the center of the ceiling, a fan shaped like large tropical leaves made lazy sweeps at the cool apartment air.

Towing my bags behind me, I noted the washer and dryer were in the kitchen alongside the fridge. What I'd anticipated to be a hallway was more like an extended doorway into the bedroom. The white tile continued, as did the white walls and white curtains. A ceiling fan matching the one in the living room was currently motionless. More of the orange-red wood had been used to build the bedframe and two dressers, as well as an entire closet structure in one corner. Draped over the bed was a royal blue and aqua striped bedspread. The pillow covers were printed with kitschy beach house phrases like, "Life's better at the beach!" or "Enter a tropical state of mind." A red, ladder back chair sat in between the closet and the bed. Directly to my right, there was another doorway that opened up into the bathroom.

Taking a quick glance in, I saw a glass brick shower and a blue tile backsplash mosaic with bits of sea glass and shell. More of that orange-red wood formed a sort of sink cabinet and shelves that were lined with blue bath towels and aqua hand towels. The toilet was just a toilet. Nice.

I set my luggage on the red chair and made use of the facilities. After I'd dealt with nature's business, I realized it was after four in the afternoon. I'd somehow managed to miss lunch. Again.

*Never misplace my keys, but can't remember to actually feed myself,* I sighed and pulled my phone back out to do some research on local grub.

HALF AN HOUR LATER I was making my way through my own private mountain of conch ceviche. I'd never had ceviche before, though I'd heard of it. Food that cooked itself chemically was pretty fascinating. I've always been fond of seafood, spicy stuff, and citrus. Allowing that I was already a few hours overdue for lunch, I don't think anything could've been better for my first meal in a foreign country. Conch was a new experience for me. It had a texture similar to, but not the same as, scallops. Of course, the only scallops I'd encountered in Kansas had come from the local Red Lobster, so maybe not the best comparison.

I broke a tortilla chip in half and scooped up another mouthful of what basically amounted to seafood salsa, but before the chip reached my mouth, something odd happened. That sensation pulling me toward the interior of the mainland *surged*. I'm not sure how else to explain it. Whatever was out there had seemingly noticed our connection, tugged on the cord between us, and sent a jolt of electricity my way. Not a lightning bolt, but one hell of a static shock—like I'd worn fuzzy socks on a trampoline, built up a charge, and then touched the springs. My entire body jumped, loosing the broken chip from my grasp. Ceviche splattered on the wooden deck beneath my table. A pair of opportunistic gulls jumped at the gobbets of conch that were suddenly fair game.

Looking around, I sent a silent prayer of thanks out into the universe that no one was really paying attention to the weird American girl throwing food off her plate. I wanted to come back to this place, maybe even become a regular at some point. I'd been the local weirdo for most of my life, so I didn't want to maintain my reputation in a new country.

Waiting for a second surge through the connection, I wished I could call someone to talk to them about this weirdness. There was nothing I could compare it to, and nothing Aunt Shay had taught me prepared me for this kind of thing. I found myself staring at the two parachute cord bracelets she'd left me in the office of her shop.

"I wish I could call you," I whispered. For the first time in a long time, I could feel the tears welling up. I'd expected them when I closed up the house in Kansas for the last time, but maybe I'd been on an adrenaline-related time delay on my way to the airport. They may have come when I stopped to admire the beach at my condo, but I'd been too excited for more than a bittersweet pang. This was my first real slow down in the last two days. Even though the tears were threatening, none of them seemed brave enough to lead the pack. After a single sniffle, I resumed eating my very late lunch.

Maybe once I got back to my temporary headquarters, I could look into some online forums for causes of psychokinetic electrical feedback or something. Odds were good that anything I found would be psychobabble, but what else could I do?

*I could get ready for my date with Yuri Knowles,* my inner voice suggested.

It made a very good point. Even if my date was with someone that kept lying, I wanted to present a better front than my frumpy traveler ensemble.

*Shit... What was it he called himself?*

Well, maybe it would come to me in the shower.

---

CURTIS JOHANSON!

## 4

FRESHLY SHOWERED, I debated how to style my hair for a full minute before settling on my usual braid. I pulled on my favorite pair of brown Bermuda shorts; they had red dragons embroidered around each of the pockets and paired well with my red tank top. The whole shirt looked hand-dyed. It had a large, faded black triskele splattered across the front. Aunt Shay bought me this tank top at a Celtic Festival we'd attended the year before her accident. Wearing it reassured me that she would be watching over me tonight. I tugged on the same brown sandals with elastic backs that I'd been wearing in the plane and looked myself over to see if there was anything else I could think to do.

While it wasn't really that far removed from the worn out campus shirt and running pants I'd been sporting earlier in the day, I felt dressier. Besides, I'd come down with only two bags of essentials. I hadn't anticipated a date on my first night in town.

*Also, I'm not sure how much of a date this is actually going to be,* I thought. *He asked me to meet him after I kinda maybe hesitated too long to call him Curtis.*

Still, I was as ready as I was going to get. I snapped the paracord bracelets on my wrist, grabbed my wallet, phone, and key, and stuffed them into my brand new hip drop bag—which I'd bought because it was more secure than a purse if I meant to walk everywhere.

My hand was on the door when my phone buzzed. A message from Elena: she'd secured a promise from someone on the island to keep an eye on me tonight while I met up with the stranger from earlier. That was the entire message. I had no idea who she was sending to look after me, merely that they were a friend of Elena's and would, theoretically, be at the Coconut Cabana around seven o'clock.

The Coconut Cabana was far enough away from my condo to require another cab ride. Having all these strangers drive me around was a weird experience. I'd had my own car since I was old enough to drive. Even renting the Beast for my last two days in Kansas hadn't prepared me for not having my own wheels. First thing in the morning, I promised myself I'd look into renting a vehicle. Not that I knew my way around yet. Maybe I could leave it for a few more days.

The cab dropped me off on the side of the road next to a long stretch of sand. A little farther ahead, I saw a parking lot filled to capacity. Apparently, the Coconut Cabana was pretty popular. Music assaulted my ears before I even spotted the thatched roof and partial walls filled with neon and halogen, defying the thickening darkness as the evening progressed. I hoped Yuri and I would be able to hear each other over the live island music.

I knew Yuri was there before I even climbed up the sandy wooden steps. While our bond wasn't anywhere near as strong as the one I shared with whatever was on the mainland, the associated tension seemed to release whenever he was nearby. It wasn't long before my eyes caught up with my extra senses.

He'd started drinking without me. I was behind by half a mojito. Filing his drink choice away for later use, I began to approach his table. Before I got there, another girl, Manon—buxom, tiny waist, a veritable waterfall of onyx corkscrew curls, wearing a string bikini and some webbing that barely functioned as a cover up—sat down in the chair across from him. I couldn't hear the words that were exchanged, but she didn't seem happy with her reception. She swept past me with a sneer that told me I was definitely not her type and she didn't think much of me as competition. I shrugged it off.

There were all kinds of power plays in the world. If I wanted to, I could add a bit more oomph than most people, but it seemed like a waste of resources.

Yuri had watched Manon depart with a modicum of interest, but his amber eyes ignited when they noticed me. I wasn't sure if he was into me in a romantic sense, but I definitely had his attention. He beckoned me over to the chair Manon had recently vacated. I took the offered seat and picked up a small laminated card that served as the bar menu. It only had nine cocktails on one side, while the other side had maybe nine thousand beers and liquors.

"You want me to get you something?" Yuri was practically yelling, but I still had a hard time making his voice out over the drums.

I pointed to the margarita on the cocktail side of the menu card. He got up and went over to the bar where words and money changed hands, and then made his way back with a punch bowl of iced lime juice and tequila. They must have had a barrel to rim a glass this size with salt. As he handed it to me, I mouthed a thank you. We both sat there, sipping our drinks and making tentative eye contact while we waited for the band to finish their current set. I wondered if Elena's friend had actually made it. Every once in a while, I glanced around the bar to see if I could see anyone's eyes on me, but generally, there were a bunch of people smiling and laughing. There were a handful of dancers closer to the band, but their attention was definitely on other things. Manon shot me another dirty look as she pulled an athletic blonde surfer, Matt, with a net shirt over to the dance floor. *Yep, you win... Sure showed me...* I resisted the urge to roll my eyes. That never went over well.

I hoped Manon wasn't Elena's friend.

After the first set was finished, the band announced they were taking a break. I turned to Yuri now that it finally seemed we might be able to say more than a few words to each other. "So..."

"So…" he agreed.

Riveting…

"It was Curtis, right?"

"Curtis Johanson," he agreed.

"Did you find that friend you were looking for?" I asked.

For a long time, he merely looked at me, like he was trying to determine if I was secretly a robot. I was becoming less and less convinced that this was the romantic evening I'd been hoping for.

"He wasn't home," Yuri said after much too long a pause. "What did you say your name was?"

"Briar Egibi," I said.

"Egibi?"

In hindsight, this was a much more important question than I realized at the time.

"You want to see my ID? I brought it so they would actually serve me booze, but that didn't actually seem to be an issue." That actually got a laugh. Laughter was good. Something to build on. I tried a question. "How long have you been in Belize?"

And he was guarded again. What the hell was going on? For the first time in my life, I wished I could read my date's mind. "I've been here for about a week, I guess. Time tends to move differently down here, though. It could be closer to three and I'd never know it."

"I'm going to take a couple of weeks to see how I like it. Then I may stay," I told him. "If not, I'm going to try out somewhere else. Jamaica or Utila, maybe. Either way, I'm in Belize for a month."

"Who are you with?" Yuri asked. I could tell this was one of the questions he'd been gnawing on since I sat down. He had that look that interviewers get when their interviewee has stumbled into revealing something they weren't planning to talk about.

The thing was… I wasn't following. "How do you mean?"

"Who do you work for?"

"No one," I said. "I owned a coffee shop in Kansas, but I sold it... So I guess you could say I'm in extremely early retirement? Or maybe between jobs but comfortable?"

"Right..." He downed what was left of his mojito. "Look, I'm not sure what your mission is or who you work for, but if you're just going to yank me around..."

I wanted to say something, but I was blanking out on the name he gave me again. This wasn't going well. Why were we bound together by some sort of fate cord if I couldn't even talk to him? I tried really hard to remember what he wanted to be called, and then I decided, *Fuck it. He wants to know who I am, and I want to talk to someone. I haven't tried talking to anyone about this stuff in ages.*

"Let's take a walk, Yuri," I suggested in as low a voice as possible.

His eyes went wide, but he didn't do anything overt like glancing around to see who'd heard. With one slow, deliberate nod, he offered me his hand like we were two lovers about to bask in the starlight over the ocean. I took it.

I wasn't ready for the contact between us. Warmth that had nothing to do with the weather rushed through me, pooling in happy little puddles in places that made it hard to focus. Yuri wasn't facing me, so I couldn't tell if the warmth had flooded him as well. He may have been too focused on finding out how I'd learned his name. Again, I wished I could take a quick peek inside his head. But he might be imagining how a night with Manon would've gone if I hadn't shown up. Best to stick to my actual powers.

Despite the situation—my date not showing any romantic interest and our exit from the bar being meant to distance ourselves from the noise more than actually stargaze—I couldn't help but take a deep breath of ocean air and lose myself in the galaxy stretching above us. Wichita wasn't the worst city for light pollution, but the sky in Kansas was still nothing like this. I felt the urge to run out into the dark, rolling waves. Not one of my witchy urges, only the natural pull of the ocean.

"I had no idea it would be so gorgeous down here," I whispered.

"It took me by surprise, too, my first time here. Pictures don't do it justice." For a moment, Yuri seemed on the brink of smiling. Then his features tightened again. "So, who are you? Who sent you? Why do you know my name?"

"I'm Briar Egibi. I'm a former coffee shop owner from Wichita, Kansas. And I'm a witch. Last in my line."

This wasn't the first time I'd told someone my secret. I'd made the mistake of telling a few people when I was younger. Generally, I got called Hermione or Sabrina, was told to grow up, and then, inevitably, they would ask me to *prove it*. Whether I did try to prove it or not, every single one of them stopped talking to me after. Witches aren't very popular in Kansas. My Aunt Shay ended up talking to a few parents that were concerned about her "troubled" niece, and that was when she decided to talk to me about the importance of secrecy. *Sorry, Aunt Shay*.

"Truly? A witch?"

I nodded. "A witch."

My earlier experiences with confessing my powers did not prepare me for Yuri's reaction. Denial, anger, accusations, anything along those lines would've made sense to me. Instead, he seemed to relax. His grip on my hand loosened. He started laughing. "An American witch. Cor, that's such a relief..."

"What's that supposed to mean?" I asked. My hackles were on the rise. There was a part of me that would've preferred him to tell me to prove it.

"That came out wrong," Yuri said, sobering immediately. "My apologies. I just thought you were someone very different."

"How do you know I'm telling the truth?" I asked. "Couldn't someone other than a witch claim witchdom? Witchhood? Witchiness..." There may have been a touch more tequila in that punch bowl than I usually ingested, and though I'd had a late lunch, I hadn't eaten dinner.

"Someone could, but the people I'm worried about know better," Yuri said. "That kind of claim is dangerous in my line of work."

"What is your line of work?"

"I'm a Reliquarian," Yuri said. He paused expectantly while I digested that.

The moon, climbing its way into the vast darkness, was casting silver shimmers over the water and the sea spray gathering on Yuri's features. I must have been glowing with the reflected light. I looked into the eyes of the man smiling next to me and said six little words.

"What the hell is a Reliquarian?"

Seconds of silence were counted out by the waves hitting the sand.

"I deserved that," Yuri said. "You're legit not messing with me right now? You really don't know?"

"I really don't know," I confirmed. I couldn't help but notice that even when his grip relaxed, Yuri hadn't actually dropped my hand. This was starting to feel a little more like the date I'd been anticipating.

He sighed and pulled his glasses off. Examining them in the moonlight with one hand, I got the impression he was considering his answer more than the ocean water adhering to his lenses. "You've heard of objects of power, yes?"

"Excalibur, the Spear of Destiny, Mjolner, etcetera?" I asked.

"Right idea, only they don't all have names. Say you have a medallion that was worn by a man in ancient Rome. This man held this medallion every time he prayed for the wellbeing of his family. A little bit of power got injected into the medallion during every prayer. Then, when he died, the medallion was passed along to one of his children who did the same thing. A couple of generations down the road, this medallion, just a worn piece of metal, has healing properties for that man's bloodline. Something happens to the bloodline, and the medallion is lost, but it has enough power to have a tiny bit of awareness. It's only meant for a certain family, so it starts to harm other people attempting to use it."

Kicking the sand out of my sandals, I thought about this accrued power. "Is it only objects that this happens with, or are there places of power, too?"

"Definitely," Yuri said. "But that's not my arena. I deal with the small bits, the relics, that get left behind. I'm part of an organization that makes sure relics don't fall into the hands of people looking to misuse them."

I stopped in my tracks and held Yuri at arms length. Because I was a witch, I could tell every word he'd uttered was true, but even so, it seemed completely insane. "There's an entire organization?"

"More than one, I'm afraid," Yuri said. "Not all of them want to protect people. One of our rival organizations may have beat me to Belize."

Looking out toward the horizon, I spotted lights moving way out on the water. I could barely make out the line of a cruise ship in the black backdrop of the sky. When I tried harder, I could see two others even farther out. I watched the ships as I considered everything Yuri had told me. "Your friend. The one I helped you track down in the cab. What happened?"

"Gone," Yuri's voice conveyed his worry. "He's a professor at the university here. His flat was completely trashed. I have no idea where he might be."

My head was spinning and, this time, it definitely wasn't due to the tequila. "Why are you telling me all of this?"

"You trusted me enough to tell me you're a witch," Yuri shrugged. "That's not something I take lightly. I've known a witch or two. And if I'm right about the type of object I'm here to collect, I'm going to need help."

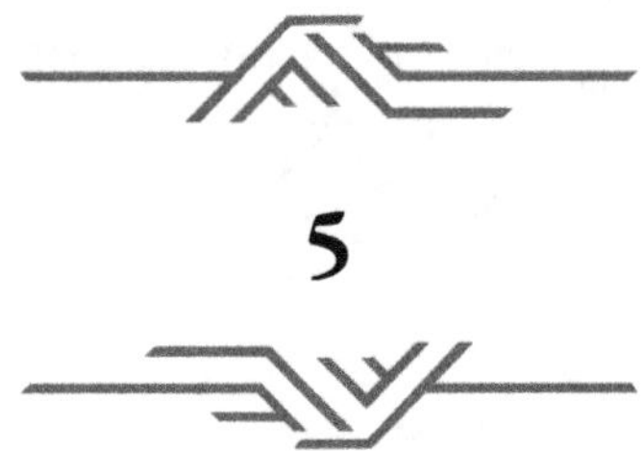

# 5

AT THAT MOMENT, SERENADED by the ocean's constant song, my stomach decided to add its own melody. Cacophony, really. *Perfect timing, body.*

Yuri looked around like he was trying to figure out what monster clam or octopus had burbled its way onto the sand. "Perhaps it's time for us to get back to a more populated area."

"I'm okay," I said. "I just haven't eaten anything since lunch."

"We can definitely find you some food once we're in a more secure location," Yuri glanced over his shoulder again. "But we've picked up a shadow."

I grabbed Yuri's free hand so that I had both of them and walked backwards in front of him like I was being playfully flirtatious. It wasn't like it was hard to pretend. This was a thing I'd been day-dreaming about since he asked me to meet him at the Coconut Cabana. Too bad I was busy looking *past* him instead of *at* him.

There was a lone, hulking figure—Jonas Ical—walking over the sand about eighty yards away. When I say hulking, I mean this guy was big enough to have his own zip code. It was like seeing a professional wrestler slow-walking their way across a ring, except I was on the inside of the ropes.

"Does the name Jonas Ical mean anything to you?" I asked.

Yuri shook his head. "Not really."

"Elena was supposed to send a friend to keep an eye on me. Maybe this is him?" I suggested. Even as I said it, I felt a twinge of falsehood. *Damn it.*

Before I had a chance to convey this to Yuri, he halted entirely. His grip on my hands tightened, more reflexive than intentional. "We've got incoming from the other direction, too."

Spinning us around so I could see the new person, I was met by another moving silhouette. This one was also about eighty yards away, but closing much faster. Where Jonas Ical was large and lumbering, this figure, Alex Smith, was slim and graceful. He moved like a dancer over the loose sand.

I looked toward the road and saw a shadowy figure in that direction too. It was shorter than the other two closing in on us. Practically unassuming in the casual way it walked toward us. But this one scared me far more than the walking mountain named Jonas Ical or the graceful dancer that was Alex Smith. For some reason, the shadow coming from the street *had no name.*

"Yuri..." The fear in my voice conveyed full sentences of alarm. My teeth started to chatter like the temperature had dropped into the negatives despite the tropical heat. Something was wrong here. So very, very wrong.

"How well can you swim?" he asked.

A part of me wanted to make some quip about how witches float, but No Name's shadow was getting closer and I couldn't do it. "Only okay," I admitted. "Probably not ocean-at-night good."

"That's what I was afraid of," Yuri said.

Just when I was certain we were out of time and options, I felt a stillness rush through my system. I was warm, and not from external temperatures. Something deep inside of me switched on and radiated through my veins. Words formed in my mind, wanting to be spoken. I didn't see them in English in my head, but I heard them as English when I spoke them aloud. *"Show me the way."*

Between Jonas Ical and No Name, a path lit up in the sand. Gripping Yuri's hand I took off at top speed, willing him to trust me. Alex Smith was only a few yards away from us when we started running.

Given the shouts we left behind, whatever I'd done had left them confused.

"Where did they go?!"

"You were right there! How did they get past you?!"

"They went for the water! There's no chance they can stay out there all night."

"I didn't hear a splash."

"Where else could they be?"

There were a few times when Yuri tried to yank me toward the road, but I *had* to keep my feet on the path. The path was the only thing keeping us hidden from No Name. I could feel it pulsing through my legs. As long as I stayed on the path, no darkness would touch me. Only once we were back at the stairs to the Coconut Cabana did the light fade, taking my sense of safety with it.

"What just happened?" Yuri asked.

I opened my mouth to tell him that I had no idea. Another voice broke in and said, "Oh, good, you made it."

An older, stout Hispanic man—Eddie Velasquez—pushed himself off the wooden steps. The patchy light from the beach bar revealed grey hair that crept up from his sideburns into his shoulder-length curls and created shadows along the well-worn laugh lines framing his mouth. He was holding a mostly empty beer bottle, with a few more empties scattered next to the spot he'd been reclining. "Elena said you would be here, but I didn't see you so I figured either she got the day wrong or I did, or maybe you'd decided not to come. But since you're here and I'm here, I can tell her I did my job."

Yuri and I exchanged confused looks. I knew exactly what Eddie was talking about with regards to Elena, but was Eddie responsible for the path that had saved our asses? My truth detector was unusually silent on the matter.

After I bought Eddie another beer and said a few goodbyes, Yuri pulled me into a cab and we made our way to a restaurant on the other end of San Pedro. Even though it was close to the place's listed closing time (maybe half an hour), I wasn't too worried about keeping them late. We grabbed the last open table and ordered a couple of plates of Boil Up. I had no idea what it was, but Yuri assured me it was a must-try for any first-time traveler to Belize. It was tempting to forget we'd just run for our lives across sand on a path of light only I could see.

Even if I could still feel it in my thighs.

The moment of peace didn't last very long. Yuri's gaze sharpened. He folded his hands as he leaned toward me across the two-person table. "So what happened back there?"

"I really don't know," I sighed. "That one guy... That last one, coming from the road, didn't have a name. I was more scared than I've ever been in my life. Just when I thought we were toast, there was this weird sense of calm. The words to a spell I've never encountered before appeared in my head. I'm not even sure what language that spell was in. When I cast it, a path of light appeared. It was instinctual at that point. I knew we had to stay on the path or those guys would see us."

Our food arrived on plates that curved up at the sides like huge saucers. I saw bits of carrot, pineapple, chicken, fish, some sort of starchy vegetable that wasn't a potato, and something else that looked like red peppers, all smothered in this brown stew or sauce. It felt a little weird to look at this and not be given some bread or rice to go with it, but Yuri attacked his plate with nothing but a fork. I followed suit.

It wasn't speaking to me the way the ceviche had earlier, but I wasn't mad. There was a lot of sweet and a lot of spicy and a lot of a lot. I wasn't sure if this would make it onto my list of favorite dishes, but I liked it. Especially when I found an egg. It was a fantastic egg.

"I've never heard of such a thing before," Yuri said. He stuck a bit of fish with his fork and it practically melted apart. "But then, I'm not specialized in spells. I'm much better with relics. I can make some calls tonight when I get back to my hotel."

"I'd appreciate that," I said. He'd mentioned needing my help while we were on the beach, but I still didn't know anything about him, his organization, or his goals here in Belize. Any of it. "Do I ever get to know who you work for? Or what I'm supposed to be helping you with?"

"I want to tell you right now, I really do... But this is not the situation I thought I was walking into when I met you at Coconut Cabana. I thought you'd have your own clearances and your own people. I wasn't anticipating running into a..." Yuri hesitated, glancing around to make sure no one was listening. "Gifted civilian. While I'm making calls, I'm going to see if I can get you written in as a temporary recruit. If that's approved, I can give you a full briefing tomorrow."

"Tomorrow," I repeated. "When tomorrow?"

Pulling out his cell phone, Yuri opened his calendar app and looked at it intensely for a few moments. This entire situation was completely batshit, but I *knew* he was telling the truth. It seemed like something out of a movie from the 1980s. They always had the weirdest plots: try to avoid making it with mom while trying to get her together with dad, a building designed by an ancient cult summons an evil god who summons a huge marshmallow to terrorize downtown New York, create a mannequin that becomes an ancient Egyptian girl and then fall in love. *Travel to the tropics and get recruited into a magical archeological spy society by potential love interest.* It tied in nicely.

"How about we meet for burgers around noon at the place across the street?"

"Well, this has probably been my worst date ever, but what the hell! I'm game for more," I grinned at Yuri as I said it, hoping to take the sting out of my words.

He had the grace to blush.

BACK AT THE CONDO, I kicked off my shoes and fell across the aqua sofa. I was very aware that I'd been up since six o'clock in the morning. A lot of my relaxing time had been taken up preparing for the date-that-wasn't-a-date. It was between ten and eleven p.m. now, but my body was convinced it was closer to two. Moving to the tropics was not going at all as I'd expected so far. Well, the food was on point. But the rest...

As much as I wanted to change out of my date clothes and climb into the bed, thoughts of No Name wouldn't stop. What if that thing found out where I was staying? What if it was standing out there on the beach watching my door this very moment?

I peeled myself back off the couch and went into the kitchen. It didn't take much poking around to find a mostly-full salt shaker. This was a quick-fix solution, but it would work for tonight until I had a chance to figure out a better warding system for my temporary shelter. I sprinkled a line of salt across the threshold and applied a sprinkling to each of the windows. For good measure, I included all of the outlets and pipes, tossed a bit around the toilet, and even in front of the washer and dryer. That thing was not drifting into this condo like a spirit anytime soon.

Checking the locks on all the doors and windows one last time (because it would suck to ward out spirits only to have someone walk in), I finally felt secure enough to change into my pajamas. White and blue plaid boxers and a loose, black yoga top. I threw my date outfit in the washer with my travel clothes from earlier. Since there wasn't a hamper, I figured that was the logical place for them. I would add detergent and run it when I started running low on stuff. While a part of me was still fighting to stay awake, I turned off the lights and slid between the sheets on the queen-sized bed.

*Welcome to Belize*, I thought as I sank into the comfortable darkness of sleep.

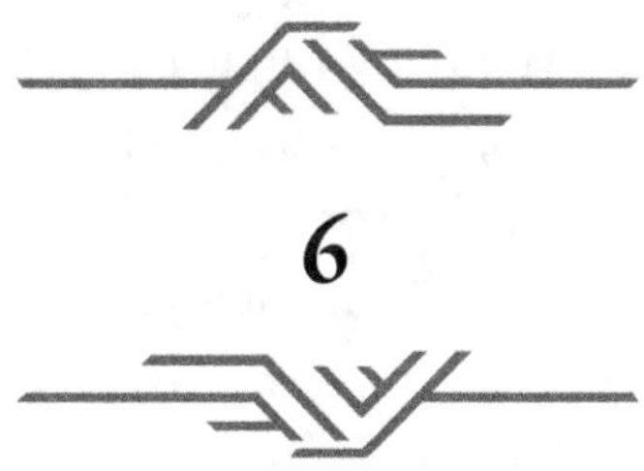

# 6

WHEN I WOKE THE NEXT morning, a lot of what had happened the previous day felt like a dream. I pushed the covers off and planted my feet on the cool tiles. The sun was still below the horizon, though the dove grey twilight was bright enough to light the interior of my residence. Time to find out if this place had a coffee maker.

I was in luck. The coffee maker only had a two cup pot, but it was large enough to fill my morning mug. The coffee available was a disappointingly generic brand, widely available state-side, but generic coffee was better than no coffee. Mmm... Coffee.

There were a few creamers stashed in the fridge. I wondered if the coffee and creamers were leftovers from a previous guest, because they were also a state-side staple. I would have to check out the local coffee scene and compare notes with my aunt's shop. If something was interesting enough, maybe I'd ship a few samples to Debra. She'd probably really like that. There wasn't any sugar in the condo, but I did find some agave nectar. That would work for the time being, but I needed to go shopping soon.

Coffee brewed and doctored, I took my mug with me out onto the front porch. Sipping hot caffeine and watching the sun rise over the water, I felt more like I was on vacation than anything. It was tranquil out here. My fears from the previous night were a whole other lifetime. Wispy puffs of cloud branded the sky with pink and orange fire while the ocean watched. Eventually, I ran out of coffee and wandered back indoors.

My phone was sitting on the counter, its screen lit up with unread messages. Several of them were from Elena, asking how things went with my date and whether I'd actually seen Eddie or not. Those had arrived around midnight. Another was an email notification, alerting me to ten or twelve bits of junk mail. I would delete most of that later. Taco Rancho had a 2 for 1 margarita special! Damn. Of all the things to get homesick about. The last message was a text from Yuri. I assumed it was him because he'd signed the bottom with a "—Yuri," but the number was anonymous. Not a random unknown. Anonymous.

*Odd*, I thought. *I don't remember giving him my number.*

Not that finding a phone number off of someone's name was impossible. There were only so many Egibis listed in Kansas. Only one living, to my knowledge.

The full message read, "Something's come up. Can you make it back to Coconut Cabana by 10AM? —Yuri."

Something was off. Why would he want to meet that close to where we'd nearly been ambushed the night before? It was still incredibly early in the day, so I washed my used mug and left it to dry while I took a shower.

Showers are great for thinking. Soap smell, scrubbing, water running. Almost as important a ritual as my morning coffee. I tried to process what was bothering me about the Yuri message. Number one: My truth sense didn't work on electronics. Magic and technology played by weird rules. But I'd never done something like the address reading the day before, so maybe there was something I could try? Number two: Why would he text me from an anonymous number? If he'd gotten me the clearances he'd mentioned last night, wouldn't I be trusted with his phone number? Number three: If he was going to text me, why hadn't he asked for my phone number? Or contact info of any kind? Why arrange in person meet-ups only to break phone etiquette with a new meet-up location?

The more I gnawed on it, the less I liked it. A new thought occurred as I was plunging my face into the water and scrubbing all the last vestiges of sleep from my eyes. I hadn't checked the time stamp on that last message. What if it came in last night while I was making my salt wards? I silenced my phone at night when I plugged it in. I wasn't generally one to do late night browsing. Sometimes, I would read a book, but last night I'd barely hit the pillow before I'd started a REM cycle.

I exited my shower feeling much cleaner, but no less troubled. As soon as I was dry enough not to track water everywhere, I wrapped my towel around my torso and hustled over to my phone. No new messages this time. The time stamp on the message supposedly from Yuri had arrived at 11:27 p.m. Damn. That didn't help. Not only had my salt wards been in place, I'd already been deep into unconsciousness. Anyone with my number could have sent the text. Anyone with my number that knew Yuri's name, anyway.

Before I got dressed, I snapped my paracord bracelets on. I missed my aunt. If anyone would've known how to deal with something like this, it would've been Aunt Shay. At least, I liked to think she would've had some insight.

I'd packed two swimsuits for my initial month in Belize. Both were tankinis: one had a blue/purple ombre top paired with black shorts, and the other had a white top with giant palm fronds and pink flowers paired with jungle green shorts. I pulled on the blue and purple suit and covered the black bottoms with a pair of grey linen capris. Even when you wear swim shorts, uncovered swimwear still feels like I'm running around in my undies. Maybe that's just my insecurities talking. But I wanted to be ready for anything today, including the possibility of jumping into the big blue ocean. I belted my hip bag into place, checking it twice to make sure I still had all of my necessities within. My skin was crawling by the time I stepped out the door.

This was such a bad idea.

It was still well before the text-designated meeting time. I could always go, get myself settled nearby and see who showed up. If it was Yuri, good. If Yuri didn't come, then I was getting texts from someone that wasn't Yuri and knew his name, and that was bad. Extremely not good. I'd called him by name on the beach last night... Jonas Ical, Alex Smith, No Name: any of the three could've heard me. How they would've gotten my information, though, that was harder. It was dark on the beach. Not like they could've snapped a pic and done a face search without me noticing. Maybe witches weren't the only ones with the ability to glean names.

As I locked the condo, I hoped I wasn't about to walk into a trap.

SAN PEDRO ISN'T A VERY large city. It's only about one mile wide and a mile and a half long. Since the Sun was out, I decided walking to the Coconut Cabana was preferable to another taxi ride. It gave me a chance to poke around on the beach where Yuri and I had our narrow escape.

Belize's beaches were pretty quiet in the early morning hours. I encountered a couple of joggers and one or two beachcombers, but no one raised my inner alarms. None of them were Jonas Ical or Alex Smith. All of them had names.

I didn't see anything unusual when I got to the right section of sand. When we'd been walking on the beach the night before, I'd been half-lost in visions of the sky and starlight, hoping that Yuri's hand-holding meant more than keeping our cover. Not a lot of attention paid to sand placement, or how far away the bar had been. I didn't *see* it, but I definitely *felt* it.

An invisible bomb had been detonated, obliterating the energy in this section of the beach. Even the joggers sensed something was off in that area. I watched a guy named Antonio jog part way through it and then run into the ocean. Slogging through the water, he fought against the surf until he was comfortable enough to get back on the beach, nearly losing his soaked shorts. He smiled half-heartedly at me as he passed. "Sometimes you've gotta get wet, right?"

"Right," I agreed with a shaky smile of my own.

This section of beach screamed at me to do something. On the visible layer of the world, everything was fine. Just another peaceful stretch of sand on a long beach that was full of similar stretches of sand. Underneath the visual layer, it was jagged and unnatural, sharp like torn metal. Someone had ripped away the very essence of what made it a *beach* and left this place hollow. I couldn't leave it like this.

Magic isn't an unlimited resource. Like a muscle, it requires stretching, practice, and repetition to do something well. It also requires talent. Someone with a talent for basketball isn't likely to make a name for themselves as a professional hockcy player. I mean, they might. But that's going to take even more time and practice. Healing magic isn't my strong suit. I was always better with minor incantations. Refilling a battery, making sure the tire lasts for an extra mile until I get to the auto shop, not letting my soda go flat or keeping the ice cold a tad longer, that was the kind of thing I found easy. This was almost half a football field worth of torn reality.

*Maybe if I look at the beach as a much larger battery?* I thought. *That... might work...*

Wishing I had a better idea, I started walking around the edge of the tear. Someone that recognized the rift might have been able to tell that I was a supernatural entity at that point. Though, if they knew enough to notice a tear in reality, hopefully I wasn't the first thing they would focus on. Once a yard, I ducked down and drew a glyph in the sand. These weren't strictly necessary for me to cast, but the glyphs were amplifiers. Given that what I was trying to do wasn't exactly a healing spell, I didn't want to run out of juice after I'd only restored a foot or two of sand. I also didn't want to be drained for the rest of the day. Or maybe even the rest of the week, given the size of this sucker.

After outlining the entire area with my footprints, I drew a big plus sign on one side and a large minus on the other.

Walking around in this space, I felt something trying to syphon away my power. Not that I would let it. The first thing I was taught, when it was obvious I had the family gift, was how to shield myself. Trust me when I say the last thing a parent wants to deal with is a leaky teenage witch.

*Here goes nothing*, I thought.

Positioning myself directly in the center of the "battery," I put one hand out toward the positive side and one toward the negative. I imagined the power that had been, reminded the space how it felt to be full, and coaxed it to reawaken. My own magic flared to life, flooding into the empty sand and threading its way into all of the hollowed out nooks that had formed inside this shell of a beach. It reminded me of butter on an English muffin. My magic was soaking into the ground beneath me and saturating every inch. The beach around me extended itself and the power of the ocean joined in, threatening to rip me away from myself. This shit didn't happen when I filled a battery. I wasn't braced for the natural world to aid me. My magic was all that anchored me to the spot, but once the empty space filled, my anchor would pop out. The ocean was stronger than one witch and one little beach. It was the very essence of *water* and it could wear away entire continents.

A flare of heat encircled my wrist. It burned like the nine hells, but I was suddenly back in control. My paracord bracelets... Of course Aunt Shay would've woven protections into them. She knew better than anyone that her niece was more impulsive than intelligent on occasion. (Who isn't?) She'd managed to save me from myself more than once, and she'd now managed to do it again. Post-mortem.

I tied off my spell and breathed in gulps of salt-soaked air. That was too much. Far too much. I needed to examine the results, but all I wanted to do was collapse. Maybe sleep. Maybe eat an entire pot of Boil Up. Maybe heave up a lung. I checked my skin under my bracelets for burns but, as hot as it had felt during the spell, there was no physical damage. How many spells my aunt woven into these things, anyway? Was the path of light her work? It hadn't felt like her work, but I couldn't discount the possibility.

I focused on nothing but breathing for a few minutes before I realized I was on my knees. I'd fallen at some point during the spell. The fact that I hadn't flat-out face-planted surprised me. I was pretty sure that someone or something would come investigate the magical thunderclap I just set off. I had no idea exactly when the original energy detonation had occurred, but it had to have been after No Name realized we'd slipped its grasp. I didn't want to know what it would've done if it had caught us. Who knows what it would've taken to undo that damage...

A slow clap worked its way into my exhausted attention. In movies, the slow-clap builds to applause. Real life slow-claps very rarely lead to those grandiose moments that you're eager for people to witness. They're much more likely to accompany a moment that you'd rather forget. Like slipping on spilled pudding in the school cafeteria while you're in a skirt and having your entire class see your unfortunate last-day-before-laundry undies. For the record, witches cannot alter memories. This was one of those bad slow-claps.

My eyes met with those of a man. Or, at least, it looked like a man. If a living shadow could be a man. There were vague impressions in my mind of something masculine. He was possibly average height with nondescript features, but those impressions didn't quite mesh with what my eyes were telling me. *Living shadow with eyes that burn*. It was No Name from the night before.

Everything in my body tensed. I wanted to run. I wanted to fight. I wanted to melt into a puddle and slide into the ocean until the thing went away. The energy wasn't there, though. I'd burned myself out fixing the damn beach.

"I did wonder if you'd actually come," No Name cocked its head at me as it spoke, like it was about to approach a skittish dog. "Most of those working for the IACI are bright enough to stay hidden after the first encounter."

"What's the IACI?" I asked. It didn't sound flippant, just tired. It helped that I really had no idea what No Name was talking about.

"The IACI... Your organization. The one that sent you here," No Name said.

"Dude, I owned a coffee shop in Kansas. You think someone needed Belizean coffee bad enough to buy me a ticket?" Okay, I was starting to sound flippant. I didn't have a plan or anything. I figured if I kept the thing talking, I might eventually regain my legs or help might arrive. "I have no idea what the IACI is."

"Then why were you out here with Mr. Knowles?"

"You mean my date?" I asked. "The guy who didn't even walk me home after we almost got jumped?"

No Name blinked a bit as though it were trying to recalibrate vectors and all that it could get was an image of a smiley face. I seemed to be messing with its notion of how this encounter would play out. As long as I could keep No Name off-balance without getting it pissed off, maybe I could talk my way out of this. The very beach I was kneeling on was a reminder that I didn't want to push this thing too far.

"You are not a member of the IACI," No Name said. "But you are dating one?"

"Maybe?" I acknowledged. "We didn't exactly exchange life stories last night. It was our first date."

It began pacing across the sand I'd fixed. Its figure shimmered a bit as it touched the fresh magic, like a mirage on a desert highway. Goosebumps rose on my arms and I fought the urge to jump up and start running. Without a path of light to hide me from it, running would be my last mistake. I could sense it in No Name's unwavering gaze. A much less human voice hissed from between its teeth as it approached me. "How did you *escape*?"

"A spell," I said. I'd been telling the technical truth about everything so far. I didn't want to risk that this being was able to feel falsehoods. "I don't know the source."

No Name was close enough to me now that I could feel its breath moving the air above my head. Fear was bubbling through my chest like foam. Any moment, my blood could start boiling on the inside of my body. My teeth were threatening to crack from how hard I was clenching my jaw. The smell emanating off of No Name was as bad as the most rancid, spoiled-egg dog farts to ever chase a family out of a dining room. *Don't run. Don't run. Don't run. Don't run. Don't run.*

"You're a witch!" No Name said. It sounded delighted about this discovery. "It's been a very long time since I smelled one of *your* bloodline."

"My bloodline?" I wasn't sure how I got the words out. All I wanted was to go back to when Yuri had gotten into my taxi and let Elena shoo him out. I would've wondered what happened to him for maybe the rest of my life, but I wouldn't be here, facing this thing that had uncovered my secret in a matter of seconds by smelling me. So gross.

Also, I was pretty sure I was about to die. That'll make you wish a lot of things had happened differently.

7

NO SHIT. THERE I WAS...

Okay, seriously, everyone should get to start a story like that at least once.

No Name was standing over me, smelling me like a freaking stalker-monster, while I knelt in a helpless, burnt-out, witch heap on the beach. There was no doubt in my mind that I was about to be reunited with Aunt Shay and my parents. Either this thing was going to chomp down on my head, or it was going to blow me up with the same energy bomb it had set off on this section of sand the night before. Possibly even a third, more horrible, option.

Running wasn't on the table. Even if I could get to my feet, which I wasn't positive I could, I was more likely to piss No Name off than make any real distance. Thank you to Peter S. Beagle for some unexpected real world advice. I could easily imagine that No Name was something immortal.

Then the ocean surged and I was floating away in waist deep water. No Name was standing on the beach exactly where I'd left it. Neither it nor the beach looked any different than they had only seconds before. The only difference was that I was being swept out to sea. There weren't any terrified screams or walls of water hurtling toward the sleepy island. The ocean had seemingly reached out with a watery hand and scooped me off the beach. While I was happy for the save, I couldn't help thinking, *Great, now what?*

"Oh, good, you made it," Eddie Velasquez said. He was sitting inside a small fishing boat in a folding deck chair. He was wearing his greying hair in a ponytail. Covering his torso, he had an aged tank

50

top that had probably started white but was now a few shades more beige, and covering that was a red and yellow Hawaiian shirt. His khaki shorts had seen almost as much life as his tank top. Yellow plastic sunglasses were barely clinging to the end of his nose. A few empty beer bottles were sitting around him while he worked on another. With a grin and a wink, he said, "I wasn't sure if you were coming. I figured maybe I got the date wrong, or maybe you did."

As I approached the boat, the water carrying me slowed and then stopped. Eddie leaned forward to grab me by the wrist and haul me out of the ocean. "I... I don't understand," I said. "You're Elena's friend, right? The one she sent to keep an eye on me last night?"

"Yeah, that's me," Eddie agreed. "You want some cerveza? It's in the cooler."

I took a beer out of the cooler and thanked him before popping the top and chugging nearly half the bottle in one gulp. I was having a day so don't judge.

"Elena is dating my niece, so that makes her family. But when I was asked to keep an eye on her new American friend, I wasn't expecting it to take so much effort. Most of the tourists we get through here, they might booze too much and maybe go down the wrong alley after flashing some tourist cash or some shit. You took the bull by the balls your first night here, huh?"

"That's one way of putting it," I agreed. "Thanks, again, for the beer and I'm guessing the rescue?"

"Which rescue, chica? I saved your ass twice now... Don't you know not to toy with the children of gods?" Eddie knocked back his own beer, finishing the bottle. I grabbed him another since I was still next to the cooler.

It took a few moments for his words to sink in. Once they did, I was very happy the boat had two chairs. I plopped down into the empty seat, the chilled beer barely staying in my suddenly shaky hands. "Children of the gods?" I echoed.

Eddie studied me for a long moment, though he was still side-eyeing the beach. No Name was pacing back and forth on the sand patch I'd nearly blown myself out trying to refill. It approached the waves and put out a hand. There was an odd flash of light at No Name's fingers and it jerked away as though stung. After a few minutes, it started walking toward the Coconut Cabana parking lot.

"Demigods, chica. Walking the earth just like they did in ancient times."

I took an absent minded chug from my beer bottle. The beer was cheap, but refreshing in its own way. Could've used a lime. Not that I was about to complain about free beer right now.

"I think there's a lot of shit that I wasn't prepared to encounter when I left Kansas."

"I know that's right," Eddie agreed. "What's your story, then? How come you seem powerful enough to put things together, but ignorant enough to walk right back into the shadows?"

With a sigh, I downed the last of my beer and told Eddie about growing up as a witch in the breadbasket of the United States. I told him how my parents had died before I started showing signs of the family gift. I explained how Aunt Shay had taught me some basics to help control things, but my magic hadn't quite functioned like hers. I wasn't as good at a lot of standard witchy things. And then, she died, too. "I'm not sure if my lack of magical education is because she didn't trust me to be able to handle it, or if she genuinely didn't know. Kansas wasn't exactly teaming with magic. We spent a lot of time trying not to be noticed."

On the beach, we could see the Coconut Cabana bartender drive up and park. Neon signs within the palapa turned on one by one, barely visible in the morning light.

"So, you're a witch?" Eddie said. It seemed like a rhetorical question, as he immediately continued, "I guess that makes sense. I don't really know anything about witches outside of the movies, and they probably get that as right as they get anything else."

"What about you? Are you a demigod?" I asked.

Eddie laughed. It was a full-bodied roar of a laugh that made the entire boat shake in the water. "Me? Oh, hell no, chica! Heaven forbid I have to deal with that kind of power every day. That's the kind of shit that'll drive you mental. One of the unwritten rules: power seeks power. The children of the gods, they're born to power, which means they never stop seeking. Get yourself another drink."

I was tempted to refuse, but I didn't want to insult my host. I grabbed another bottle out of the cooler and cracked it open, but I restrained myself to sipping this one.

"No, I'm not a god's chico unless my mother's got more secrets than she's let on. Which, to be fair, isn't impossible. She could keep the universe in a cupboard and not tell anyone, my madre. I am from a long line of shamans though. Not great at the spiritual side of that, but I've seen some shit," Eddie said. "A few people like that guy that's after you, for starters."

"I've been calling it No Name in my head," I admitted.

"For the best," Eddie raised his bottle to me. "Some names aren't worth mentioning."

He set down another empty bottle and turned in his seat to yank the motor pull. With the motor happily buzzing, Eddie sat up and grabbed the rudder handle, steering us toward a distant boat dock I hadn't seen until we were in motion. "I think we've let enough time pass that your No Name has moved on to other things. Either way, you probably want to go make sure your phone still works. Sorry I had to dunk you all sudden like that."

"No worries. I appreciate the hell out of it," I said.

My hip drop bag was supposed to be water resistant, but Eddie did raise a good point. I'd want to do a maintenance charm on my phone as soon as I had the energy. Also, I still had to meet up with Yuri. I was sure he'd want to hear about my morning.

I ARRIVED BACK AT MY condo with barely enough time to change and leave again. It was hard not to think of it as my place, despite the fact that just this morning I'd been feeling more like I was on vacation than moving. The condo was supposed to be my house-hunting base.

*When am I ever going to find the time to do THAT*, I thought. Only my second day here, and I'd done more in Belize than I had in my last year in Kansas. Granted, it was Kansas. Not a lot happened in Kansas outside of tornadoes and crop growing.

My ombre bathing suit and grey capris joined the pile already forming in the washing machine. At this rate, I'd be doing laundry tomorrow. According to my early, state-side calculations, I'd packed enough to get through eight or nine days. Even though I had come to Belize looking for an adventure, I'm not sure I'd actually anticipated finding one. I pulled on the green and white tankini and found an old pair of cut-offs. They weren't my cutest shorts, but if I ended up taking a dive again, I wouldn't mind these getting stained or soaked. I was half-tempted to raid the washing machine and grab my travel clothes. As hot as Yuri was, I was getting over my need to primp for him in a hurry. Too many shenanigans.

I checked my phone and wallet inside of my hip drop bag. They were completely dry, no worse at all for my unexpected trip through the water. Huzzah! This thing was going to get a stellar review.

Once more unto the beach.

Door locked, sandals on, hip drop bag and bracelets in place, I made my way back to the restaurant-laden street Yuri had taken us the night before. It was less crowded in the daytime, but not by much. I spotted Yuri heading toward the burger place only a breath before he noticed me. His mouth parted into a wide smile. Shit, he had the cutest dimples. Why had I forgotten the dimples when I was getting dressed?

*Because you nearly died this morning*, my inner-reason reminded me.

Oh, yeah. That'd do it.

Yuri's outfit was basically the same as the one he'd worn the day before. Professor glasses, clean tank top, Hawaiian shirt with various shades of green leaves and vaguely tribal imprints, and more khaki cargo shorts. My brain went a little fizzy with a memory of what his eyes had looked like in the moonlight. *Stop it, Briar,* I told myself. *Remember that it wasn't a date. This isn't a date. He's looking to recruit you into a secret organization or something. Make sure it isn't a cult.*

"Hello, and how are you today?" he asked.

"What's the IACI?" were the first words that came out of my mouth. Not something like, *I'm fine, thanks for asking. Do you have any idea what I'd like to do to you behind a closed door?* But secret hush-hush acronyms right out on the street. Smooth, me. Real smooth.

"I... think we might need to find someplace else to talk, huh? Maybe get some burgers first?" Yuri's smile barely moved, but the warmth behind it had diminished visibly. Me and my big mouth.

"Yeah... Yes... Sorry. I just... I've got a lot to tell you about my morning," I felt my shoulders sag. "I didn't mean to say that, or sound like I was attacking you. Food would be great."

Some of the warmth returned to Yuri's expression along with a current of understanding. "Okay. We'll get some burgers, you'll tell me about your morning, and then I can tell you about what I managed to get done last night. After that, we can get to work."

"Yes," I said. "I like that order of operations."

Yuri chuckled. I hadn't meant it as a joke, but I was too pleased that he was happy again to really care.

We stepped into the burger place and got slammed in the face by the smell of BEEF. It seeped into the pores and left you feeling like a fifteen year old that hadn't discovered face cream. If you stood in one spot for too long your arteries would clog on principle.

Glorious.

After checking to see what I wanted, Yuri ordered two cheeseburgers with extra pickles and mustard. They came with fried plantains instead of french fries, which seemed weird to me but I was game to try something new. We were told to sit wherever we liked, and they would bring out our food. As much as I enjoyed the thick meat smell that we were wading through, I dragged Yuri out onto the patio to find a table. He chose one that was still against the wall, but surrounded by other patrons. Probably so the surrounding conversations would muffle our voices? Or to make it harder to shoot at us? I was still adjusting to this espionage mindset.

"Okay, so, tell me about your morning," Yuri said. He leaned toward me across the table and I had to remind myself, again, that this was not a date.

Starting with the weird text message, I told him that I'd planned to go early and hide myself to see who showed up. I described the entire scene at the beach and getting ambushed by No Name. Then I told him about the ocean grabbing me off the beach and towing me to Eddie's boat, though I did leave out Eddie's name and background. I referred to him as a local magic user. Eddie hadn't given me permission to discuss his abilities, and it seemed wrong to out him to whoever it was that Yuri worked for without consent.

Yuri turned out to be a very good listener. He only interjected once with, "And then what happened?" But he never interrupted me. Nor did he call me a dumb ass for going into a questionable situation on my own. I *had* been a dumb ass, but he didn't call me one. I appreciated his discretion.

"That sounds like quite the morning," Yuri said once I had finished talking. "Frankly, I'm surprised you came to meet me for lunch after that."

"Not like I could call you up and cancel," I shrugged.

"You could've called the restaurant and asked them to relay the message," Yuri said.

"Dammit, why didn't I think of that?" I grinned to let him know that I wasn't serious. "At this point, I think I'd be disappointed not to see where this takes me."

"Good news for you, sir!" At that moment, one of the restaurant workers—Ivanita—arrived bearing two plates on blue and white cloth napkins. The way she pronounced the word *sir* made it sound like the *r* had rolled out of bed and taken a leisurely stretch. "Wish more of my dates were that open! I can't seem to keep 'em hooked! Have a wonderful day, you two, and enjoy!"

My burger was gigantic. It only had one patty, which was fortunate because it looked big enough for two people. Accompanying it on the plate were the fried plantains, rice, and what appeared to be a pineapple salsa.

"I hope you're hungry," Yuri said as he took in his own dish. "I'm never prepared for the actual portion sizes. Every time I go abroad, it's either too much or too little."

"Please tell me this is the too-much end of the spectrum," I pleaded.

I was rewarded with another laugh. When Yuri laughed, his entire face seemed to light up and those killer dimples made a showing. The things I would do to this man, if he let me...

*Easy, girl, easy does it. Still don't know if he's even interested in anything more than a colleague. And he might be in a cult. Even if his organization is legit, there's nothing saying he can't also be in a cult... He might recruit you for a job, and then throw you in a volcano later. That way lies death. Death and madness. Behave!*

Sometimes my inner voice could be a real ballbuster.

To distract myself from thoughts about dimples and cults, I popped one of the fried plantains into my mouth. Well, I was obviously going to eat those as often as possible. Fried plantains were apparently a dessert hiding in the main course, and I'm always on board for that. Between the fried plantains and the pineapple salsa, my sweet tooth was about to be very, very happy.

For a few blissfully quiet moments, I was eating a burger with a very attractive man and no one was trying to kill anyone. It was the best I'd felt since my morning coffee. And there were fried plantains, so bonus!

"Just so you know," Yuri said, managing to chew and talk without showing me a half-masticated cow. "I would not send you a text like that. Not without some sort of prearranged code word or phrase... Something more concrete than merely my name, anyway. I can see where you wouldn't have known that this morning, though. That's entirely my fault, too. I was being so cautious about what I was telling you that I didn't even think about what I *wasn't* telling you."

"Given what I went through this morning, I think if I did get a text from you without more verification, I'd tell you to shove it," I said. Perhaps that was a crass way to put it, but the reminder of my morning adventure had popped my blissful bubble of denial.

"That's fair," Yuri admitted. "Still, we should come up with something while we're on the way to the mainland tomorrow."

"We're going to the mainland tomorrow?"

With a nod, Yuri pulled a worn leather journal out of his cargo shorts. It was one of those unbound journal coverings where the paper insert could be removed and exchanged for a new booklet. Bright pink, blue and yellow sticky notes stuck out of the edges like it was a mouth with a thousand little tongues. "I got the clearances I needed for you to tag along as a temporary ally. I wanted to offer you a position straight out, but even with your extra abilities, the higher ups want to see how you do with a field test."

I felt like I'd been demoted from possible Bond girl to potential office intern in the space of only a few seconds. How did this turn into a job interview? "I'm sorry, but I still don't even know who these people are. I agreed to the possibility of helping you yesterday, which I would still like to do, don't get me wrong... But before we get to clearances and positions and field tests, why don't you tell me who it is you work for?"

Yuri nodded, and placed the journal on my side of the table. "You're right to ask, and I'm sorry for all the obfuscation. But this should clear up a lot of your questions."

I wiped my hands with the cloth napkin so I wouldn't get burger grease on the leather. Finally, I was going to get some answers!

# 8

AS I OPENED THE JOURNAL, protective wards tickled the tips of my fingers. If I didn't have the owner's permission, the sensation wouldn't have been nearly so pleasant. Yuri tried to give me some privacy by watching the people walking up and down the city streets. There were plenty of touristy stores and diving shops nearby so there were plenty of people to watch. Maybe it was less innocent than that and he was watching for No Name and his human associates. (If No Name was a demigod, it seemed wrong to keep referring to him as an *it*.)

The first sheet inside of the journal wasn't originally part of the inner book, but a glossy pamphlet with full color pictures that reminded me of the posters they put up next to the Bursar's Office when I went to college. One of the pictures looked like a stock photo archeologist that had watched Indiana Jones too many times, while another one looked like a movie poster for "The Alchemist" by H. P. Lovecraft. If I'd found this under different circumstances, I would've thought it was a joke.

*We are the IACI— the International Anti-Cataclysm Initiative,* I read. *It is our job to keep the world safe from ancient powers and magical threats. From our team of Reliquarians that handle the artifacts and relics left behind to our R&D lab that creates tools used to keep us safe in the field, we all do our part to ensure tomorrow comes.*

"This reads like a recruitment ad from the 1950s," I commented.

"That may have been intentional," Yuri said. "Though I'm not sure if it's meant to be funny or not."

I flipped the pamphlet over and saw a bunch of positions listed: the aforementioned Reliquarians, several lab jobs (research scientist, biologist, botanist, mystic botanist, alchemist, research assistant—ideally someone with medical and military experience (*Wow...*)—and technician), archaeologists, anthropologists, architects, office management, mathematicians, *oracles*? This list was intense. It was starting to make a lot more sense to me why Yuri had seemed unphased by my being a witch. I'd always assumed that my aunt and I had been part of an endangered species, one that was effectively extinct. Now I was awakening to the fact that we'd merely been on the reservation too long.

Moving on from the colored leaflet, the first page of the journal held sketches of a few different artifacts. I wasn't sure what I was actually looking at. Mezo-American? Mayan? Aztec? Olmec? I had an interest in history, but that wasn't the same as training. My instincts said Mayan. They were helpfully labelled with carefully printed words, etched in the same pencil that they were drawn with. One of the drawings was of a stele, another was a stone head, a third was some sort of plate or dish, and the last drawing was a knife.

The knife drawing drew my attention, and not because it was drawn in more detail or because it was the most dangerous looking thing on the page. As soon as my eyes landed on it, I felt another of those surges through the connection stretched between me and the mainland. It wasn't as strong as the surge I'd felt the day before, while I'd been making my way through a pile of ceviche, but it was insistent. Like a pulse. The longer I looked at the sketch, the quicker the pulse beat. I felt the thrum of it in my ears and couldn't hear anything else until the journal was pulled from my grasp.

"What? Huh?" I felt like I'd woken up from a restless sleep.

Squatting next to me, Yuri had one hand one my shoulder and the other was holding the journal down on the table. "Are you okay?"

"I'm... I'm fine... I think. What just happened?"

"Well, you got this really intense look on your face, so I asked if you saw something disturbing. You didn't say anything. You stopped breathing. I tried calling your name and shaking you awake. It wasn't until I took the book away that you even started breathing again. I know this thing isn't hexed. It's protected against that. What do you think happened?"

Blinking a few times to try and get my bearings, I shook my head. "I'm not sure. I turned the page. There was a sketch of a knife and then, this rhythm in my head... It was like a heartbeat, but it kept getting faster..."

"Have you experienced this before?" Yuri asked.

"Not exactly, but I felt something sort of like it yesterday," I told him.

He looked away from me and checked our surroundings. "I don't think this location is the most secure place to talk anymore. We've drawn a lot of attention. Do you trust me enough to walk you home?"

*This is how kidnapping movies start*, one part of my head warned me. "Should I trust you?"

The question was a trap, and we both knew it. There was no way that he could lie to me. If he said yes and it wasn't true, I would be able to tell. If he said no and it was true, that was a pretty solid hint not to let him anywhere near me. If he didn't answer at all, that was also going to be interpreted as a *hell no*. "I mean you no harm, Briar Egibi. But that's not the same as being able to guarantee your safety. If I walk you home, there could be complications. I swear I will do all in my power to keep you out of harm's way."

*True*, my power confirmed.

*Still, that wasn't exactly a yes*, my inner voice grumbled.

I told it to hush and let the nice man walk me home.

AS I WAS UNLOCKING my door, I still wasn't sure this was a great idea. Yuri and I hardly knew each other, and I was ridiculously attracted to him. Holing up in this tiny condo while I was dying to rip his shirt off with my teeth wasn't the brightest move. But he was right. We needed to talk in a safe space, one where we weren't constantly in danger of being discovered or overheard.

Walking me home after I had a public episode made way more sense than having me go back to his place, wherever that might be.

The leather journal was back in one of his many pockets. His penchant for cargo shorts made a lot more sense now that I knew he was carrying around a journal that size. He was stuck with either cargo shorts or a messenger bag. Having decided to go purse-free myself a few years back, I could appreciate the need for massive pockets. In that respect, Yuri was lucky that he was a guy. Women's pockets are a joke. Not a good one.

I walked in the moment the door was open and enjoyed the instant relief of air conditioning. There was something comforting about air conditioning, like a taste of home. Again with the homesickness!

*I haven't even been gone two full days*, I huffed at myself. *You're being ludicrous.*

Yuri hesitated at my door. For a moment I was afraid my salt wards or the innate magic of thresholds was holding him back. Was he a vampire? Was he an evil warlock? Was the only thing holding him at bay the lack of an invitation? Of course, the moment he walked in without an invitation, I felt entirely nonsensical. My cheeks blazed with embarrassment.

"This is a really nice condo," Yuri commented. His eyes lingered on the brilliant orange-red wood that made up the kitchen and found its way into so many of the living room's accents. "I may have to ask for an upgrade if they send me to Belize again. This looks like they used Jobillo."

"Jobillo?"

Yuri ran a hand over the door frame as he said, "A tropical hardwood."

"Why'd they send you to San Pedro?" I asked, not all that intrigued by the type of wood they'd used in my current residence. "It's not exactly the beating heart of the country. Wouldn't Belize City have been easier for you to get around?"

"Honestly, they didn't initially book me out here. My original location got burned, but I've still got a mission. I relocated to a less centralized base in the hopes I wouldn't be followed," Yuri said.

"But then we ran into No Name and his goons almost immediately last night," I said. "I sincerely hope they didn't follow us here. I'm not an agent. I don't have the resources to go condo-hopping all willy-nilly like that."

"Then let's get to work," Yuri's voice was solemn as he locked the door behind him. The move gave me shivers, and not the sexy kind.

I wasn't really hungry or thirsty, but I needed something to do with my hands. Dumping the used filter out of the coffee pot, I started prepping a fresh batch. "Would you like some coffee?" I offered.

"No, thank you. I never touch the stuff," Yuri said. He sat down on one of the bar stools hidden under the kitchen island and watched as I poured water and coffee grounds into the machine. I nearly tripped as his words penetrated my brain. *Who doesn't drink coffee?*

Everyone has their flaws, I guess.

"So, you said that you've been experiencing these... you called them *surges*... since you arrived in Belize? Has something like this ever happened to you before?"

That wasn't a question I really wanted to answer, but it would be dishonest to try and avoid it. "Not exactly the same, but yes, I've felt pulls and pulses and such for most of my life. The last time something was this intense, Aunt Shay died. I had to wait two hours for the call. They verified I was her niece and told me how it happened. Car accident on the highway. A semi-truck didn't see her while merging, and there'd been a pickup on her other side. The pickup held a family of four, including a toddler in a booster seat. They all survived. My aunt must've only had time for one safety spell and I'm sure she spent it on them. The mother from the pickup told me that she exchanged a look with my aunt just before it happened and felt an odd sense of calm wash over her."

A tear fell into my empty coffee mug before I even realized I was crying. This was the first time I'd gotten to tell anyone what happened in the car crash that had taken Aunt Shay away from me. I was proud of her, insanely proud. It was very like her to do something ridiculously selfless like that. But why did it mean I had to be left alone? Aunt Shay had been my only family, my only friend, for so long. I'd been completely lost and I couldn't tell anyone.

Arms wrapped around me and I felt a cheek resting against the top of my head. This close to Yuri, I was wrapped in his scent—a mixture of tea, men's body wash and... tobacco? Odd. He didn't smell of smoke at all. I hoped he didn't chew.

"I'm sorry," he said. "I didn't realize what I was asking. I'm so, so sorry."

As tempting as it was to stay within the cocoon of Yuri's embrace, I pushed back to a safer distance. If he held me that close for much longer, my body might give in to its baser desires. We had work to do. *Damn my sense of propriety.* "It's okay... Well, it's... It is what it is. That happened two years ago. Honestly, I'm just glad I finally got to tell someone."

"Your aunt sounds like an amazing woman. I would've loved to meet her," Yuri said. He was letting me go, but it felt reluctant, like he was enjoying our closeness as much as I had been.

*Try not to read into it*, I told myself. *He might be afraid you'll burst into tears again. Or, with the way things have been going, he might think you're about to spontaneously combust.*

With a deep sigh and a shake of my shoulders, I shrugged the sadness back. It wasn't totally gone, of course, but I was functional again. "Okay, so obviously it's a bad idea for me to go poking around in your journal again. We're alone here. Want to walk me through it?"

"You effectively got stuck on the first page with the drawings, right?"

"Right."

"Those drawings are potential artifacts in this area that may have awakened powers," Yuri explained. "Our team can narrow things down to a certain region, and then people like myself have to go take a look. Unless we have an oracle on staff, this step can be hit or miss for a Reliquarian like myself. I have no powers."

Deep brown liquid was starting to pool in the bottom of the coffee pot, filling the condo and all of its apparently-jobillo accents with the rich, earthy smell. Coffee soothes the spirit. I was starting to feel better already, and I hadn't even gotten around to drinking any yet. "So how did you end up as a field agent guy if you don't have any magic? Isn't this organization of yours designed to suss out power?"

"Actually, the majority of us don't have any inherent abilities. People like yourself tend to be a rarer breed, and they aren't always interested in aligning with the IACI's goals," Yuri said. "There are days that I'm not sure I wouldn't do things differently if I could, but the IACI fights against the world's end. Ultimately, that makes us the good guys."

I was pretty sure my face was red and puffy from my earlier cry, but I turned to look at Yuri anyway. He was at the edge of the kitchen island, leaning rather than sitting. It looked like he was on the verge of jumping up and hugging me again. He was watching me with those beguiling, concerned eyes. "What do you mean?"

With a deep sigh, Yuri crossed his arms and looked away. "What I mean is—the way we keep these powerful artifacts out of dangerous hands isn't by taking them to a warehouse and storing them. Sometimes, when we're lucky, we can place the relic or object with a museum or university that takes the proper sort of precautions. Some items, though, they're too dangerous. Occasionally... often... they have to be destroyed."

Wincing, I turned back to my coffee pot. Destroying something because it had too much power... I could definitely see why other witches might hesitate to join that kind of organization. While the witch trials of the past hadn't been successful at finding actual witches, the sentiment behind them was still frightening. Not to mention prevalent. People rarely liked things—or people—that they didn't understand.

"I'm suddenly second-guessing my own desire to sit in on your mission," I admitted.

"My degree is in archaeology," Yuri said. "I was top of my class in Durham."

I had no idea how impressive the name Durham was supposed to be, but he said it with the same sort of gravitas as someone name-dropping Harvard. Even if it had been a middling school, being top of the class was pretty outstanding. But then it started to sink in... An archaeologist—someone who specialized in searching out hidden relics of ancient worlds—making the call to destroy a link to the past. "Ouch."

"Ouch," Yuri agreed. "But I believe that what we do is important. So I keep accepting missions."

We both let the silence breathe for a few moments while I poured and doctored my coffee. I'd always assumed I was weird because of how comfortable I found these quiet spaces. Most people either kept talking like they couldn't let the stillness win or turned on music to drown out the tranquility. Yuri seemed as happy as I was to let the hush have its say.

The moment had to break eventually. I took a sip of my liquid support blanket and steeled myself before asking, "So what's the pay like?"

9

"YOU'RE STILL INTERESTED?" Yuri immediately brightened. "I thought for sure that was going to be a deal-breaker."

Using a universal slow-down gesture with my free hand, I said, "I believe your bosses wanted me to go on some sort of field test first. Initially, I was a little insulted that they thought I might not be good enough, given what we went through last night and this morning, but they didn't know about this morning. And I didn't know that I might have to help destroy something precious. So let's all take this one step at a time. Just to be sure, this isn't an unpaid internship, right? This temporary agent thing is more like a consultancy?"

Yuri raised an eyebrow at me.

"Business major," I said. "Plus running my aunt's coffee shop for a couple of years. You always want to know you're about to get paid for something, especially if it's dangerous."

Flipping through the pages of his journal, Yuri pointed to a number. "This is the standard offering for a temporary agent. You don't have access to our expense account, but I'm authorized to make purchases on your behalf assuming I think they're appropriate. I don't think you're the type to try and buy out a shopping center on the IACI's credit, but it wouldn't be the first time a Reliquarian misread a potential recruit."

I almost gave Yuri and his journal a coffee shower. Coffee burned my nasal passages as I choked back my beverage hard enough that it tried to escape through my nose. Not a method I recommend for experienced coffee drinkers. It took me a solid minute to get my lungs back under control.

"That... I... Where do you guys get your funding?"

Yuri laughed at that. "I've never been a member of the financial team, but as I understand it, we get some of it from the various museums and universities that house artifacts. We have some backers that did field work before they retired. We've made some wise investments, and I think a chunk of it may even come from the United Nations... Assuming our current mission goes well, and you decide to stick with us, I can arrange for you to speak with that department and ask whatever questions you have for them."

I'd been on the brink of asking about benefits, vacation, sick days, and expected duties. All of the things that I'd been primed for by my degree, really. I had my aunt's old investment firm taking care of the cash I'd pocketed from selling her business and her house. I was getting so caught up in the flow of things, I needed time to really think about this. When I'd been planning on moving to the tropics, I'd intended to hang up my barista apron and maybe pick up a cocktail shaker or tell fortunes for tourists. Something that would pass the time, cover my day-to-day spending cash, and keep me comfortably occupied. Even though the IACI's offer was more than generous, I didn't *need* that kind of money.

*It could put palaces back on the table*, my inner voice suggested.

No. I would keep an open mind while I was helping Yuri with his current mission, but I was not going to make up my mind based on numbers. Nor would I make it based on the painfully sexy man currently obstructing my exit from the kitchen. He wasn't blocking me in, but it would be a bit of a squeeze to get past him. I wasn't in that big a hurry to get away at the moment.

"How long have you worked for the IACI?" I asked.

"Since I graduated from uni," Yuri said. "I guess that means I've been with them for roughly ten years now."

"You've been globe trotting and doing this magical James Bond thing for ten years?" I didn't mean to echo him, it was just that he didn't look old enough to have ten years under his belt at a job that I knew first-hand could get very stressful. Stupid freaking No Name.

Grinning, Yuri shook his head. "No, I haven't been doing field work for that long. I started in the archaeology department. Back when they recruited me, I'd never heard the term Reliquarian. The archaeology job was pretty much what I'd dreamed of finding after leaving uni. I went on digs, did research, and went to meetings with some of the best in my field to collaborate on findings. I wrote research papers on discoveries and sent them up the chain. It didn't occur to me until I'd been with the IACI for a few years that none of my papers were being published. None of the people I was meeting with seemed to know me by reputation. As nice as it was not to fight to fund digs, I wasn't happy with the discovery that I wasn't actually getting my name out there as a member of my field. When I voiced my concerns to an older colleague who'd been with the IACI for a very long time, she laughed at me. She arranged for me to meet a Reliquarian. That was when I realized I wanted to do more than dig. It took a few years of training and tests before they let me out into the field. I've only been on this side of things for three or four years."

After hearing how long Yuri had been working to become a Reliquarian, I felt like a heel. I was on the shortlist and they hadn't even seen me in action, really. I let that sink in. Given that all I brought to the table was a meager list of powers and a business degree, I couldn't understand why I was being offered a position in the first place.

"Why am I being given preferential treatment?" I asked. I couldn't help it. I had to know if this was going to cause a rift between us at some point.

Yuri met my eyes. We stood there, in my tiny kitchen, gazing into each other's cores for what seemed like a small eternity. He'd lied to me when we first met, we'd escaped from a trap on the beach under the stars, we'd eaten together twice... There was so much about him I didn't know, so many gaps in what I'd gleaned—but I trusted him.

Damn if it didn't seem like I'd known him for centuries. This connection between us was so bizarre. I wondered if he felt it.

"I'm the reason you're getting rushed through. I asked if I could recruit you as my partner."

Well, fuck. So much for my ability not to be swayed by a pretty face. *We still have to get through his current mission, and then there's the field test,* I reminded myself. *One or both of us could change our minds before this is done.*

For a few heartbeats, I felt like the tension in the room was causing the temperature of the entire condo to rise. But then the air-conditioning kicked in and I realized the actual temperature was rising. The gust of cold air was as almost as effective as a cool shower.

"Okay," I said. I broke our eye contact and began rinsing my coffee mug. Much like making the coffee, this was more to distract my hands than anything else. I didn't have a lot of dishes piling up. It was the same mug I'd used that morning. But I needed something to redirect my attention before the air conditioning turned off. "You mentioned going to the mainland tomorrow, right?"

━━━━┼┼╟╘┼┼━━━━

AFTER YURI AND I HAD nailed down our plans for the next morning, he departed and I was left to my own devices for the rest of the day. My condo seemed awfully empty the moment Yuri walked out the door.

It was strange how easily I'd adjusted to having someone in my life again. After Aunt Shay had passed, I'd gotten used to living alone. Having to keep so much of myself hidden from other people, none of my friendships from high school or college had really stuck. I thought I was going to be alone for most of my life. I found myself thinking about Elena and how I'd asked to be her friend. She'd agreed so easily, like it wasn't a big deal. Then she'd even followed up on sending someone to keep an eye on me. I wondered how much she knew about Eddie's abilities. Given her check-in message last night, I knew Eddie hadn't called her after he'd seen me.

I didn't know much about Elena. Eddie told me she was dating his niece, so I knew she had a girlfriend. (No judgement here. I'm maybe a two on the Kinsey scale?) She obviously drove a taxi and lived in Belize. And she really liked Belize. And nails.

Rather than driving myself nuts worrying about the new friend I'd recruited on a whim the previous day, I did what most people my age would do. I started scrolling through her socials.

Elena's girlfriend, Eddie's niece, was a trans woman named Sylvia Velasquez. Sylvia was short and stocky. She had her uncle's eyes, a sharp nose and a sultry mouth. It looked like she and Elena shared a love of vibrant colors, as most of the pictures of them together were filled with splashes of red, royal blue, yellow and orange. They'd moved in together only two weeks before I got down here. First thing after their move, they'd adopted one of the cutest puppies I've ever seen. He looked like some sort of corgi-german shepherd mix. For some reason not disclosed on Elena's account, they'd decided to name the pupper, "Chicken."

Not wanting to be a weirdo cyber-stalker, I stopped myself when I got about a month and a half back. I decided the next step I needed to take with this being-a-friend thing was to suggest that we all hang out. Figuring out how I was supposed to ask was intimidating. Was I supposed to message her and say, "Hey, let's hang?" or was it supposed to be more formal? Could I admit that I'd seen pics of her dog and her girlfriend, or was that weird?

"I definitely should've paid more attention to this socializing thing when I was younger," I said as I twiddled with my paracord bracelets. Aunt Shay would've known what to say. She was always good with people. That was part of why she'd liked running a coffee shop. It had been as much about her customers as it had been about her coffee.

Finally, I decided to bite the bullet and typed out a message that read, "Your puppy is the cutest! Eddie told me you were dating his niece. We should all grab lunch or something soon." I hit send before I could stop myself.

*There you go, Aunt Shay. I'm trying.*

# 10

IT WAS FAR TOO EARLY in the morning again. What was it about being in Belize that woke me up before the sun even rose? Yuri and I were going to meet on the dock for the ferry back to Belize City at 7:45. He told me not to show up too early because Belize time tables were generally more like suggestions than hard deadlines, so a ferry that was scheduled to leave at 8:00 might not arrive until 8:15.

My morning cup of coffee used up what few supplies had been left in the condo. I would have to stop by a store before tomorrow, or I'd be an absolute beast to the first unfortunate I ran into. If my aunt hadn't dubbed me a Tacomancer, she may have described me as a coffee cultist. All hail the holy caffeine bean.

I watched the sun ignite the sky again. Instead of jumping into the shower immediately, I put on my green and white bathing suit and trotted across the sandy beach that was my front porch. I craved some sun and sand untainted by the memory of No Name reaching down for me. The waves were rougher than I'd expected, but not scary.

With the exception of my unanticipated dip the day before, the closest I'd been to the ocean was a waterpark wave pool. I was very cautious about going any deeper than my waist when the waves were at their trough. Not once but twice, the crystal blue waters seemed to reach up and slap me in the face. When I felt I'd had enough beach time, I began the trek back out of the water. The water slapped my ass on my way out. Cheeky Poseidon.

I added my green and white swimsuit to the growing load and started the machine. There was no way I could be this close to the ocean and not have a clean swimsuit. I should've bought a few more when I was making my plans. Not that it would be hard to buy some more suits here in Belize. I'd seen three or four swimwear shops when I'd met Yuri for burgers.

After my shower, I grabbed the outfit off the top of my suitcase. A black racer-back tank top with a stripe of rusty orange bleach stain across the center, kind of like a reverse tie-dye, that I paired with some army green shorts. The shirt had Sit-a-Spell Coffee's logo emblazoned across the chest in white. It was a test product I'd been experimenting with using as store merch during my two years of running things. I hadn't had much luck with the merch, but I'd been designing to my own tastes more than that of the existing clientele. Still, it was a memento of my time running a coffee shop. My usual additions of bracelets and hip drop bag, and I was good to go.

I checked my phone and realized it was almost an hour before I was due at the dock. At least there weren't any suspicious messages this morning. Elena hadn't gotten back to me yet, but I wasn't too worried at this point. My brief perusal of her feed told me that she liked to stay busy.

Given the lack of java my condo was experiencing, I decided to check out a local brew shop on the way to meet Yuri. He didn't like coffee, but maybe I could pick him up some tea or fruit juice. What was the morning equivalent of a mojito? Peppermint tea? Lime spritzer? Then again, that would be like assuming that since I loved coffees and mochas, I was a mudslide girl. (Not a good assumption. Something about coffee liqueur makes me queasy.) Best to play it by ear.

As luck would have it, there was a coffee house between the condo complex and the water taxis. I pulled on my sandals and started walking.

The line was longer than I expected at this hour but, given that the shop apparently opened at 6:00 a.m., I shouldn't have been that surprised. I grabbed myself a coconut caramel frappuccino and I picked a pineapple-banana smoothie made with coconut milk for Yuri. If he didn't like it, at least I got points for trying, right? Between the line and how long it took to make the drinks, I made it to the dock right on time.

Despite his warning not to show up too early, Yuri was already waiting for me on a bench. Today's Hawaiian shirt was bright blue with orange and yellow tiki masks and his cargo shorts were a darker tan, almost camel. I extended the smoothie toward him as he stood to greet me. "What's this?" he asked.

"Pineapple-banana smoothie with coconut milk," I said. "You said you didn't drink coffee, so I guessed based on the way you inhaled the fried plantains and pineapple salsa we had with our burgers."

For a moment, I swear I thought Yuri was going to cry. He stared at the drink and then at me for what felt like a solid minute. "You didn't have to do that," his voice seemed oddly thick.

"I didn't *have* to. But I *wanted* to," I said. "What's wrong? Has no one ever bought you a coffee substitute before?"

"No, it's not that..." Yuri said. "I just... it's weird that we recently met, you know? I've never had someone accidentally bring me my favorite smoothie before. It's not exactly the menu standard."

He was lying to me. I wasn't sure exactly what he was lying about, but I really didn't want to press him on it right now. At the same time, I didn't feel right not addressing it. Lying might be a necessity given his line of work, but he should've known better than to lie to someone he wanted to recruit as his partner. "I can tell that's not entirely true," I said. "I'm going to let it go just this once, but in the future, I'd much rather you tell me it's something you're not ready to talk about."

Yuri seemed to snap back into himself. "Right, you're right. Sorry. For a second I forgot…"

Neither of us needed to say what he'd forgotten. I wished like hell I hadn't told him I would let it go, because I was dying to ask questions. Instead, I pushed the whole thing to the back of my mind. I would prod at it later, when I was alone on my condo porch, gazing at the ocean.

I tried not to stare at Yuri's lips as they sought out the smoothie's straw. Men with full and shapely lips were definitely an understated turn on. Although, the fact that he'd lied to me again helped to keep my libido in check. Or perhaps, *barely restrained* was a better description. It had been a while since I'd liked anyone enough to sleep with them. A couple of years.

No wonder I was fighting a losing battle.

*Focus, Briar. You two are here for a reason.*

Right. We were going to Belize City to try and pick up the trail of Yuri's missing colleague. The man he'd been trying to find when our paths had first intersected and gotten tangled. "Do we have anything to go on besides his being a professor with a ransacked apartment?"

"Before you came along, I had a name and a poorly written address on a paper napkin," Yuri sighed. "This particular endeavor is one of the worst I've been on. It's like the mission itself is fighting me."

Before I could respond, 8:00 passengers were called to line up and present their tickets. The captain—Joseph—had a thick New Jersey accent. It sounded like I'd found a fellow expat. Well, okay—my status as an expat wasn't official yet. Still, if Yuri and I hadn't needed to talk about IACI stuff on the ride to Belize City, I'd be tempted to ask Joseph a few questions about the moving process. As he came into view, I couldn't help but notice that he had the longest dreads I'd ever seen. He'd wrapped the dreads into a ponytail that hung down his back and peaked out from behind his white shorts as the boat swayed. The ease with which he kept his balance on the bouncing deck spoke volumes about how long he'd been working on the ocean.

"What is it that you're hunting for down here, anyway?" I asked Yuri once we were seated. We'd managed to get seats that were close to the nose of the boat, where the wind would ensure that our conversation didn't travel to our fellow passengers. There weren't that many people onboard with us, fortunately.

"You saw the sketches yesterday," Yuri said. "It's either the stele, the knife, or the head. The contact we're looking for was supposed to give me more to go on. Mayans are a big subject and my focus was much more geared toward the early Mediterranean civilizations. Egypt, Mesopotamia, Greece, the Etruscans…"

I was trying to pay attention as Yuri talked, but his mention of the knife sketch brought the image back, as though he'd waved the page in front of my eyes. The feeling that kept pulling me toward the inner jungles tugged so hard that I thought I might get physically dragged from the boat. "The knife," I said, cutting through Yuri's explanation. "We're looking for the knife."

"You're an expert on Mayan relics?" Yuri asked.

Shaking my head, I tried to also shake off the feeling that was thrumming through my skin. "Not at all. It's my natural gift speaking to me. Every time this knife comes up, things intensify. It's like it knows…"

Yuri pulled out his journal and flipped through the pages. He pointed to a few notes jotted down like bullet points. The page read:

- *Possible blood-letting or sacrificial blade*
- *May or may not have decorative handle*
- *Recent use=awakening?*
- *Where?*

"Can you figure out any of this using your gift?" Yuri asked.

I wished we'd actually talked about some of this before boarding the boat back to the mainland. I'd figured today would consist of talking to a few students and maybe getting to see Yuri in action as a magical spy-man. Considering the page, I turned the prospect over in my head a few times. "I'm not sure," I said. "I can try."

Yuri snapped the journal shut. "I've been thinking about your abilities primarily as a lie detector, as opposed to an entire skill set," he admitted. "I'm sorry. I'm not trying to imply that you're a tool... I meant that I figured we would still have to go through certain channels, find people that knew about things... I'm not making this any better by talking longer, am I?"

Gently laying my hand on his shoulder, I gave him a reassuring squeeze to let him know I wasn't offended. It hadn't occurred to me either that we could've been doing more with my abilities. Scrying wasn't something I did very often, and I'd never had to think about my talents in active situations before. A spell to preserve the coffee beans from mildew, maybe. Glancing over my taco sauce, yes. Hard-enchantment, layered protection spells on my car after my aunt's death, certainly. But I'd never thought to find a missing person or a missing artifact before. This was new ground for me.

New, but not impossible. Belize was an excellent place to experiment with my strengths. "I'm not promising results or anything, but I may have a few ideas."

"IS THIS HOW THIS IS normally done?" Yuri asked.

Immediately after we'd disembarked from the water taxi, I'd pulled him along with me into one of the dozens of stores lining the port. Like those around it, this shop was largely stocked with kitschy tourist paraphernalia. A few t-shirt racks and even more shelves held Belizean merchandise of all sorts. Bags, jackets, shirts, magnets, maps, postcards, scarves, hats, wood-workings... If a tourist could want it, these stores were determined to provide it.

Unlike the stores flanking it on either side or across, this one held a full display of what I was after right next to their open door. Shelves upon shelves were devoted to Belize's best known brand of hot sauce, in all kinds of sizes and flavors. Upon entering, Yuri was practically tackled by the shop proprietor—Angelina. She'd shoved a handbasket at him while saying, "Yes, thank you," repeatedly.

I was currently debating between a smokey habanero sauce and a mango habanero sauce before I grabbed both and plopped them in the basket.

"Normally, no," I said. "This is just how I do things."

I'd never had the chance to experiment with a variety of sauces before. Would pineapple or mango make my readings more accurate? Or could the smokiness of the habanero make it better for scrying than its original flavor counterpart? I wasn't going to go nuts in here and buy all the biggest bottles of every flavor available while the IACI was footing the bill, but I was more than willing to take advantage of the sign that told me four bottles for ten dollars, while individual bottles were marked at three-fifty. Yes, I was spending more than strictly necessary, but more sauce, yo.

I can't pull off yo.

Maybe one bottle of the extra hot wouldn't hurt. But five was as far as I was willing to push the IACI's generosity with my little experiment.

After I made my hot sauce selections, I grabbed a couple of maps of Belize—one was a modern map with a Belize City inset, and another was a map of ancient Belize with the locations of known Mayan sites and cities. While Angelina wrapped the glass bottles into thick sheets of paper and Yuri paid, I walked outside the store to look around and see if I could spot a taco stand or restaurant. It was still a bit early in the day for lunch, but I really wanted to test this out on a known medium before I started ruining the maps we'd recently bought.

"Do you mind telling me why we purchased five bottles of hot sauce?" Yuri said as he handed me the bag of supplies.

"My abilities have always been a bit... unusual. Even for what I am," I said. "My aunt tried to teach me how to read tea leaves, and it never worked for me. But when I got to be a teenager, I decided to try something different."

"Hot sauce," Yuri said, comprehension flaring in his eyes.

"Hot sauce," I agreed. "My aunt started calling me a Tacomancer."

"The Tacomancer and the Reliquarian. We sound like a wrestling tag team."

I laughed as we started walking farther into town. "You're not wrong."

When Elena first escorted me to the water taxis, I hadn't been paying as much attention to my surroundings as I was today. She'd rushed through like the local that she was, and I'd been daydreaming about my date with Yuri. I hadn't noticed that the shopping section of the port was so vast. Every time Yuri and I turned a corner, we encountered another row of shops very similar to the one I'd jumped into first. "It's like we've entered the Belizean Labyrinth."

"Do you think they have a minotaur?" Yuri asked.

"Maybe, but if so, I'd imagine they'd have trained him to be appeased by the sight of shopping bags." I held up our purchases as though to demonstrate that we had a powerful minotaur-stopping charm. "We should be alright."

"Remind me to hide behind you at the first sight of anything with horns," Yuri grinned.

This was nice. Things felt so natural with Yuri that I forgot, for just a second, that we were trying to find some dangerous artifact before some genuinely scary people could get their hands on it. Of course, my moment of inattention was when we turned a corner and ran right into Alex Smith.

# 11

IT BEARS SOME EXPLANATION as to how, with a name as generic as Alex Smith, I immediately recognized this person as the same Alex Smith I'd seen on the beach. My name sense isn't exactly like sound, but it's close. If you were to put a bunch of people in a line and have them all say the same name, no two people would pronounce that name the exact same way. Some would emphasize the first letter, some would enunciate every syllable, while others would rush through it to get things over with as fast as possible. Kinda like signature analysis paired with voice recognition, though that's not a perfect simile. But with most people, their name is one of the most solid things about them. Alex Smith's name was smooth and pliable—like if he wanted to, he could bend it like wire to become something else.

Without No Name looming in front of me, eating the majority of my awareness, I couldn't miss how unnatural Alex Smith's name felt. That was much more recognizable than a tall silhouette on a dark beach.

He and I slammed into each other full speed at the corner intersection. We both took a tumble. My shopping bag bounced over the ground, the hot sauce bottles cushioned by their tightly wrapped layers of paper. A part of me started taking in Alex's features, now that I could see him in the daylight—slightly tan, with a strong Aquiline nose, and razor thin lips. His hair was brown, but cut so close to the scalp it was hard to tell. It looked like a buzz cut that was only beginning to grow out. Despite the heat, this guy was wearing a full, cream colored suit over a pressed blue shirt. The shirt matched his eyes. Oddly, I felt like people would've confused him for my brother if we stood side-by-side for long enough.

*I don't think our minotaur-charm worked.* The thought ran through my head as I fought the fear building up in my chest. A snort escaped me. Perfect timing for me to go giddy.

Yuri didn't seem to recognize the man from the night on the beach at all. He helped me up and then began offering apologies as he bent to retrieve the escaped sauces. I wanted to scream. I wanted to tell Yuri to run. I wanted the light path to magically encompass us again so Alex Smith wouldn't be able to catch us.

If Alex had been laying in wait for us there's no way we would've managed to get away from him, but he seemed as surprised to see us as I'd been to recognize him. Possibly, he was shocked someone had managed to knock him over. As soon as he was on his feet again, he regained the graceful, dancer-like poise I'd noticed the last time we'd crossed paths. It was too late for him to try anything though, as our tumble had attracted the attention of an armed guard and several shop owners.

His eyes narrowed in recognition. Our audience had him visibly biting his tongue as he restrained himself from whatever he wanted to say or do. With an irritated shake of his head, Alex Smith continued on his way, clipping me with his shoulder as he went. As he shoved past me, he hissed into my ear, close enough that I could feel the heat of his breath crawl over my skin, "Next time, watch your step."

I shuddered and reached for Yuri's arm, hardly aware I was doing it. The moment my hands fell on him, I felt tears start to form though I couldn't have said why I was crying. Something about Alex Smith was almost as upsetting to me as No Name. I ached all over, far more than I thought possible from such a minor collision.

"Are you okay?" Yuri asked. I noticed he was ushering me toward a bench on one edge of the walkway, keeping us both under the watchful gazes of our protective audience. Good. I didn't want to run into Alex Smith now that he was ready for us.

"Yuri, that was one of the guys from the beach the other night," I said. I slumped against the bench with a shudder.

He made a show of checking me over for bumps and scrapes, prolonging the interest we'd generated for as long as possible. While there was still the chance to see an injury, people lingered in shop doors and walked past us much more slowly than normal. Bending in close enough we could've kissed if I leaned forward a little, Yuri asked softly, "Which one?"

"Alex Smith," I told him. My own voice was barely above a whisper. I yearned to close that gap, to merge our mouths and see if the taste of pineapple smoothie still lingered on his tongue. The more sensible side of me remained in control, convinced there were more important things to be focused on at the moment. Qualifying rounds for the mattress olympics would have to wait. *Uuurgh...*

"*Fuck...*" Yuri swore, ducking his head and breaking the spell his nearness had cast. I shivered as my libido, rallying forces to bridge the gap between our bodies, was forcibly overruled. Not the time.

My throat went dry as Yuri stood up and took my hand to haul me off the bench. I could tell he'd gone to his mind palace. He was both here and not. I didn't know whether he was reliving something in a memory or thinking through IACI stuff that I was not yet privy too, but I felt very left out as a potential partner. He started to drag me down another tunnel in the portside labyrinth. Tugging back, but not quite pulling away, I tried to get his mind to return to the present. "What is it? What's wrong?"

For a moment, as his lips tightened with frustration and a hint of anger, I thought he wasn't going to answer me. Hell, I was afraid that he'd turn and leave me there. I wasn't sure if I'd said or done something wrong, but I was more afraid of Yuri abandoning me than I was of being alone with Alex Smith.

"I... can't talk about it here," Yuri said finally. "When we get somewhere safe, I'll explain. But not here."

I nodded and let him continue to pull me through the stores until we emerged into the unobstructed sunshine on the other side of the port center. I wasn't sure when the aches had subsided, but they'd evaporated completely by the time we left the labyrinth.

"YOU'RE NOT MY FIRST partner," Yuri said as we hid in a booth at a bar. The sandwich board outside had promised tacos. We ordered drinks at the bar the moment we'd arrived in the hopes that we wouldn't be bothered by any servers for a while. Fortunately, it wasn't the busy season for tourism. There were plenty of people scattered amongst the wooden tables in this bar and grill, but we weren't in danger of getting asked to move on as long as we continued to order. Our table was in the corner closest to the bathrooms, where we had a pretty good view of both the kitchen and the patio. Since the windows were completely open to let in the trade winds, there was only so much we could do for security. It seemed to be enough for Yuri. "Or, well, not we're partners quite yet... But you should know, you're not the first. My last partner, Kailey Callahan, was a *force*. She could bench fifteen stone. I can't bench fifteen stone. Hell, I can barely bench seven, and I whimpered the whole time. I think I pulled something. Not to say I'm a pushover, but lifting is—"

"Yuri..."

"Right, sorry. Suffice to say, Kailey could deal with most problems by punching them or threatening to punch them. She was beyond sweet, though. It seemed like she took a genuine interest in everyone that she met. We worked really well together until..."

Yuri had shrugged off his Hawaiian shirt and we'd both grabbed hats on our way here—his was a faded purple ball cap with a yellow sea turtle and *Belize* embroidered in lime green, while mine was a black straw hat with a rainbow of tassels around the band. I'd twisted my braid up onto the top of my head so my hair would look shorter. Short of heading back to San Pedro, which would mean giving up on our goals for the day, this was as safe as we were likely to get.

"Until?" I asked as delicately as I could.

"The lines blurred. We became... more than partners," Yuri sighed. "Our mission was in the Steppes of Mongolia. We went out to recover a sarcophagus with another agent. Something went wrong. A *lot* of somethings, actually. Kailey and the second agent both went rogue. The other agent, his name was Alex Smith and he was a warlock."

I felt a chill of foreboding that I couldn't rationalize. Of course I'd heard the term warlock before. Just because a lot of books and movies get shit wrong doesn't mean they're not fun to indulge in. This was the first time I'd heard someone say it like that, though. My entire body was confirming the *truth* behind Yuri's words.

"Kailey asked me to come with her. I refused. It got ugly. She told me that I wasn't the only one she was involved with, and I called her some things that I'm not proud of. Kailey told me to grow up. I'd imagined that we were in love... The sarcophagus, Kailey, and Alex Smith were gone the next morning when the retrieval team found my ass knocked out with a charm around my neck, handcuffed in a closet. I still don't know which of them took the object or if they were a team."

I swallowed, trying to calm the growing lump of fear nestled in the back of my throat. "I'm familiar with the dictionary definition, but I get the feeling that's about as accurate as what it says about witches. What's a warlock?"

"In this sense, it means he wasn't born with powers, but he acquired them through... questionable sources," Yuri said. "He was a very able Reliquarian though, and no one questioned his dedication to the IACI. Not until what happened in Mongolia, anyway."

I chewed on that mentally for a few minutes. "If you worked with this guy in the past, why didn't you recognize him back at the port when he knocked me over?"

"That's a very good question, but the thing is..." Yuri rubbed the back of his neck, embarrassment written in every line of his face. He squeezed his eyes shut and said the next part in such a rush it took me a few seconds to parse it all out. "I never actually met Alex Smith. All of our contact with him ran through Kailey. I was the fresh, young rookie on the trip, so I didn't even think to wonder about that at the time. Honestly, if there was a rule against it in the books, I probably broke it during my Mongolia mission."

There was a lot to unpack in this story. I found myself curious how much clout Yuri actually had with his organization with a screw up like that on his record. Then again, I'd seen the pamphlet. As desperate as the International Anti-Cataclysm Initiative seemed for Reliquarians, they probably made room for a mistake or two. Or perhaps most mistakes of that nature were weeded out a lot more lethally, so they were impressed with his survival? I had so many more questions, but I didn't want to grill Yuri. *Tread delicately*, I told myself.

"So... the lines blurred," I prompted.

Yuri stayed quiet. This wasn't going to be a fun question.

"Partners in the IACI aren't supposed to get romantic, are they?" I asked.

"No," Yuri said. He wasn't looking at me. "They are not."

I was right. That wasn't fun. Fuck. *Fuck.*

Our glasses were only sweating slightly more than Yuri had been while he talked about his history in Mongolia. I grabbed mine and downed half the contents, wishing that it had been something with a tad more punch, but this early in the day I'd ordered a lemonade. It was more tart than I enjoyed my lemonade, but still this side of palatable. Yuri hadn't told me he wasn't into me, but he'd definitely taken a relationship off the table. If we were going to work together. And we were working together. I'd promised to help him with his mission. "If this is the former Alex Smith from IACI, do you think Kailey's down here somewhere?"

"It's possible," Yuri conceded. He leaned back in the booth and propped one leg on my seat. If I couldn't hear the tension in his voice, I would've thought he was completely relaxed. "The two of them being down here together would explain how I got spotted so quickly... I can't imagine what Kailey is doing with a team like that though. When she was trying to get me to join her, she said she wanted to show the IACI there was a better way to do things. You said No Name was a demigod, right?"

"Something like that." This was no good. I was dwelling on the bomb he'd dropped on my daydreams, not on the task at hand. If I couldn't focus on my readings, the results would be all over the place.

"I've gotta ask... Why do you want me to be your partner anyway? I've never done anything close to this in my life. If you have zero interest in me, that's one thing, but I thought we..." I trailed off, unable to finish the sentence. *Had something* was too cliche. While I could've said *shared a connection*, I didn't. We had one, but that didn't make it anything romantic.

"Because I trust you," Yuri said. For the first time since he'd started talking about Mongolia, he met my eyes. "I didn't want to. I haven't wanted to trust anyone since that job in Mongolia. But I do."

*Well, when you put it like that...* I thought. Now I felt like a jerk. "Oh."

"I'm sorry I put you through all of this. I can clear up the paperwork, and you'll still get a payment for what you've already helped me with," Yuri said. His shoulders sagged as he projected the essence of a wounded puppy. I was such a jerk. "I can be out of your life entirely in only a few days."

"Don't," I said. "I promised I was gonna help you. Nothing has changed that. As for the rest..." With a deep sigh that I blew out through my nose, I got to my feet and offered him a weak smile. "We'll figure that out later. Now is the time for tacos."

# 12

TRYING TO FOCUS ON anything at this point felt pretty futile, but I'd learned to read hot sauce while I was in middle school. If I could read portents during the ugly days of adolescence, my recent disappointment was not going to stop me. I ordered six tacos, all fish, just to make sure it wouldn't stop me. Besides, Yuri could probably eat half.

We didn't talk much while waiting for the tacos to be brought to the table. I'd brought back a margarita and a mojito after ordering the food, hoping the alcohol would take some of the edge off our earlier conversation. At least Yuri had perked up after I'd told him I'd continue helping him. Still, this silence was not as comfortable a shared moment as a lot of our other quiet times had been.

Food arrived in the nick of time, saving us from attempts to fill the awkwardness with conversation.

"Aunt Shay's the only person I've had watch me do this," I said as I reached into the shopping bag and began peeling away the protective paper on one of my new sauce bottles.

"Do you need me to look away?" Yuri offered. He turned in his seat and made a show of looking at the other diners. "I could look over there, at the couple with the noisy child. Or I could look at the two men with matching watches. I could stare at the people working in the kitchen as they make food and make them think something's wrong..."

Despite myself, I laughed. "You're such a goof... It's okay. You can watch if you want."

The weirdness between us wasn't entirely dispelled, but things felt better after that. As much as I wanted to stay hurt and disappointed because I'd been rejected, it wasn't quite true. Yuri hadn't told me he didn't feel anything. He'd put us on this course because he'd felt something pretty damn strong. Viewed in that light, it was kind of flattering.

Okay, I was still disappointed. My crush was firmly locked in place and it didn't want to be ousted because of a little thing like IACI dating policies. Or past relationships that made those regulations necessary. But it was manageable.

"First, I usually do a general reading to get in the right mind set," I explained as I yanked at the plastic that sealed the cap. I'd managed to unwrap the extra hot first. I wasn't sure if that signified that it was going to be the best for my needs, or if I'd been the most excited to try that one. Either way, extra hot hot sauce!

It was hard to unfocus my eyes with Yuri sitting across the table from me, so I closed them, trusting to my witchy senses not to miss the taco I was aiming for. Pouring sauce from a bottle is a lot trickier than working with a sauce packet. Ultimately, I have to trust that my wrist is going to be at the correct angle, that the sauce is going to fall in dribbles instead of gushing, and that however much ends up on the taco is going to be edible without a gallon of milk handy.

When I opened my eyes, I saw that the Belizean stuff worked even better than my usual sauce packets. *Danger, adventure, heartbreak, renewal, bonds, strength, open to possibilities*—all of which tracked well with my current situation. I usually only got three to four signs per taco. Six was practically a record. "I think we're done calibrating."

"Find out anything interesting?" he asked. He pushed another taco toward me, already open the same way that I'd arranged my first one.

"Nothing new," I said. "Okay, this one... I'm going to try and focus on news about your missing professor. What's his name?"

"Professor Phoenix Gentle."

Again, I closed my eyes and tilted my wrist to what felt like the proper angle. My thoughts were on an address I'd only seen once and a name I'd never heard before. There wasn't much to go on. But that was why we were doing this in the first place.

My hand jerked, like someone else had grabbed onto it. That had never happened before. I resisted and the feeling got stronger. A person started to form in my mind. A short, balding man with a beard. His nose was stubby and even with the beard, it was obvious that he didn't have much in the way of a jawline. What hair he still had was baby powder white and stood out all the more against his burnished gold skin. I could see him standing at the front of a lecture hall, drawing out rough Mezoamerican hieroglyphics on a whiteboard. He wore khakis and a leaf green polo shirt, as though he wanted to carry a bit of the jungle with him into the room. Emotions crashed over me as I saw this inner image of who he was—regret, longing, sadness, pain. A wish that he'd never left his classroom. *"Please... Let me go..."*

My eyes flew open and I looked down at the taco. Only one symbol gazed back at me. If I could've, I would've jumped away from the table. As it was, I slammed my back up against the booth's backrest. "Shit," I breathed. "Fucking shit..."

"What is it?" Yuri asked. He was reaching for my hand but I didn't really want to touch him right now. It was too much. I wanted to accept his comfort, to have him wrap me in a big bearhug and not let go until the shaking stopped. But not this soon after he'd drawn the lines for us, and not after what I'd just seen. More than anything I wanted to run away. I wanted to take the blue pill and go back to my first night in Belize. There was always a part of me that had known this was dangerous, but I'd gotten through everything unscathed so far. No one had gotten hurt. It almost felt like a game.

Up until I saw the symbol of death staring at me from my taco and heard the last whisper of a dying man.

"He's dead, Yuri. Professor Phoenix Gentle is dead. Someone took him off your path," my voice was quivering. I could feel tears threatening to climb up out of my throat. This was all real. None of it was a game. People would kill us. We'd been lucky so far, but that was it. Luck. If we weren't careful, our luck would run out.

"Damn," Yuri's tone was so soft that I barely heard him. He took off his glasses and rubbed at his eyes. "Damn, damn, damn."

As conflicted as I felt about everything, I reached out and took Yuri's hand, setting his glasses safely away from the taco plates. This contact wasn't about romance, it was about being human together in a moment of loss. We didn't know the professor. He hadn't known us. That didn't matter right now. A life had ended too early, and we were both acutely aware of the danger this man's death signified. At least, I hoped that was what was going through Yuri's mind.

Making assumptions was a perilous business.

After a few moments of silence, we collected ourselves. While it was too late to save Professor Gentle, I still had four tacos and the maps to try and make a little more headway into our investigation. My enthusiasm for this idea had waned significantly after the previous taco, however. "I don't even know where to start."

"I know what you're going through right now," Yuri said. His hand was still in mine and he started brushing his thumb over my knuckles in an absent-minded way that didn't stay on the right side of the comfort-romance line for me. After an internal struggle with the part of my being that was still in full crush, I withdrew from his fingers and their gentle strokes. "I mean, not exactly... But I've lost contacts and colleagues before. Contacts are worse, somehow.

They're civilians. They haven't trained for this. No mental preparation, no choices, simply responding to the wrong email or query."

"Got into the wrong cab." I meant for it to sound more glib, but there was some truth to the way it came out. A little harsh, a little remorseful. I winced when I heard it out loud, but I didn't try to take it back.

The look on Yuri's face made me wish I'd kept my mouth shut. He was hurt. I'd stung him with that. "I can't say that I blame you. I meant what I said earlier. I'll absolve you from all of this if that's your wish. You'll get paid, and never hear from any of us again. I will do everything I can to make sure that you're safe and then I'll go."

*This margarita is* not *strong enough*, I thought as the deepest sigh I could make filled my lungs with air and rushed out of my nose. "No," I said. "I don't want out. I want to stop this. I don't want the people that killed Professor Gentle to walk away with a weapon that will help them kill more people. It just hit me all at once how high the stakes really are. I'm used to the stakes of doing a bad job resulting in someone not being happy with their coffee for a morning."

The two men with matching watches got up and left their table, chatting companionably about how they were going to spend the rest of their afternoon doing yoga and hiking. I'd made a similar list of things to do down here when I was originally making my plans, but something had changed in the last three days. Listening to two strangers chat about extremely mundane activities didn't instill me with a sense of longing. It sounded dull. Yoga in Belize was not really any different than yoga in Kansas. It just came with a better view.

"This job changes you, doesn't it?" I asked. It was only partially rhetorical. "Things don't go back to normal once you've started doing this."

"No, they don't," Yuri said. I glanced at him and saw him watching the men leave, too. His expression was wistful.

"Do you regret it?"

For a long moment, I thought Yuri wasn't going to answer me. He took a polishing cloth out of one of his numerous pockets and gave his glasses a quick wipe before setting them back into place. "Sometimes. I sometimes miss things being simple. I miss office parties. I miss traveling for pleasure. I miss being able to tell my family what I do for a living. Even chatting with strangers is different now."

I couldn't help laughing. It wasn't much of a laugh, given the circumstances. Just a rough chuckle that bubbled out of my throat. "I don't think chatting with strangers has ever been normal for me."

Those dimples reappeared as Yuri flashed me a quick smile. "No, I guess it wouldn't be. Honestly, we're not missing much with the office parties either. Stale, store-bought cake and weak tea."

My god, those dimples.

To distract myself from Yuri, and make the death symbol stop looking at me, I closed the tortilla over the sauce and took a bite. It wasn't bad for a death taco. We'd taken enough time talking that the fish was getting tepid, but it was coated with some sort of spicy-sweet seasoning that had caramelized on the surface. Eaten fresh, it would've been outstanding. The extra hot hot sauce was bringing a touch more heat than I wanted, but I wasn't about to breathe fire. Yet.

Whether he was hungry or trying to fit in by actually eating something at a bar and grill, Yuri snagged the other sauced taco and bit into it. "You reacted poorly just looking at a picture of potential relics," Yuri said. He gazed at the remainder of his taco for a bit, as though he was trying to divine some answers himself. "Is it really a good idea for us to do this for more information on what we're seeking? Do you think you can handle it?"

It was a fair question. Even before the death taco, I'd had some doubts. I had calmed down a lot considering that my primary tool as a witch, the thing I'd always excelled at, had thrown an unexpected gut punch. Factoring in the weird pulses from the interior of the country, my episode with the knife sketch at the burger place, practically draining myself at the beach... I was feeling kinda off my witchy game recently.

I took a deep breath and nodded. If I could find anything that helped us locate what we were looking for, maybe I could prevent another Professor Gentle from disappearing. That final *"Please..."* would likely haunt me for years. It had been so full of resignation and pain. The image I'd seen of him in the classroom, it had been his passion. His favorite place. The thing that Professor Gentle used to define himself. He loved teaching. The Mayans had been his subject of choice, but I'd gotten the impression that the classroom was even more important than his sketched hieroglyphs. "I'll manage."

Yuri studied me as intently as he had his taco. As he pushed a third taco my way, he said, "I can't tell when you're lying the way you can read me, so I'm trusting you to be able to do this."

I took the sauce bottle in my hand and closed my eyes, finding the position that felt right. *This one's for you, Professor Phoenix Gentle*, I thought. Then I pushed it away and let the picture of the ancient chipped-obsidian knife fill my mind.

# 13

I WAS NO LONGER SEEING through my own eyes. No longer seated across from Yuri in a booth. No longer in a bar in Belize City. I was standing on a trail of worn rock. Trees lurked on a ridge above me and a disconcerting amount of sunny sky left my right side completely unshielded. The path curved up the side of a mountain, while the bowl of the sky on my right led down to a canopy of trees, far enough below my current position that the leaves looked like an unending carpet. Bird song and monkey cries echoed through a world that seemed untouched by time. Unless I had teleported into the jungle in the last five seconds—somehow coming out on the other side wearing flamboyant boho pants, a leather halter top and a crochet shirt that probably could've doubled as a fishing net in a pinch—this was someone else's head. *Laura.* Several inches taller, too, and I could see blonde bangs hanging annoyingly over my eyes.

*Never had this happen before*, I thought. A dizziness brought on by panic threatened to overwhelm me and throw me straight back out of wherever I'd found myself. Then I remembered Professor Gentle again. I could do this. Whatever this was.

On the path in front of me, I could see a bearded guy, *Todd,* that had some very wavy, auburn hair that rivaled my current blonde tresses for length. He was wearing a white button down shirt, baring most of his tawny chest hair and russett bell bottoms. If I had to guess his age, I'd peg him as somewhere in his mid-twenties. Probably younger than my normal Briar Egibi self. Laura's hand reached out to steady herself on the side that hugged the hill and I saw henna trailing up the side of her arm. Neither Laura nor Todd seemed to be holding anything electronic, and there was an authenticity to the way both of them wore the dated clothing that I was pretty sure I was mentally visiting the 1970s.

*Are we hippies?*

"C'mon, Willow! We're almost there! I can see it!" Todd was grinning at me, or rather, at Laura.

"I'm coming, Falcon!" Laura said. *We are, indeed, hippies.* "I can't believe we're out here! Are you sure it's cool that we blew off that tour guide?"

"People duck out of these things all the time. If we're gonna get back to nature, we can't let the Man keep us out of the trees. Ya dig, baby?"

Laura giggled in response and took Todd's hand. I found it odd that I could sense their real names instead of those they'd chosen to go by. Normally, even if it's a nickname, I get the name that someone truly thinks defines them. These two seemed unlikely to be hold-overs into the next generation. What any of this had to do with the knife I was attempting to scry for, I hadn't the slightest.

"Mmm, this could be like our own private Eden, baby. I think we could have a groovy good time right here," Todd leaned into Laura's hair and started kissing through it into the side of her neck. Laura giggled while I became decidedly less comfortable with the entire situation. *Please, please, pleeeeease, don't have a groovy time while I'm in here.*

Todd started to run his hands over Laura's back through her barely-there shirt. I had no control over Laura's limbs and she was entirely into Todd and the idea of being his Eve on the side of this cliff. She was starting to unbutton his shirt. I was strictly here in a viewing capacity. Ugh. I would need to spend a solid week in the shower if this went much further.

I was much more relieved than the two I was spying on when a sound came from a nearby bush.

"What was that?" Laura asked. She'd gone from enjoying the moment to instantly tense. Todd was urging her to turn back toward him so he could kiss her mouth, but she and I were frozen in place.

"C'mon, baby, it's probably just a monkey. Don't go harshing my mellow for something that's just a part of nature," Todd said. He pulled on Laura's arm, coaxing her with soft murmurs about her beauty.

"Stop it, Falcon. Something's wrong," Laura said. She was tense before, but now she was scared. I wondered if she had a gift of precognition or if I'd missed something by trying not to pay attention to the make out session.

A man jumped out of the brush—*Arthur.* There was no telling when or how or why Arthur had come out here. He had the look of someone that had gone a long time without food, water, company or a bath. His clothes looked like they'd started out as hardy expedition wear, maybe even military—there were still a few tattered pockets visible on what had been his shirt. The pants were jagged at the bottoms, and his left leg held an oozing gash that must've hurt like hell. Long matted hair, so dirty and unkempt that I couldn't tell its original color, surrounded his head like a helmet, tangling into his beard so that his only visible facial feature was a set of eyes that looked on into a well of madness. Laura, taking me with her, jumped away from her would-be lover and huddled against the ridge Arthur had descended from. Arthur's crazed eyes fell on Todd and the madman leapt on the hippy with a savage scream, brandishing a glistening piece of obsidian.

I could feel the presence behind that knife. It recognized me, too. Despite the decades between us, it was *aware* of me. It wanted me to see what it could do.

Volcanic glass bit into Todd's collarbone with a spurt of blood that looked like it should have been in a horror movie. Todd cried out in pain and grabbed ahold of Arthur's arms, trying to free himself from his attacker. I could feel Laura's scream ripping its way out of my own throat. Todd, Arthur, and the knife all took a tumble over the cliff, leaving Laura emotionally scarred, but physically unharmed, on the edge of a mountain.

She picked herself up from the dirt and looked down the near-vertical slope, tears streaming down her cheeks and her arms wrapped around her own torso, as she tried to find the bodies of the two men through the blanket formed by the canopy. I couldn't blame her for shaking. I wanted to stay with her until she calmed down, even though she couldn't tell I was there.

I fought off the ending of my vision for as long as I could. My head was filled with questions about whether Laura made it back to civilization and where the entire scene had taken place. One thing was certain, though. That flash of obsidian that had driven itself into Todd's flesh... That was our missing object of power.

WE WEREN'T AT THE BAR and grill. I was laying on a couch in an oddly familiar room I'd never been in before. At first, I was scared that I'd body-hopped again and this was going to turn into a Quantum Leap situation. The panic subsided pretty quickly as soon as I felt the paracord bracelets snapped around my wrist and noticed I was dressed in my own clothes.

As my heart rate slowed, I settled into myself again. My own body had a very familiar, lived-in feel, and I was more aware of my own scent. I hadn't really noticed until I was out of the scry, but Laura had smelled of patchouli and lavender. I smelled like strawberries, coconut and mint—basically a mixture of my bodywash and shampoo. It was good to be back.

My personal scent was soon overwhelmed by that of my current location. Where had I returned to? Somewhere with a dog—that was obvious given the unmistakable scent of canine urine and disinfectant spray.

The big, purple couch I'd been draped over had a soft blue throw blanket tossed over the arm. I propped myself up on my elbows to take a better look at my surroundings. A Belize City map with a red frame hung on the wall above me. An aqua, blue, and purple woven area rug swam out from beneath the sofa, over the white tile floor. A wicker sitting chair with orange cushions was placed out of the way of a partially-open glass sliding door. The incoming wind was doing what it could to dispel the doggy odor. I could see some patio furniture out there, but it didn't look like anyone was sitting in it. On the wall opposite me, a modestly sized television sat dormant next to a shelf filled with movies, video games, and three different gaming systems. Nice.

While the sitting area stopped, the room kept going. Open concept. Five chairs, all of which looked like they'd been acquired at thrift shops or yard sales, had been reupholstered with the same yellow and white the palm leaf fabric so their seats would match. They surrounded a circular dining table. My hat rested in the middle of the table like a centerpiece. An artwork clock and a framed Belize poster hung on the wall in the dining room area. The kitchen loomed at the far end of the apartment, all white cabinets and beige granite. Except for the sea blue backsplash, the kitchen looked like it belonged in a different apartment.

As the bold colors and competing styles began to click into place, the source of the doggy odors scrambled out of a hallway, clickety-clacking his nails across the floor, and lunged onto my lap. My face apparently looked like an ice cream cone, because it was immediately covered with enthusiastic licks.

"Nice to meet you, too, Chicken," I laughed as he tried to squirm his way past my restraining hand. He was happy I was giving him scritches, but not happy enough to stop trying to give me more pup-py kisses.

"Chicken, you behave. Gyal, weh do you?" Elena came into the room from the same hallway that Chicken had barrelled out of. Her hair was up in another bun. Wearing a bright pink top with darker pink floral embroidery worked onto the shoulders and blue shorts covered with dots of pink, orange, green and yellow, she was the embodiment of a living firework. Her nails were bright yellow with purple tips. She was scowling at me, but not like she was mad at me. It was more like the look my aunt used to give me when I'd lied to her. As though to say, *We both know I can see straight through you, so why even try?*

"I'm sorry... What?" I asked. I wanted to answer her, but I wasn't even sure what her question had been.

She shut her eyes and leaned back with a bit of a sigh. "It's kinda Creole-Beliezean slang. What I mean is, what's going on with you? I get your message that you want to hang out, but next day, I find you passed out in a restaurant with the same man I warned you on from day one."

"Where is Yuri, anyway?" I asked. "And how did I end up here?"

"That man..." the way Elena said those two words spoke volumes of her disdain for Yuri. Somehow, during only two interactions, he'd managed to get on her shit list. I wondered if he'd said something while I was busy watching a hippy couple get jumped by a mad man. "He accompanied you here, carried you in, put you on my couch, then said he had an errand to run. Sylvia took him out in my car, because I didn't want you to wake up in a strange apartment all by yourself. Now, tell me what's happening."

I wasn't sure what I was supposed to say. The IACI seemed pretty secretive. Then there was Professor Gentle, who'd died because people didn't want Yuri to meet with him. What if Elena had put herself in danger by taking me into her home? What if I'd put her, Sylvia, and Chicken into danger because I wanted to make a friend?

Shit.

If I'd had the three years of Reliquarian training, maybe I'd be prepared for this sort of thing. There was no helping it, though. With Yuri gone, and no one save a fiercely wagging puppy between me and Elena's gaze, I had to make the call on what to tell her.

I opted for the truth. All of it. Well, most of it. I kept out the IACI's name and the more magical aspects of Eddie's role.

It wasn't the smartest thing I could've done. My potential job was, in all likelihood, over the moment I decided to open my mouth. But I couldn't look Elena in the eye and lie about what she'd taken into her home and put on her couch. She needed to know the dangers and risks involved. I wanted her to protect her home and her family. Chicken deserved a long, happy, tail-wagging life.

For her part, Elena asked very few questions. Her gaze left my face and landed on Chicken, who'd stopped demanding attention for a few milliseconds to romp in circles as he pursued his own tail. Even his limitless puppy energy wore down and he curled into a ball on the rug.

"So you're being recruited by this mysterious agency because you were born with special abilities, and you're looking for some sort of magic knife out in the jungle?" Elena summed up my entire story in one question.

"Yes," I said.

We were both quiet after that. I'm not sure if that silence lasted for only a few seconds or if it lasted for a few years. I couldn't imagine what was going through Elena's head. There wasn't anything to prepare me for what she was about to say.

"Get out."

I blinked at her as though I hadn't understood her. As though she'd spoken in Creole again. "What?"

"You claim you want my friendship on your first day in town, but I know this for what it is now. You want my help, but you're just out to use me and my resources. Maybe you hoped for some free fairs or something. I take you into my home after finding you unconscious at a bar with a man you barely know and when I ask for an explanation, you think you gonna be a big woman and feed me some lies. This is how an American treats their host, is it? I don't have to open the door for you. You're gonna leave, and I'm gonna block you on my socials. I don't have time for liars."

"But..." I started to protest that I wasn't lying. I'd really wanted to make a friend, only to have a complicated mess of a situation blow up around me. But somehow, knowing that I'd been telling the truth, I felt worse. I'd knowingly pursued getting to know her despite the caution Yuri had taken in all of our meetings. Elena could throw me out because she thought I was a liar, or she could throw me out because I'd knowingly endangered her. Either way, I didn't deserve to be here. I closed my mouth and got up.

Chicken woke up as I stood. I grabbed my hat and walked toward the door. He stayed in his spot and gazed at me with raised eyebrows, as though he were asking what I'd done to make his mama so mad. I wished I could explain it to him.

With my hand still on the door knob, I realized there was one thing I could do to make amends for my selfish behavior, even if Elena had no idea I was doing it. Aunt Shay had excelled in protection spells and hiding magic, and I had been her protege. I couldn't make the apartment entirely invisible. But I could enchant the place so that anyone intending my friends harm couldn't find the apartment. This spell was less effective than a salt ward, but it was the best I could do on short notice.

I hoped it was enough.

# 14

WHEN YURI AND SYLVIA returned, I was sitting by myself on a curb in the parking lot. For the record, sitting in a parking lot in Belize feels a lot like sitting in a parking lot just about anywhere else. Happily, I'd chosen a hat with a brim to keep the worst of the sun off of my face.

Sylvia's eyes passed right over me without taking in that I was there. She was wearing a bright orange sundress and leather flip flops with frosted glass beads. Her raven hair was swept back into a casual ponytail. If things had been different, I'd have been waiting to meet her while playing with Chicken in the living room of her second story apartment. Instead, I saw Eddie's niece scowl slightly, as though she could sense she was being watched. Interesting.

Yuri spotted me the moment he was out of the car. He came straight to me and then turned in confusion as Sylvia headed up the stairs without pausing. "What just happened?"

"She couldn't see me," I said. "Or, rather, I wasn't important enough to notice."

"You can do that?"

"I had almost a full half hour free to concentrate on very little else. My aunt could make herself practically invisible in less than five minutes during a conversation," I sighed. "I'm not sure if Elena called her while you two were out, but I don't think I'm going to be invited over again."

"Does it always take you a half hour to do something like that?" Yuri had his thoughtful look on. He was probably more interested in the don't-notice-me spell than my personal tiffs with friends that didn't like him.

Tough. I was going to have to tell him about it. Because I'd been dumb.

"It's easiest if I'm motionless and get to concentrate for a while. Buildings and objects are much easier. They don't tend to move much. That's not really important right now."

Yuri was scandalized. "It's definitely important. Do you know how impressive something like that really is?"

"Yuri, I told Elena. Not *everything*-everything, but almost everything. I told her I had powers, I told her we were secret agent types, and I told her that helping us would put her in danger!" Most of that came out in a breathless rush as I fretted about how he was going to react. After having told one person the truth and it ending horribly, I'd have developed a little more in the way of self-interest. I couldn't do it though. I wanted to deal with this head-on and get it out into the open as soon as possible.

There was a pregnant pause. Even the wind lulled, like the entire world was waiting to see what happened. I expected Yuri to dismiss me. To tell me that I'd fucked up everything—it was time for me to pack up and go home. Not that he had the power to expel me from the country, but it was hard to imagine staying put after the day I'd had. Rejected. Learning about one death, and then witnessing another. Rejected again. Even high school hadn't been this bad.

Without saying anything, Yuri reached out a hand. I hesitated before reaching up to take it. Before I had time to register what was happening, Yuri had yanked me off of the ground and into his arms. I wasn't sure where my hat had gone—knocked off, crushed, evaporated—and I wasn't sure I cared. Burying my face into the thin, white fabric of Yuri's tank top, I soaked in the comfort he projected. Added to his personal scent mixture of tea, fabric softener, cinnamon and tobacco I'd noticed the day before, there was the musky smell of sweat. It was the second time in as many days I'd found myself on the receiving end of a Yuri hug. They were pretty addictive.

"Does this mean I'm not fired?" I finally asked. My voice was muffled because my head was still smooshed into Yuri's torso, but I really didn't want to move.

Yuri's chuckle did more to reassure me than anything he could've said in that moment. "Do you not remember me telling you how my first mission went all to pot? It'll be okay. We're not KGB or anything. There are people that deal with obfuscation."

"Is Elena gonna get hit by a flashy thingy?" I began to extricate myself from the wonderful, warm circle of Yuri's arms. I wasn't sure how I felt about being told they might mess with Elena's memories. Especially if they were messing with her memories because of something I did.

"I... What? Why would we flash her?"

"No," I felt the urge to laugh, but it didn't quite overpower the other emotions that were still swarming my system. "Not... Not flashing her. Flashy thingy. It's from a movie. A couple of movies at this point. But it's these guys that wear suits and protect the world from aliens. They have to do so secretly, so they have this tech that they point at people and it makes them forget things."

"Oh!" Yuri said. "Yes, I saw the first one! I don't think that's how it works, but I could look into it more if it'll make you feel better."

My hat was hanging in one of Yuri's hands. I grabbed it and placed it back on my head, concealing my braid and smoothing my flyaways out from between my forehead and the hat's band as I did so. Hats are generally too much work, but I wasn't wearing it for style. "Please do. Also, she thought I was lying, so it may not matter. But I don't think that's the point."

We began to crunch our way over the pavement back toward the road. After the way I'd been kicked out of Elena and Sylvia's apartment, it was pretty obvious they wouldn't be driving us anywhere else for the rest of the day. I half-expected someone to show up on the balcony and start yelling at us to get out of the apartment complex before they called the authorities, but we managed to leave without any further drama.

At the end of the lot, we turned and started walking further into town. I wasn't sure where we were going, but Yuri was striding with purpose so I figured he must have had a destination in mind.

"Where did you go with Sylvia while I was unconscious?" I asked.

"We stopped by the university to check and see if there'd been any news on Professor Gentle. I was hoping to verify what you'd already seen, but also wanted to muddy our tracks in case there's someone checking up on us. If they think we're still looking there, maybe they'll think we don't know what's happened yet."

I flicked my hat with my middle finger and thumb and raised an eyebrow as though to ask why we were wearing the things if we were being followed anyway.

"Just in case," Yuri shrugged. "A lot of what we do is designed to convince the other groups out there that we don't know as much as we've figured out."

It made a certain amount of sense. Spy work was a lot like poker. Hiding what you had in your hand was almost as important as deducing what the other players at the table were holding. I didn't play much myself, but Aunt Shay and I had enjoyed watching poker tournaments when they aired. It was like our own version of the Super Bowl. We'd make a table of snacks, choose our favorite player for the day, and wager chores on match outcomes.

"Where are we going now?"

"I think it's time to take a water taxi back and finish what we started at lunch. You can tell me what happened with that last taco during the ride."

IN SPITE OF EVERYTHING, or maybe because of it, I remembered my need to replenish coffee supplies at the condo. I view coffee shopping the way fashionistas view shoe shopping. I'm not really on board with uncomfortable art that gets crammed onto my feet and may or may not improve the lift of my posterior. It's not a part of who I am. Coffee, on the other hand, I can get lost in. Cold brew, frappuccino, cappuccino, espresso, mocha, latte, Americano, black, Turkish, Cubano, flat white... The list goes on. Flavor shots can add missing notes, but nothing beats getting the right roast on the right blend. I didn't enjoy owning a coffee shop though. Too much of a good thing, maybe? Or maybe because Sit-a-Spell Coffee was always Aunt Shay's shop, even after she died.

After the first ten minutes of being in the coffee section of the local market with me, Yuri told me he'd meet me outside the store. I'd been taking boxes and bags of brands that I was unfamiliar with, sniffing them, and replacing most of them. The majority of the coffees on display were imported. I was disappointed to learn Belize wasn't really a great place for coffee growing, so my daydreams concerning the local blends weren't likely to pan out. Oh, well.

I came out of the market with a bag full of coffee grounds, some bottled sodas I was unfamiliar with, raw sugar, and coconut milk. Before I found Yuri, I felt a familiar burning sensation around my wrist with the paracord bracelets. There was a sharp twist in my gut as I spotted the massive form of Jonas Ical standing next to the store entrance. His head was pointed in the opposite direction from me and his body language was tense, as though something had managed to catch him off guard.

*Shit... Where is Yuri?* With Jonas right there, I was immediately scared that No Name and his compatriots had already managed to snatch Yuri and cart him off somewhere to be tortured. Or maybe to reunite him with Kailey Callahan.

The burning sensation around my wrist strengthened. I needed to get out of here. If Yuri had been caught, getting myself taken wouldn't do either of us any good. Despite my urge to hunch and slink, I kept my spine straight and maintained my normal walking speed as I turned away from the distracted slab of muscle.

Once I was well away from the entrance, I ducked behind a nearby golf cart and stuffed my hat into the shopping bag. I wasn't sure if they knew to look for the hat or not at this point, but it seemed unlikely my long brown hair would draw as much attention as the band of rainbow tassels when I was trying to hide behind a golf cart. Golf carts were as prevalent in San Pedro as normal cars and blocked a lot less from sight. They were basically windows on wheels.

My advantage here was that I'd spotted Jonas, while he didn't know I'd snuck past him. It gave me my first real chance to look the man over.

I'd been able to tell he was large in the moonlight, and he didn't look any smaller with the sun overhead. I don't think he had gigantism, but I wasn't sure. That was out of my scope of expertise. But the guy was brushing the upper echelons of six feet, if he wasn't a cool seven feet tall. Jonas Ical's skin reminded me of leaves in the fall—reddish brown with golden undertones—while his hair was so black that it almost seemed blue. He had a broad, flat face which made his hooked nose look a bit like it had come out of a pop-up book. His mouth was set in a perpetual scowl. Even though he was wearing jeans and a t-shirt, he projected power in almost the same way that Alex Smith did. With these two backing No Name, I was even more impressed that Yuri and I had made it off of the beach during our first meeting. What kind of power was Eddie packing? Why couldn't I sense it?

The burning around my wrist was starting to ebb. Jonas Ical checked his watch and walked away, leaving me alone with a shopping bag and no idea of how to proceed. I still didn't have Yuri's phone number, so I couldn't call him to see if he was okay. Following Jonas to wherever he was heading seemed like a horrible idea. But if Yuri had been nabbed, this might be my only chance to find him. I was gathering the courage to start trailing the big, scary man when a hand settled on my shoulder.

I almost, *almost*, yelped like a chihuahua.

Gazing into Yuri's amber eyes, my heart skipped a beat. I was so relieved to see him, and so relieved that I didn't have to follow Jonas through a strange city, that I wanted to pull Yuri down and kiss him. Alright, so I'd wanted to do that from day one anyway. But the urge was stronger than normal.

"Where were you?" I asked. My voice sounded a little hoarse, which I hoped came off as more husky and sexy than like I'd swallowed a frog.

"Hiding," Yuri said. "I may not be able to identify everyone at a glance like some people, but that silhouette is hard to mistake."

There was no denying that. Jonas Ical was hard to miss.

AFTER THE BRUSH WITH Jonas Ical at the supermarket and the run-in with Alex Smith at the docks, I was almost surprised No Name wasn't waiting for us in my living room. It seemed like everywhere we turned, someone chasing Yuri was waiting for us. Mercifully, the salt wards were intact and there weren't any strangers camping out in my temporary home.

For the first time since I arrived in the Caribbean, I lamented the lack of a bathtub in my bathroom. After a day like the one I'd had, I could've gone for a good, scalding soak. As excited as I'd been about my coffee purchases, even a cup of joe didn't sound all that soothing.

"Yuri, I know we need to get a move on with this, but I need a break. A nap, a shower, a movie... I don't really know. It's been a wild, gut-wrenching day. I need some time."

For a long time, Yuri didn't say anything. I wasn't even sure he heard me. He seemed to be looking out the front window. I followed his gaze, one-hundred percent certain that I was going to see someone or something horrible looking back at us, but the only thing outside was a gorgeous view of the beach.

After a while, Yuri finally said, "This isn't normal for most people, is it?"

I didn't have to ask for clarification. This constant motion, jumping from one threat to the next, not getting to form any attachments—this was a world Yuri had lived in for years. I was only beginning to get a taste of it. "I've never been a great gauge for normalcy, but no, this is not it."

"This is the third time I've asked this today," Yuri said, breathing in and sighing so deeply that it almost looked like he'd started to deflate. "But I've got to be sure that you're really committed to this course. Do you want to pursue this kind of life?"

Three is a powerful number. Even with the line of work he was in, I wasn't sure if Yuri was aware that asking the same question for a third time was akin to offering me a contract and a needle and asking me to sign. It wasn't written on his face anywhere that he was aware of the binding nature of his question. I had to consider my answer very carefully now, because if I said yes, I couldn't back out, and if I said no, I couldn't change my mind. Ever. The magic in my blood wouldn't let me.

"At the very least, I want to finish this mission and see what happens from there," I told him.

# 15

YURI WATCHED A HOUSE hunting show in my living room while I took a nap. I hadn't actually intended to fall asleep, but there was something soothing about having someone in the condo with me. I'd fallen asleep wondering why someone who worked as a magical tomb raider would choose something so mundane. The people on the show never seemed happy with the size of the kitchen or tile floors. Yuri responded to them outloud with things like, "How many people do you need to cook for? Why do you need more than two ovens?" and "Are you having the Queen in to inspect your floors? The tile is fine!"

As I drifted off, it occurred to me that Yuri was trying to reconnect with the average person. No action sequences, no tragic deaths, and the most drama these people were subjected to was their potential view including a parking lot. Even if these shows were staged, they were safe.

Only three days in his world and it was taking a toll. Already, I'd nearly forgotten my original purpose in Belize was my own house hunt. I was supposed to be one of those people, complaining about the small sinks and the lack of dishwashers. I'd come to Belize to find my place in the world.

*I think that may be what I'm doing, though. Maybe I wasn't supposed to find a house. Maybe I was supposed to find a calling.*

That was my last conscious thought before my brain shut down for a pleasant and dreamless rest.

A TRULY HEAVENLY AROMA coaxed my tired brain back to life. It wasn't coffee, but it was just as enticing in its own way: pizza! The overwhelming scent of pepperoni and cheese teased my nose and sent my stomach into high alert. I was pretty sure Yuri could hear the rumbling on the other side of the bedroom wall.

"Briar? Are you awake?"

"Barely," I answered. "But I'm working on it."

"I took the liberty of ordering out. I got one pepperoni and one ham and pineapple. I wasn't sure which way you took it," Yuri said. Despite the fact that I'd left my door open, Yuri was being very respectful of the invisible barrier that separated my bedroom from the condo's public space. He wasn't even looking at me from the other side of the door frame.

Whatever brownie points he'd risked on ham and pineapple pizza evened out with the ones he earned for not sticking his head uninvited into a sleeping girl's room. Very decent of him. Extremely proper. Doing nothing to help me get over my crush. I didn't even care if other people liked ham and pineapple as long as I didn't have to eat it. So that didn't even help. Damn it.

But maybe he wasn't trying to peek because he wasn't into me at all. I couldn't discount that possibility.

*Fuck it, this is turning into a rabbit hole that I don't want to go down. Pizza time.*

Nothing heals a broken heart faster than pizza. Don't let the movies and shows fool you. Ice cream has its place, but pizza is magic. We didn't have ice cream parties at school. We had pizza parties. People know pizza is magic, but they don't realize that they know.

I went into the bathroom, had some very self-conscious toilet time (the noises that come through walls and doors while your crush is within earshot is like a cruel joke played on us by creator gods), and did some cursory hair smoothing after washing my hands. When I finally emerged, Yuri handed me a plate. His plate was still empty and unmarked by grease. Aw, he waited for me.

Uuuuurgh.

"How are you feeling?" he asked.

Without meeting his eyes, I began slipping slices of pepperoni pizza onto the teal ceramic dish. Red, teal, and white. Vibrant colors in a vibrant setting. I was not feeling as alive as my plate looked, but on the whole, I was starting to feel human again. As human as I ever did. I decided to condense my answer. "Better."

"Good enough to try with the hot sauce again?"

"I'm not putting hot sauce on my pizza," I said.

Rather than speaking, Yuri gestured to the two maps that had ended up on the counter at some point after we'd come in. The idea that I could use hot sauce as a scrying tool. Right. That almost felt like another lifetime.

"Yeah... I think I'm up to it, now." I opened the fridge and pulled out a grapefruit soda. "Would you like one of these?"

"Sure." Yuri opened his own box of monstrosity pizza and piled slices onto his plate. We'd gone light on the lunch tacos. Unless he'd eaten something while I was visiting the 1970s, he was probably as hungry as I was. I set a soda can in front of him and grabbed myself another.

We sat on the bar stools and ate at the kitchen island, close enough that our legs brushed against each other from time to time. Neither of us chose to speak until we'd managed to inhale an entire slice apiece. I was happy to note that Yuri was a crust eater like me. Our toppings might not mesh, but we still had some common ground.

"Did you find out anything at the university?" I asked.

"Nothing we didn't already know, really," Yuri said. He took another bite and chewed quickly, trying to gulp it down before he continued. "They've noted Gentle's absence. The students seem more concerned than the school. There were fliers about trying to organize search parties from a club he sponsored."

"What kind of club?"

"World Mythology," Yuri answered. His focus was still centered on putting more food into his mouth, but I could see his expression shift. "I really hope that no one thinks they know anything. They're practically still kids."

"We're not exactly old ourselves," I nudged him playfully with my shoulder, trying to hide how much the thought bothered me. The people we were up against, it wouldn't matter how young someone was if these guys thought there was information to be gained. "The faster we deal with this thing, the safer everyone will be, right?"

By the time I'd managed to down a third slice, my stomach seemed much more content. While I could've eaten two more and not been miserable, I wanted to put my words into practice. We had to start moving and I'd already delayed us. Yuri ate a fourth slice before he picked up both plates and began to wash them in the sink.

I got off of my stool and started flipping on light switches. The sun wasn't quite down outside, but shadows were stretching their way across the sand as the waves grew darker. I pulled the maps out of their plastic sleeves and spread them out on the floor. Both maps fit in the space between the kitchen and the living room. My arms could reach every section without the danger of slamming into anything. This was probably better than my initial restaurant table idea. With my eyes shut, I reached into the bag of hot sauces and pulled out the first thing my hands came into contact with. It was one of the wrapped packages. A large scuff mark marred the crisp, cream paper—a reminder of my collision with Alex Smith.

The bottle proved to be intact, but the glass had changed from clear to an odd honey-topaz hue. I checked the label to be sure this was the same bottle I'd selected in the store. It was the smokey habanero sauce, and the expiration date was the same as the bottle of extra hot I'd unwrapped earlier. I tore the paper off of the remaining three bottles to make sure that I wasn't misremembering. They'd all been clear to start with, right? The other sauces looked as I would've expected: clear bottles, seals intact, sauce colors consistent with flavor labels.

After Yuri finished washing dishes, he stuck the pizza boxes in the fridge and returned to his stool. He watched me examine things like he expected me to give a test later.

Maybe I would test him.

"Yuri, does this look weird to you?" I asked.

"Does what look weird to me?" he replied. "I'm watching someone arrange condiments to throw at a map. Even for IACI, this isn't exactly your average Tuesday."

Fair point, even if it didn't answer my question. I picked up the bottles and handed them over, trying my best not to linger on any particular one. If he was colorblind, I wasn't sure if this was going to work, but I didn't want to coach him into seeing the same thing I'd noticed.

I watched as Yuri turned the bottles this way and that, holding each one up to the kitchen lights before setting them down and examining the labels. Even as he worked, I was certain he couldn't see the discoloration of the glass on the smokey sauce bottle. This was confirmed when he shrugged and said, "I give up. What am I looking for?"

"The smokey habanero bottle... It's glass is darker than the rest of them. I'm seeing it as almost being that amber color that floods antique stores," I said, accepting the bottles back into my custody.

Yuri scowled. He beckoned for me to give him back the bottle in question, as though another bout of evaluation would reveal what he'd missed the first time. I handed it over. I doubted that he'd see anything differently with a second run, but science was all about confirming results. So what if it's magic? I can use science on magic. They're not completely separate circles. It's more like a venn diagram.

"It looks clear to me," Yuri sighed. "I can't tell any difference."

Interesting...

Concerning.

I wasn't sure what to do with the knowledge that I could see something weird about this bottle and Yuri couldn't. That scuff mark on the paper hadn't been on any of the other wraps. Maybe Alex Smith had done something to mark it? Should I even be handling it if that were the case? My magic had led me to choosing the altered bottle when I wanted the best one for scrying, though.

It was moments like this when I really wanted another magic user to talk to. I knew nothing about warlocks, nothing about demigods, and nothing about objects that functioned as power reservoirs. I'd always thought that my own abilities were rather lame, even when they behaved properly. Now I was wishing I'd asked my aunt a lot more questions. Maybe she'd have known why contact with a warlock would change the color of glass. Maybe she would've told me warlocks were a thing. I was out of my element.

"I don't suppose you have any other witches or warlocks on speed dial?" I asked.

Shaking his head, Yuri grimaced. "None that I could chat up at this time of night. It's almost two o'clock in the morning back home."

"What kind of secret organization keeps office hours?" I was only half-joking. I couldn't keep the frustration out of my voice entirely, but Yuri chose to ignore it.

He scrolled through his phone, despite what he'd told me. "The problem is that the people I know aren't on the Reliquarian side of things. As I said before, most magic users aren't comfortable with the way that some antiquities are dealt with."

That made sense. I still wasn't sure how well I'd take it when the time came. The erasure of the undesired. It reminded me of nightmares I'd had about Salem as a kid. Not that the actual witch trials dealt with many actual witches, but that didn't matter to tiny me. I was a witch. They'd hunted witches. It was a simple math equation. At the moment, I missed that time of simplicity.

Okay, so things boiled down to two options: use the scary bottle for the best results, or use a different bottle and hope it wasn't too inaccurate to help.

Before I had a chance to make my decision, a third option knocked on my front door.

# 16

"HEY, CHICA, YOU OKAY?" Eddie's voice reverberated through the door along with the heavy thuds of someone that used the side of their fist rather than their knuckles against the wooden surface. "You want to talk about it?"

Exchanging a confused look with Yuri, I got up and hopped over the maps I'd laid out. My first thought was that Eddie Velasquez had somehow heard my plea to the universe for someone magic to bounce ideas off of, but he wasn't a mind reader. To my knowledge. I peeked out of the tiny peephole to confirm what my ears had already told me.

He smiled at the peephole as though he could tell I was looking. Which he probably could, given that I blocked the interior light with my head. "I brought cerveza!"

Well, it was definitely Eddie. I went ahead and opened the door.

"Eddie, what are you doing here?" I asked. "Not that you're not welcome," I added hastily. I hadn't forgotten that he'd already saved my bacon twice.

Wearing an old pair of cut-off jeans, a faded t-shirt with his preferred beer brand, and a pair of well-loved flip flops, Eddie stepped in and lifted up two of the promised packs of cerveza. I didn't even know that glass bottles of beer came in twenty-four packs. Then again, beer was never really my go-to. Maybe I'd known and just forgotten.

"I got a phone call from Elena telling me that I wasn't supposed to interact with you or your boyfriend anymore because you were a liar and phony, so naturally I had to come check on you," Eddie said.

He glanced curiously down at the maps on the floor and sidestepped past them as he made his way to the fridge. "Hola, boyfriend! Good to see you again!"

"I'm not—"

"We're not—"

"Not exclusive? Why would you be? You only just met," Eddie said, not letting our attempts to interrupt phase him. "So, you wanna talk about it?"

"I..." Stealing a glance at Yuri, my mind rushed to find a way to balance everything that was happening in this room. I hadn't told Eddie about Yuri's connection to the IACI, and I hadn't told Yuri that Eddie was the local magic user that had saved us on the beach. Neither secret was mine to tell. But Eddie's presence could help me solve the mystery of the bottle if I could speak openly.

Eddie tore open the first beer case and began stuffing bottles into the fridge. Forty-eight bottles takes up a lot of space, and the fridge in this place wasn't as big as my fridge in Kansas. It was probably a good thing I hadn't settled in long enough to do any actual grocery shopping yet. "If you're concerned about what to tell your boyfriend about me, it's okay," Eddie said. "He can know that I'm a legacy shaman. It's kind of an open secret in this area. Most figure I'm either that, or an alcoholic. Shamanism requires the mind to be altered, and I've never been a fan of the hard stuff."

With that thrown out in the open, I breathed a small sigh of relief and turned back to Yuri. "Eddie was the one that sent me the path of light on the beach. He's also the local that dragged my ass away from No Name the next morning."

Yuri popped up out of his seat and clasped Eddie by the hand and drew him in for a bro hug, complete with two solid thumps on the back. "Cheers, mate. It's good to get to say that in person."

"I was actually really wanting to talk to a fellow magic user right now," I admitted. Beckoning Eddie over to me, I handed him the altered sauce bottle. "What do you make of this?"

He let out a low whistle and his laugh lines went slack as he peered through the yellowed glass. "That's some work, that is. Lucky you brought it through your wards before you tried to open this one. Burnt out the hex before it could do its damage."

*Fuck.* We'd been carrying around a hexed bottle for most of the day? I hadn't noticed the spell energy in the bag. Hell, I hadn't even felt the cast and I was practically touching Alex Smith for that whole encounter. According to what my aunt had taught me, magic in motion was the hardest to hide. Assuming that Alex Smith was the one responsible. The bag had been with me or Yuri all day though. At least, I thought it had been... I had been out cold for almost an hour, and I didn't have any idea what Yuri had been up to while I shopped for coffee.

Returning to his stool, Yuri took off his glasses and rubbed his eyes with his free hand. It was like he was trying to rub away another close call in a day already full of them. I couldn't blame him. Despite my nap, I was starting to feel tired all over again.

"But is it safe to use?" I asked.

"Oh, yeah. For sure," Eddie said. He handed the bottle back to me before walking over to one of the two sitting chairs in the living room. Twisting it around to face the kitchen area where Yuri and I had arranged ourselves, Eddie plunked himself down and got comfy. "I wanted to tell you, chica... Telling Elena what you did, I know that took guts. My Sylvia, she agrees with her tio. Give it some time and Elena will come around. If she's not the type that would, then she wouldn't be good enough for my Sylvia."

I was touched. Truly, deeply touched. Eddie and I hadn't known each other for long, and I'd only caught a glimpse of his niece. It meant a lot that he'd come here to check on me after being told never to speak to me again. "How did you find me, anyway?"

"We've connected through our magic twice now," Eddie shrugged. "It's not hard for me to track you."

"Can anyone that's tangled with her magic trace her that way?" Yuri asked. He'd voiced the question before I could, but I was certainly curious about the answer. The last thing we needed was to get cornered in my condo, with only one door between us and No Name and his warlocks.

"I don't think it's an issue," Eddie reassured us. "Intentions matter with that sort of thing. Since I've only ever been out to protect her, her magic lets me find her. If I were to up and hit her one day, even if it was an accident, my difficulty finding her would increase because the trust would shift."

Odd, but good to know. "So... is your tracking anything like my scrying?"

"You'd have to tell me, chica. You're the first witch I've met, remember?" Eddie shoved himself back out of his chair and went to the fridge. "Damn. Not cold yet. Warm cerveza no es buena."

Despite his complaints, Eddie came back with two beers and sat back down in his chosen chair. I knelt down between the two maps and tried to resume the mindset I'd been in before Eddie came in. I'm not sure what edicate says about casting spells in front of guests. It's probably frowned on at the very least. Asking Eddie to leave felt wrong though, and I didn't want to waste more time now that I knew it was safe to use the best bottle of hot sauce for the job. It was no use. Either Eddie's presence was disrupting my mojo, or I was spent from a day full of close calls and heartaches. I got up and grabbed myself a tepid beer and spent a pleasant hour chatting with Eddie and Yuri.

Yuri and I seemed to have reached an unspoken agreement that today's agenda was a wash. When Eddie got up to leave he offered Yuri a ride home.

"I wouldn't want to impose..." Yuri started to protest, but Eddie pointed out that he could mask Yuri's presence in his car. With a shrug to me, Yuri followed Eddie out of my condo. I watched the two men amble past my windows through the dark.

After the longest day I'd had in years, I wasn't sure if being alone was a relief or not. I straightened the used chair out and pushed Yuri's stool in. I moved the laundry from the washer to the dryer, hardly believing it was the same load I'd started earlier in the day. The maps, I left out. I didn't know what time Yuri intended to show up in the morning, but I knew he was coming. We hadn't worked anything out, but I knew he was coming with as much certainty as I knew I was about to take an extra long shower.

I WASN'T DREAMING. Not exactly. It felt closer to when I found myself looking through Laura's eyes in the vision of the 70s. Which I was still thinking of as a vision, but I guess was more like an astral projection to the past? Was that a thing? *I really could've used a magical school when I was growing up*, I thought with a huff.

A huff that misted the air in front of me. Interesting. The air here was cold. Much colder than my air-conditioned condo could account for.

Looking down, I saw my own body, wearing my favorite pair of jeans. They were long discarded, due to a number of holes, rips and stains. Also, I'd outgrown them during college, so I doubted they'd even clear my hips anymore. But they'd been my favorites because they had a big green dragon embroidered down the right pant leg, and they were an odd color for jeans. Practically brown denim instead of the usual blue. More like a tint than a full dye, though. They'd been pretty unique despite finding them in a local department store. I was also wearing my red triskele tank top. Also my favorite, but my ownership of the two hadn't overlapped. A burgundy jacket I'd stolen from my aunt covered my arms. I hadn't worn it since her funeral because it felt wrong without her there to make faces at me about it, but it was my favorite jacket. I sensed a trend developing. At least, regarding things on my person. Cold, however, was never a thing I'd sought out.

It was dark, wherever this was. Not pitch black. More like one of those grey days, when the sky is extremely overcast but refuses to rain. I could see the fog of my breath, and I could see my own body. At my feet, rolling mist obscured the ground I was standing on, but the whirling pockets and eddies would sometimes reveal bits of asphalt or slate. Basalt? Black.

The smell was off. This place should've had a dankness to it, or maybe a petrichor. Perhaps even the sharp odor of frost. Instead, all I could make out was the scent of fire. Not the pleasant smokiness of a campfire. This was like all the worst parts of a house fire. Mattresses and sofas. Other things.

"Hello?" I called out into the darkness. No one responded.

Rather than continue to stand in one place and hope that answers would come to me, I started walking. A figure began to emerge from the darkness. I almost jumped when I saw it—a pillar rising up from the haze—but then I recognized the shape as a person's silhouette. "Hey? Can you hear me?"

I stopped cold when I recognized them. It was Professor Phoenix Gentle. He looked exactly like I'd seen him in his mind, only his skin had a greyish cast to it. His eyes were dull and lifeless. Even when I grabbed him by the shoulders and shook him, he didn't respond to my presence.

"Professor Gentle? Professor Phoenix Gentle? Phoenix!" I tried every variation on his name I could think of and still got nothing.

Out of desperation, I slapped him. Not even a flinch.

I didn't want to leave him here, but he wouldn't budge when I attempted to pull him along with me. There were no landmarks to mark his location.

An idea occurred to me. Because I couldn't think of any other options, I went ahead with it. I reached into the back of his shirt and pulled off the manufacturing tag. A piece of something will always remember where it came from. "I'm very sorry, sir," I told him, even though I was pretty sure he couldn't hear me. "I'd ask for your consent before doing something like this in a normal situation."

Once more, I ventured out into the mist. Two more figures rose out of the darkness. Both of them were as still as Professor Gentle had been when I'd approached him. They were far enough apart that I couldn't actually examine them at the same time. I would have to look at one and then move to the next.

Following my intuition, I chose the one that was further to my left, even though they were slightly farther away. Clean shaven with much shorter hair, I almost didn't recognize Todd. He was wearing a spotless white ringer t-shirt with red bands at the collar and cuffs. His pants were brown corduroy bell bottoms. This version of Todd was much less hippie and much more moderate college student. It was surprising how different this version of him seemed. Like Professor Gentle, he had a lifeless greyness to him.

If I hadn't seen Todd first, I don't think I would've recognized Arthur at all. Even with my gift supplying Arthur's name, it took me a while to equate the man I was seeing with the crazed killer that had plunged an obsidian knife into Todd.

His matted cloak of hair and beard were gone, replaced by a mop of tousled, sandy brown locks that came to rest along Arthur's jawline. He had a super thick, but neatly trimmed, mustache that was a shade or two darker than his hair. Older than Todd, judging by the crow's feet that crinkled the corners of his eyes. Arthur's skin was so pale that the greyish pallor that merely rested over the other two made him look like he'd been carved out of marble. Wearing blue jeans that only hinted at a flare near the ankle and a sensible green button down shirt, I could only guess at what had brought this man into the jungles of Central America. Maybe he'd been an archaeologist or a treasure hunter?

Whatever he had been, I was starting to suspect I knew where we both were. Somehow, I'd gone inside the knifeYuri and I were hunting.

*Yes... You've recognized us.*

The voice, if it could be called that, vibrated through my cells. There were several layers of resonance, as though I was hearing a room full of people all speaking in unison. Or... attempting to speak in unison. I was catching the meaning, but it sounded as though the voices didn't all speak the same language. The voice surrounded me, tore through me, as it spoke to me. I hated it.

I wanted it to keep talking.

*What the hell is wrong with me?* I was covering my ears with my hands and crouching as close to the ground as I could without actually sitting down. I couldn't even recall moving.

*You are drawn to us, and we are drawn to you. You are the one that will wield our power.*

"No!" I shook my head, still crouching and holding my ears. It wasn't helping, but it was impossible to fight the instinctive urge to curl into a ball. "I don't want this! You take life! People have died!"

*They serve.*

Thoughts flashed through my mind faster than I could vocalize them. No Name and Eddie were at the forefront. The things Eddie had told me about the demigods and how they sought power. Eddie's own abilities and others that were born closer to this thing's home. Why would it have sought me out when I was half a world away?

*The shamans guard against us. They've seen us rise before. The Other would use us as a tool. Drain us. Discard us. You will wield us.*

"I don't want you," I said. My vision was blurring around the edges as I felt my body stir many miles away. Soon I would wake up. I'd be free of this place and its lifeless, staring bodies. I could scry the location of the blade and let Yuri destroy it.

Even as I woke, I tried to tell myself that I hadn't felt a lie cross my own lips.

# 17

YURI SHOWED UP WHILE my coffee was still brewing. It was the longest I'd managed to sleep since arriving in Belize, so I tried not to begrudge the interruption of my morning routine. I wasn't sure if his presence was a relief or not. On the one hand, I wasn't being left alone with my thoughts. On the other hand, Yuri wanted to talk about finding the knife. I wanted to *avoid* thinking about the damned thing.

"Ready to give it another go?" Yuri asked the moment I opened the door.

I just looked at him. On a normal morning, I'm pretty sure the look would've translated into, "Don't talk to me yet." Today's look probably translated into, "I will incinerate you whether you're standing in the orphanage or not."

Holding up his hands in a show of surrender, Yuri revealed that he'd arrived bearing gifts. A white paper bag with the crest of one of the local bakeries. Between baked goods and the pizza still cooling in my fridge, I waved him in. The man had fed me on multiple occasions. He'd earned himself a reprieve. "I brought along chocolate croissants," he said.

Okay, he'd earned himself a few reprieves.

"Sorry," I said, as I led him into the kitchen. "I had a rough night."

Tossing the bag of croissants onto the island, Yuri pulled out the stool that he always seemed to sit in. He had a paper cup of something as well. I glanced at it questioningly.

"Chai latte," Yuri said. "I also like Darjeeling, Oolong, and Earl Grey. In a pinch, I'll drink matcha but not with milk."

"And here I thought that whole British tea thing was a stereotype," I shot a semblance of a grin at him to show I was teasing as I pulled the bag of croissants open. They were still warm. If Yuri were open to the idea, I'd marry him on the spot. There's very little that can't be cured with a warm chocolate croissant.

*That knife wants blood.* The thought pierced the happy little bubble of normalcy that I was trying to insulate myself with. *It will try to kill more people. It wants you to wield it while it does. Why on earth would you want that?*

I had no answer ready for that. I'd tried my best not to think about it while I was filling the coffee maker. Before Yuri showed up, I'd hoped to put that dream or vision or whatever out of my head entirely.

My coffee had stopped dripping. I tried to remove the pot, but my hands were shaking. The harder I tried to pull the pot out, the more it seemed to catch on the rest of the machine. I was practically banging the machine against the counter in the attempt to extract my coffee. "C'mon, let go! Let go, you stupid piece of..."

"Everything okay over there?" Yuri asked.

"It's... it's fine," I said, gritting my teeth. "I... I'm having a little trouble."

Yuri stood up and came into the kitchen behind me. He slid the coffee pot free of its cradle and poured it into my waiting mug, leaving an inch and a half for my sugar and coconut milk. There was a heat simmering between us that had nothing to do with the steaming mug sitting on the counter. "You know you can talk to me, right?"

Every time I'd opened my mouth lately, it seemed like something got worse. And this... this was pretty damn bad. How could he trust me if I told him I was drawn to this thing? I didn't want to kill people! But the knife was right... It called to me. I'd come to Belize to find it. It was the thing pulling at me from the mainland.

"I..." I took a step back from Yuri, crossing my arms as I did so. "I still need to take a shower."

Trying my best to ignore Yuri's kicked-puppy face, I raced back into my bedroom and shut the door behind me. I would have to come back out eventually and face the cooled coffee but, for the space of a shower, I'd have some time to think.

WHEN I RE-EMERGED, feeling much cleaner in many ways, I found Yuri on the teal couch. His leather journal was out and he was flipping through it like it was a magazine—very casually perusing each page, but not really reading. Yuri didn't look at me as I entered the room, but he did jerk his head toward the kitchen. "I poured your coffee back in the pot. I didn't think you'd like it tepid."

"I'm really sorry about that, Yuri. I'm... I'm not good at this. I've never had friends. I barely had a family. Sometimes, I have no idea how to deal with shit," I said. It came out kind of rehearsed and measured. Not surprising given how many times I'd gone over it in my head while water trailed down my back. But it had the benefit of being true.

"I do mean it, you know?" Yuri said, finally setting the journal down. "If we're going to be partners, we're going to have to trust one another."

With a nod, I took a deep breath and shoved the words out of my mouth. "Last night, I dreamt I was trapped in the knife with the souls of Professor Gentle and the two men that I saw die in my vision. During the dream, I pulled the shirt tag off of Professor Gentle's clothes. When I went back to my room to shower, I found this on my pillow."

In a blur of motion, Yuri was on his feet and next to me. He took the faded scrap of material that I had pinched between my finger and thumb and held it against the sunlight streaming in through the condo's front windows, as though he could verify its authenticity. I had a pretty similar reaction while getting dressed. While I'd known that my dream was more than a dream, there was no part of me that had anticipated bringing back a souvenir.

"Good gods, Briar... Are you okay? What happened?"

I told Yuri most of the dream. Everything about the mist, the lifeless bodies and my attempts to wake them, and my decision to grab the tag off of Professor Phoenix Gentle, I included. I may have skimmed over what the knife actually said to me, but I did tell Yuri that I'd heard its voice and that it had freaked me out.

"I'd ask if you'd fancy a cuppa, but you've coffee ready. Here, you sit there, and I'll get you settled," Yuri escorted me over the stool he normally sat on and made sure I was sitting before he got out a fresh mug and poured in coffee, coconut milk, and a spoonful of sugar. He stirred it three times and then set it in front of me and then set one of the once-warm croissants on a plate next to the mug.

"I'm... really okay," I protested. The protest was a little late considering that the plate and mug were already in front of me, but it took me that long to grasp that someone was taking care of me. It had been a while. "Thank you, though."

"It's how my nan would've handled something like this," Yuri said. "It's what I tend to fall back on when something worries me."

I nodded. Aunt Shay's remedy for worries were lessons on traditional witchery, which rarely worked right, but definitely took my mind off of things. Taking a bite out of the croissant, I regretted my earlier freak out more than I already did. These things were freaking amazing. If I'd eaten them when they were still warm, my brain would've melted and I wouldn't have been worried about talking knives anymore.

Once I'd downed most of my coffee and Yuri and I had decimated the sack of baked goods, I got down to business. Sinking onto the floor between the two maps, I grabbed a hot sauce without looking—and I ended up with the smokey habanero in the yellowed bottle again. Noted. I clamped the pilfered shirt tag between my palm and the hot sauce.

In traditional witchery, I would use a pendulum for this sort of scrying. Pendulums were a lot like the rest of the traditional tools for me—unpredictable at best. The last time I'd attempted to make a pendulum behave for me, the bob had spun fast enough to produce a breeze before breaking its chain and vanishing. We never actually found the thing.

Time to test out my title as the world's only Tacomancer.

This felt very similar to my readings on tacos. The moment my wrist hit the correct angle, I moved my hand without really paying attention. I could tell that the spread was bigger and my arm extended much further from my body than normal, but it was working. Before I even opened my eyes, I had a destination in my head.

The Belize City map was completely clean except for one tiny blotch, while the ancient road map had a big blob of sauce on one location. I exchanged a look with Yuri as he bent down to look over the maps with me.

"Caracol," I said.

"What is this smaller bit on Belize City?" Yuri asked. He pointed at the tiny blip of smokey habanero, being very careful not to dab his finger into it.

"I'm not sure," I admitted.

Yuri whipped out his phone to check the address. It turned out to be Explorers Unbound, a tour company advertising Caracol visits on their website. Something about that sent up a small warning bell. "That seems awfully convenient. My gift isn't normally my travel agent."

"We could rent a car and drive out on our own," Yuri said. "I'm not the one with the special abilities here. If you think this isn't the best road, I'm behind you."

Great... I was being given free rein to make a call on an under-developed talent. *Maybe I shouldn't have said anything,* I thought. If I hadn't said anything though, Yuri still could've thrown the decision my way. I didn't know if he was testing me or not. Nothing he'd said was a lie, but it was worded in a way that had many truths. "I don't have enough experience," I said after a few moments. "This is the first time I've ever tried this. Maybe my gift has been wanting to act in this capacity for ages and is only now getting to do so. Or maybe it's telling me one possibility to get out there because it felt like it. Perhaps that's how Professor Gentle went out there and his shirt tag helped me track his path. It might be a random blob." My senses all flared against me in protest. "Okay, not that last one."

Leaning one elbow against the kitchen island, Yuri took his time digesting what I'd just uncovered. His eyes roved from the two maps back to me and back to the maps again. "Let's make a go of it," he said. "Grab your stuff. We need to get back over to the mainland."

IT WAS THE LEAST SUNNY day I'd seen since touching down in Belize. As the water taxi cut through the waves, I started to see why they handed out barf bags on every trip. The surf was choppier than I'd ever seen it. Other people on the boat were using the barf bags, and the noises were making me feel a bit green in the gills myself.

When we disembarked at the Belize City port, I stumbled over to the nearest bench and hung my head down between my knees. Waves were still crashing around inside my skull even though I wasn't on the boat anymore. The sudden onset of clouds was accompanied by some unhappy winds. Ocean spray was slapping against my skin while I sat immobile on the dock willing my body to get back to normal.

I hadn't noticed Yuri leave, but he was suddenly pushing a Sprite at me. "This'll help. Trust me."

"Thanks," I said. I took the offered can, popped the top and sipped gingerly. It did help after a second or two. I shivered. Now that my stomach was no longer rebelling, I was very aware of how damp I was and how the wind was still picking up. "We should get off the dock, I think."

The water taxi crew was throwing lashes and securing the boat to the dock with increased fervor. They hadn't run ashore themselves yet, but they were growing increasingly agitated with their tasks. I noticed that the bustling tourists and shop owners from my previous visits weren't visible. Even the restaurant where Yuri had acquired my drink was being shuttered and locked as we watched.

"Definitely time to get moving," Yuri agreed.

The rain held back until we'd managed to find cover in the same shop that we'd purchased hats in only yesterday.

"Back for more, eh?" the proprietor, Isamir, said. She chatted with us good naturedly for the better part of an hour while we waited for the skies to stop falling. To thank her for our shelter, and relieve my shivering, Yuri bought me a fresh set of clothes. I found a light blue tank top and matching sweatpants that both said, "You'd better Belize it!"

I'd worn worse. The bigger problem was what to do with my wet clothes. Yuri assumed we'd toss them in the nearest trash can when we got the chance. While I'm not one to be hung up on fashion, I tend to get attached to the clothes that I wear. I'd packed a lot of my favorites to come along on my trip to Belize. He wanted to ditch my heather-green tank top, printed with three yellow triangles arranged in a pretty recognizable symbol, and one of my comfiest sets of camel-brown shorts.

"There do come times when you have to burn clothes," he said. Yuri's voice was strained, like he was struggling to maintain a reasonable tone.

"When that happens, I'll deal with it. But those are just wet. We haven't been seen and I don't have enough clothing with me to toss stuff," I said, yanking my shorts back out of his grasp. "I will buy myself a backpack. But I'm not throwing my clothes away."

"A backpack marks you as a tourist," Yuri argued.

In response, I gestured to my brand new ensemble.

Defeated, Yuri left the shop as I purchased a boho drawstring backpack.

# 18

THE RAIN HADN'T STOPPED, merely paused. We used our brief window to climb into a taxi, one that wasn't driven by Elena, and make our way to the touring company. As soon as we stepped inside, a wall of rain slammed into the mainland.

Explorers Unbound wasn't much to look at. The entire place consisted of two rooms. Three, if you counted the bathroom. We'd entered a lobby with wainscoting from the seventies. An office was visible through a glass wall with a door. A cash wrap counter inserted itself between the uncomfortable chairs of steel and plastic in the waiting area and a full view of the old metal desk standing vigil over the empty office. Glowing in the corner of the cash wrap, a single computer monitor cast a blue light against the glass. Tinito Cowo, the lone employee in the office, looked as though he was wearing an odd, rectangular halo.

"We're not doing any tours today," Tinito told us. He was a short guy. I'd thought he was sitting on a stool when we first entered the tour center, but he'd been leaning on his elbows. He straightened up when he saw us and I realized he was a full head shorter than Yuri and myself. With his broad shoulders, toned muscles, and barrel chest, he looked like a wrestler or street fighter. "Too dangerous with the rains. You can try again tomorrow."

I turned back toward the door. It wasn't the first time that I'd misread something. I was gearing up to apologize to Yuri when I realized he hadn't turned with me. He'd continued to approach the counter and pulled out a billfold of some sort. Did he have an official IACI badge? Why hadn't he shown it to me? Despite my questions,

I felt like I should be doing something to signify that he and I were in this together so I flipped the Open sign hanging on the door to Closed and shuttered the blinds. I didn't mess with the locks, though. That felt like a step too far for what was basically theatricality on my part.

"Sir, we're in pursuit of a rogue agent that we believe crossed your borders from Guatemala. Our agency has every right to commandeer one of your vehicles, but we'd rather this all stay civil. If we are able to pose as tourists, it is much less likely the rogue in question will attack on sight. Now, can you help us with this? Or should we borrow one of your busses? You will be compensated, of course."

Tinito Cowo leaned forward and squinted at the billfold Yuri held. Those toned muscles tensed. I hoped he wasn't about to throw a punch at Yuri; despite his being some sort of magical secret agent, I wasn't sure Yuri could take this guy in a fight. "I've never heard of the IACI. Whose authorization do you have?"

"We're fully sanctioned by the UN. Now, I can get all the paperwork sent to you and you can spend a few days recovering from a hand cramp while you fill out all the forms in triplicate, telling a heavily bureaucratic agency why you're entitled to money for a brand new bus that may or may not arrive by the end of the next decade, because you know how fast governing bodies are, or..." Yuri let the pause hang in the air. Tinito Cowo leaned forward in his seat like he was witnessing a fight with one person on the ropes. I wasn't sure if he believed Yuri or not, but Yuri wasn't lying. With his free hand, Yuri pulled his IACI credit card out of his pocket and slid it toward Tinito. "...we could rent a private tour and you could get us where we need to go."

"A private tour?" Tinito Cowo studied the card in front of him and looked over at me. I looked like a wide-eyed tourist. With my gift shop attire and my big, blue eyes, there wasn't much else I could convey. Tinito gave off a condescending little chuckle as he jerked his head toward me. "Is she part of your cover?"

Okay. I take it back. I could convey anger pretty damn well. I didn't do anything flashy like turning the lights on and off without touching them or jangling blinds and door chimes with telekinesis. If my power were a visible substance, like red smoke for example, it was as though I'd poured enough of it into the room that Tinito wouldn't have been able to see any other color as he choked to death on the fumes. While my power isn't as tangible as smoke, Tinito went from chuckling to swallowing nervously in a hurry. Struggling to pick up Yuri's card, he mumbled that he was going to run it through the machine. "Private tour. You got it. Renting the whole bus plus gas, and you're wanting a driver and a tour guide?"

"If we're really gonna sell that we're a couple of tourists, that would be best," Yuri said.

I let my power surge dissipate into the background noise of the storm. I'd let my temper get the better of me and I couldn't help but worry who might've noticed. With No Name and the two warlocks still out there somewhere, that kind of display was as bad as holding up a big, neon sign pointing right at me.

"That's gonna be about one thousand, four hundred dollars, Belize," Tinito Cowo said. He started to take on an over-practiced cadence, as though he was slipping into something that he'd had to repeat thousands of times before. "Tips for your driver and guide are separate and given at the end of the tour. Should you have any complaints, please stop in and see us any time."

His brain caught up with him after that last bit, and Tinito stole a glance at Yuri as the receipt started to print. "Actually, you're making us go out in this sort of weather. You can keep your complaints to yourself. I'm going to have to pay my team double just to get them to come in."

"Then I'm surprised you didn't charge more," Yuri said.

"You think this is the first time I've had to deal with government work?" Tinito asked. "I made your reasonable expense on credit. Now where's my incentive to keep quiet?"

I waited for Yuri to look at me, to ask a question so I could confirm whether this guy would keep that kind of bargain. That moment didn't come, though. Without a word, Yuri pulled a small stack of clipped bills out of one of his many pockets and pushed it across the counter. Tinito whisked the entire clip into his own back pocket. If I had blinked, I would've missed the entire thing.

"I need to go make some calls," Tinito said. He went through the glass door behind him.

"Why didn't you ask me if he was actually going to stay quiet about this before you paid him?" I asked, keeping my voice low so it wouldn't carry too far.

Yuri didn't respond to me for long enough that I was starting to think he hadn't heard me. When he finally did, it was simply one word, "Later."

Okay. Spy stuff reasons. He was the one with the training here, so I kept my thoughts to myself and continued to glare through the office wall whenever I caught Tinito looking at us. I wondered how sensitive he was to magic. Most people had a bit of perception where magic was involved, but Tinito was acting much jumpier than any of my classmates had when I'd lost my temper back in high school. Maybe it was because he was already dealing with government agents. Maybe he had something to hide. Maybe he had some sort of magic himself.

Maybe I was jumping at shadows.

The rain whipped up toward the office windows and the lights flickered. It took everything I had in me not to jump away from the door. There are reasons that kind of thing is used so much in horror movies.

Tinito came back out of the office only a few seconds later. "Okay, I found a team that's willing to chance it. They said they'd be here as soon as they could."

"I guess we'll take a seat," Yuri said, giving Tinito a smile that even I found off putting. It had the desired effect though. Tinito went right back into his office to wait us out.

Yuri beckoned me to sit next to him against the far wall. I mentally began weaving the threads around the two chairs in question to make us less noticeable, the way that I'd hidden myself in Elena's parking lot only the day before. I didn't think it would really work against Tinito. He'd been too badly shaken already, so his senses were on high alert. I figured it might buy us a moment or two of reaction time against anyone who might come looking for us. Couldn't hurt to take precautions.

"Ready to tell me what that was about earlier?" I asked as I sat down.

"Wasn't worth letting him know we didn't trust him," Yuri said. "He already suspects we don't trust him, but right now, it's not confirmed. As soon as he *knows* we don't trust him, he won't feel any need to respect the deal."

"So, basically, you don't want me to confirm whether he's trustworthy or not because that way he'll probably be more trustworthy than he would be otherwise?" I was glad that the cash wrap was now between Tinito and myself because there was no way I could keep the confusion off my face. "That... That's... I don't even know what that is."

"It sounds weird, but basically there are two options—either he's trustworthy, or he's not. But a lot of trustworthy people can still do bad things if they get put in a bad position. The other side could offer better money, they could threaten his family, or they could hurt him to get him to talk. If any of those things occur, and he knows we already expected him to out us, he's less likely to hesitate to betray us because, in his mind, we deserve it for doubting him. This is one of those things that they cover a lot in training, but it's hard to believe until you see it first hand," Yuri sighed. "I've been betrayed by some good people because I pushed too hard. And I've been surprised by some real stand-up schmucks."

Rather than trying to wrap my brain around people and their puzzling behaviors, I leaned back and listened to the rain as it rampaged outside. The lights flickered again. I wasn't sure they were coming back on this time.

Splashing sounds hidden in the rain were too regular to be anything but footsteps. Footsteps were followed by muffled voices and shadows moving along the windows.

"Are you sure we should be goin' out in this?"

"We need the money, especially with what happened to the cab."

I couldn't believe it. Even as the door opened and they shuffled in out of the rain, I felt like this wasn't really happening. Elena and Sylvia were shaking collected water off of their raincoats and patting themselves dry with hand towels they'd stashed in the pockets of Sylvia's purse. Both of them were wearing the Explorers Unbound employee uniform: neon green shirts with logo and name done in hot pink, and khaki shorts.

"I get a bad feeling about anyone willing to pay Tinito enough to go out now," Elena said, clicking her tongue for emphasis.

Yuri leaned in and whispered, "Did you know it was going to be them?"

With a helpless shrug, I looked at him with wide eyes. I didn't know what to do in this situation. When Elena had thrown me out of their apartment, I'd thought that would be the end of it. I'd never anticipated seeing her or Sylvia again. Even with Eddie's checking in on me, I didn't think anything would come of it. Given that Elena seemed to already be in a less than charitable mood to her potential employers, I didn't feel equipped to deal with this. For longer than I thought necessary, Yuri watched me for signs of dishonesty.

I almost, *almost*, forgot that I'd put up a glamor to lessen Yuri and my visibility. Even so, Sylvia got that look on her face that she'd had in the apartment parking lot when her eyes passed over our spot against the wall. It was the look of someone who could almost remember something or was trying to read a billboard that was barely out of range. *She's as sensitive as Tinito,* I realized. *Maybe even as magical as her uncle.*

"Oh, good," Tinito came out of his office with a sneer on his face. "My *favorite* team is here. The lesbian and her *boyfriend*."

"The only team you were going to get out on a day like today, so be a little grateful," Sylvia said. She kept her voice even despite the anger I felt coming off of her in waves. It almost matched Tinito's level of distaste. He wasn't even bothering to hide his sneer.

"It's the two of you that should be grateful. Your kind is only barely tolerated here, and I wouldn't have called you in today if I could've helped it. As it is, you're going to be getting double pay and whatever you can scrape out of this pair as a tip. Once they set eyes on *you*, I can't imagine it'll be much," Tinito's voice was something between a yell and a hiss.

If I hadn't already disliked Tinito, that little speech would've sealed it. The anger rolling off of me was almost a match for Sylvia's ire. *Fucking transphobic asshole.* "I wouldn't say that, Mr. Cowo. I think they'll work for us just fine."

He'd managed to forget about us long enough for my spell to affect him. I could read it on his face. Not only had he forgotten we were there, but he'd been caught treating his employees like shit when he thought no one was looking. Sylvia and Elena were also looking at me with varying levels of anger and disbelief. Well, okay, all the anger from those two flowing in my direction was really coming from Elena. Sylvia's expression was more disbelief and assessment.

I had interrupted a row between unhappy people and at least half of them looked ready to turn on me.

"Assuming they are still interested in accepting the job," Yuri stepped in, breaking the tension with his reminder that there was money on the table.

"We're up to it," Sylvia said. She reached out and squeezed Elena's hand. "We're the best team he has, in any case. A fact that has kept us employed here and not taking *other* offers."

Tinito's eyes and nostrils flared as he swallowed words that were likely not fit for polite society. "They do have the best ratings of all of my teams," he admitted. Though I could tell he was telling the truth, it was costing him something to do it. He did *not* want to praise them in any capacity, but he also didn't seem willing to alienate people that brought him revenue. "Bus Five. Watch for floods. I'd hate for anything to happen to the bus."

Backhanded truth. This guy was an asshole and a half.

If not for Yuri's restraining hand, I'd have followed him into his office and rectified that half an asshole situation for him by ripping him a new one.

Before Elena had a chance to turn on me, Sylvia all but shoved her toward the cash wrap. "Grab the keys for Bus Five before Tinito comes out here and changes his mind. You know he usually reserves that one for Mike and Cari. Once we're out there, we can all talk about everything."

Elena muttered under her breath as she followed Sylvia's instructions. She managed to keep herself moving until we'd all run through the rain one more time and were shedding water like pet hair over the plush padded bus seats. Bus Five was definitely not an economy model. It had a lavatory in the back, air-conditioning vents over every chair, and headrests. These seats even had armrests. It wasn't a big bus though. With only fourteen spaces plus the driver's chair, there wasn't much chance of pretending that we couldn't hear each other from anywhere on the bus.

As soon as the doors closed out the rain, Elena turned on me. "I TOLD YOU I WANTED YOU OUT! That meant out of my life, not just out of my door! Why the hell are we here?! Did you know where we worked?! Are you some sort of weird stalker gyal that latched on to the first body she saw?! Is this bally really even a stranger to you?!"

"I had no idea you guys were getting called in!" I protested. My hands raised in surrender almost of their own accord. "I swear, I had every intention of staying away from you after you told me you wanted me gone! Yuri and I were strangers when we met in your cab. I promise!"

I could feel Yuri's presence behind me, but he was wisely keeping his mouth shut. There was very little he could say that would improve Elena's view of either of us. She'd not exactly been warm to him from the start.

"Are you the witch that my uncle recently befriended?" Sylvia asked.

It seemed like the temperature of the entire bus dropped a notch as Sylvia and Elena both waited to see what I would say. I'd already told Elena that I was a witch once. She hadn't believed me then. I wasn't sure she would now. Either way, I didn't see any point in lying about it. "Yes. Unless Eddie's met multiple witches within the last few days, that's probably me."

Sylvia and Elena exchanged a look that I couldn't interpret, and then Elena slid past her girlfriend and into the driver's seat. "Let's get this mess done," she said as she turned the key in the ignition and Bus Five clamored to life. "And you'd all better hope no one has to get out and push."

# 19

KEEPING A PROFESSIONAL distance between us, Yuri opted to sit behind me rather than next to me. I tried to pretend that didn't bother me, but after finding myself face to face with Elena's animosity again, I wasn't having much luck.

My powers were doing odd things here in Belize: tying me to a man that only wanted me in a professional capacity, continuing to throw me into the path of someone that wanted nothing to do with me, and the coup de gras—linking me with a blood-thirsty knife that had chosen me to wield it. During the first few days of learning about this wider world of power, I was so relieved to find out I wasn't alone that I didn't want to go back to my life in Kansas ever again. Less than a week into learning about everything past my immediate scope, I was regretting the decisions that had led me to Belize. Maybe life had been a lot less interesting in Kansas, but I'd never woken up inside a knife with a bunch of dead men either.

"Since this is a private tour, would you like me to do the guide talk or do the two of you prefer a quiet trip out to the ruins?" Sylvia asked.

I wasn't sure if Yuri was leaving it to me, or if he hadn't realized we were being spoken to, but I answered after a second. "I wouldn't mind hearing the tour speech."

Anything was better than continuing to be alone with my thoughts.

With a nod, Sylvia launched into her tour guide voice. It filled every inch of the bus. Despite it only being Yuri and me, she was projecting her voice on a level that could've been heard over several smaller conversations on a much larger bus. "Welcome to Belize! I don't know if you're first timers or not, but let me assure you that there is plenty to love about this Caribbean nation so you'll be extra sure to come back! As you can see, this is the rainy season. Despite that, Belize has many more sunny days than rainy throughout the year."

I had to give it to the stout Hispanic woman—she had a radio voice. Very clear articulation. There was a slight hint of accent here and there, but not nearly as thick as Elena's tended to get. Her facial features held a strong resemblance to her uncle—they had the same nose and cheekbones. Sylvia's hair was still entirely raven black, while her uncle's was greying, but I could've mistaken Eddie for her father if I hadn't been told otherwise. Intelligence flashed in those dark brown eyes and her lips curved up as she talked, like she was sharing a private joke with everyone that listened to her. It was easy to see why Elena had fallen for Sylvia. She had the kind of personality that would leave entire tour groups feeling a little enamored.

"Psst, hey!" Yuri's hand touched my arm through the gap caused by the armrests. It was only when I felt his touch that I realized that I'd been on the verge of falling asleep.

"Hmm?" I leaned toward the gap. Yuri was trying not to draw attention to the fact that we were talking, so I didn't want to risk anything more overt.

Sylvia wasn't looking at me. She was directing us to look out the windows to the left of the bus to try and catch a glimpse of something through the rain. I turned my gaze far enough that my ear was almost on Yuri's lips. If not for the thickness of the bus's cushions, we might have made contact.

"These two might be in danger once we get to the ruins. The knife isn't the only thing in this area to be aware of. There've been reports of Guatemalan guerillas crossing the border into the surrounding jungle in recent months," Yuri said. "I know I already asked once, but please tell me you didn't bring them out here on purpose."

*Shit.* A chill of fear ran across my arms making my downy, little hairs stand on end. "I had no idea. And when were you going to tell me about the possibility of guerillas?"

"I was hoping I wouldn't have to," Yuri said. "With your ability to fade us, I thought it wouldn't be that big an issue."

If I'd had the blood knife with me right then, I think I could've stabbed Yuri in the foot. Not somewhere vital, but definitely somewhere that caused him a lot of discomfort. This was the kind of thing that I hated about being a witch. Even people who understood what I was didn't really *know.* "That's a concentration thing. I have to be able to hold it in place. If I've got a bunch of semi-automatics being waved around in the immediate vicinity, or if someone looks long and hard enough, the way a trained soldier might, I'm not sure I've got that kind of staying power."

There was a pause from Yuri's direction. I was on the verge of sitting up again when he said, "I suppose that's going to make this a very interesting endeavor."

I didn't need any gifts of premonition to know that was one hell of an understatement.

IT WAS A ROUGH RIDE out to Caracol. We slid in a mud patch at one point. Later, there was a spot where Yuri, Sylvia, and I had to get out of the bus to meet Elena on the other side of a bridge she didn't trust to handle the entire load. Taking the bridge on foot, with flood waters roaring underneath, was bad enough. I couldn't imagine driving over it. Around noon, we emerged from the worst of the storm. The rain tapered off and the wind softened into a breeze.

We made a brief stop for lunch at a local place. (I had a johnny-cake sandwich, which was a bit like a sandwich made with a cornbread biscuit. I've eaten worse things, but in the future, I'm going to steer clear of johnnycakes.) By the time we reached the ruins, the afternoon sun had broken its way through the clouds. The rapidly rising humidity made me happy that I hadn't let Yuri throw out my clothes. Sweatpants were going to get uncomfortable out here in a hurry. Before we even left the bus, I changed back into my brown shorts.

I debated leaving the backpack on the bus. If we found the knife and couldn't—or didn't want to—destroy it, I didn't want to risk touching the thing. Better safe than sorry. It wasn't like the knife would fit in my hip drop bag.

Yuri took Sylvia aside to ask a few questions about the ruins. Their conversation picked up an academic tone and they started talking at a higher level than I was able to follow. In a general studies way, I can tell the difference between a Mayan pyramid and an Egyptian pyramid. Both are pretty amazing. But when it comes to time periods and the various tribes of Central America, I get lost fast. I wandered back to the bus to let them geek out in peace.

Elena opened the luggage compartment on the side of the bus and pulled out an ice chest hidden inside. It was filled with water bottles and a layer of water that may have been ice at one point. Hissing through her teeth, Elena's eyes seemed to roll back into her head. "Cari did it again! She left the ice in the water case yesterday! My god, that gyal! Why's she even still working here!"

Even with the bottles being room temperature, I accepted one when Elena passed it to me. Before I could chicken out, I made myself ask the question that had been bothering me since we'd been in the Explorers Unbound office. "What happened to your cab?"

So many expressions crossed Elena's face that it looked like her eyebrows were at war. The idea struck me as absurdly funny and all of the sudden I was fighting not to laugh. But I didn't want Elena to get any madder at me than she already was. Both the moment and my fit of humor passed. With a sigh, Elena passed me two more water bottles before shutting the chest and using it as a stool. "Someone burned my taxi. They were looking for Sylvia and me, but when they couldn't find us they lit my livelihood on fire."

"Holy shit," I said. Any vestiges of laughter that lingered rushed out of my body. "I'm so sorry. Do you know who they were? Or why they were after you?"

Looking more defeated than I'd ever seen her, Elena shook her head. "At first, I thought they might have been one of the local hate groups. There's always going to be those that try to hurt people who are simply trying to live their truth. It's why Sylvia moved in with Eddie in the first place; her family threw her out when she told them she was a gyal. From what she's told me, her old neighborhood in the U.S. sounds just as bad as the stuff we deal with down here. But the men didn't leave when they heard the sirens coming. The two of them stood there, talking about how maybe the fire would make us come running. And then they'd be able to ask about our visitors."

*Fuck*. That was the last thing I wanted. I'd been so convinced that Elena cutting her ties with me had put her out of danger, it hadn't occurred to me the danger was already aware of her. Somehow, I'd still managed to drag her and Sylvia into my mess.

"I wanted to believe the worst in you, you know," Elena said, interrupting my descent into self-recrimination. She leaned against the bus doors and met my eyes. It was the first time in a few days her face didn't hold a spark of rage when she focused on me. "When we showed up to the tour office today and I saw you there, I wanted to believe that you'd known what was going to happen the whole time. But I had time to think on the drive out here. Sylvia said she sensed some sort of protection laid on our apartment. When Tinito was trying to push us around, you stood up to him. I need to be angry for a bit longer, but whatever's going on with you, I know you're not a bad person. Maybe I won't block you from my socials quite yet."

It wasn't the nicest thing anyone had ever said to me, but a gigantic burden lifted from my chest. I hadn't even been aware that I was carrying that much weight around until it vanished. All of a sudden, I could breathe again. Managing a weak smile, I swallowed back the urge to launch myself at Elena and hug her. It would probably strain what little grace I'd managed to win back.

Elena heaved herself back to her feet while I stashed the water bottles she'd handed me into the backpack. She picked up a couple more that she'd placed on the ground. Added to the bottles she'd already given Yuri and Sylvia, it seemed like overkill on water for only four of us. Then again, there wasn't a store of any sort out here. No restroom, either. Not even an admissions stand nearby. (There'd been an admission booth to the national park that housed the ruins, but we'd passed that a few miles back.) This was the most secluded place I'd ever seen. Perfect for someone wielding an ancient murder knife to prowl around. Also, guerillas.

"How safe is it for tourists out here normally?" I asked. There was a bit of a lump forming in my throat as we walked into a large green square. Step pyramids rose on every side of us. While they weren't monolithic in the sense of being carved from a single stone, they dominated the landscape, pressing on my mind like living mountains. I could feel the eyes of ancient deities following me as I crept across their grounds. Even as a witch among mortals, I'd rarely felt more alien in my own skin. The presence of the knife was growing, too. We were close to wherever it was hiding.

"It's usually pretty safe out here. There's snakes and things, though. Not usually too many jaguars. They prefer to be left alone so they don't normally attack people. Of course, not crossing paths with anything wild is best," Sylvia said. Neither she nor Elena looked overly concerned by the idea of crossing paths with snakes or a deadly jungle cat, but the lump in my throat seemed to grow a whole extra size. Kansas didn't have much in the way of big predators and I'd been raised in what passed for the city. The closest I'd been to any wild animal had been within the confines of the local zoo.

Yuri started toward the largest of the pyramids with purposeful strides. "These pyramids are climbable, yes?"

"Yes," Sylvia said. "The largest structure is often called the Sky Palace. It likes to surprise you with how high it is. Be ready, because the top is at least one hundred and ninety-two steps away."

I trailed along at the back of the group. That feeling of being watched was getting heavier. Eyes were burning into me from every-where and I couldn't shake the sense that I was being tested. Weighed. Judged.

Yuri seemed confused by my lingering at the back of the group, but I wasn't sure how to tell him what was going on with Sylvia and Elena between us. He kept turning back to check on me and I waved him on. I could tell him what was bothering me once we were at the top of the pyramid. I didn't need to tell the entire park that I felt the burgeoning weight of gods watching.

The way the steps of the pyramid were constructed, we were re-quired to bow and scrape our way to the top. We reached something like a flight marker once and we were only halfway up. We kept mov-ing. My legs ached as though I hadn't been exercising daily since I'd arrived in the tropics. With the humidity leaving me breathless and the discomfort of being on this ancient temple, I probably looked like the living dead.

"Hey," Yuri said, giving me a hand as I stumbled over the final step of the base level. Now that we were up here, I saw that the steps we had been climbing actually led to a second grassy square with three miniature stepped pyramids reaching even higher toward the heavens. No wonder they called this a palace. "Are you alright? You're looking kind of rough there."

I started to let him lift me, and then decided to pull him down to sit beside me instead. Our guides took the hint and went to sneak a sweet moment to themselves on one of the upper structures. "This place is a bit overwhelming," I admitted. "I'm not sure who was worshipped here, but I don't think they left when their people did."

Yuri let my words sink in. It was nice that he could do that. So many other people felt the need to be heard that they talked over me instead of actually taking the time to listen. "That's possible with these old places. That's part of how we get things like the demigods. A tourist or visitor will strike an old god's fancy and they'll take a form to attract the visitor's attention. If they're nice about it."

Remembering some choice tales about the Greek gods from an elective mythology class, I didn't have to ask what Yuri meant by that. Seduction was common in the mythos, and I couldn't imagine that other ancients would be much nicer. "I really hope that's not the type of attention I'm drawing," I said.

"Honestly, with the Mayan gods, we're probably okay," Yuri said. "They aren't as forgotten as some of the others, which generally means they've evolved along with the practitioners of their faith. But then, all religions have forgotten pieces of their lore and hidden knowledge. If it's one of the forgotten gods, there's no telling what they might be after."

"There's more," I said. It was hard to drag this part out past the swelling that clogged my voice box. It was as if a hand was clutching my throat and trying to choke the words away. "The knife is nearby. It's not in this complex, but we're very, very close."

At that moment, hands came down on both of our shoulders and we found ourselves looking into Elena's worried eyes. "I don't know what actually brought you two out here, and right now, I'm not gonna to ask. We've got company and we need to hide. Turn your phones off. A ring or a buzz carries farther than you think."

I tried to swallow past the choking sensation. The three of us scrambled as quietly as we could away from the steps and into the shadows of the Sky Palace's upper levels.

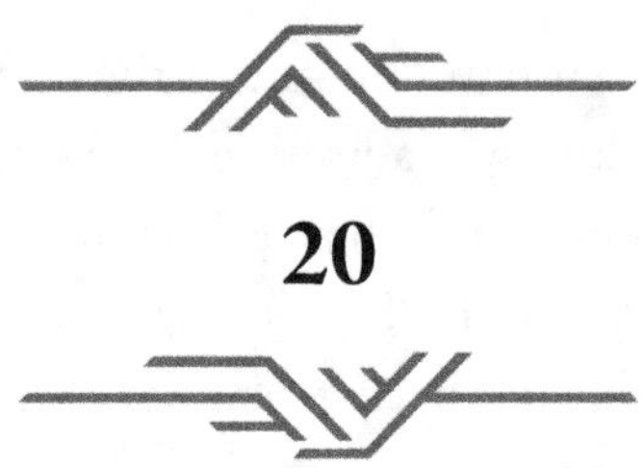

# 20

MOST OF THE HIDING options provided by the Sky Palace would've been struck down as too obvious by the average six-year-old. There were a couple of dark doorways leading into dead-end chambers, a few open-to-the-sky rooms at the feet of the upper pyramids, and of course, there were the tops of the upper pyramids. Elena and Sylvia were all for hiding in one of the dark no-escape chambers, but Yuri refused to go in. All four of us had reached an unspoken agreement not to talk until the threat had passed, so Yuri's refusal was mostly given in hand gestures.

I still hadn't seen or sensed the threat that caused Sylvia to retrieve us from the steps. Being watched by gods overwhelmed all of my supernatural senses. All but the link I had with the knife. Even my connection to Yuri was duller out here. My curiosity was stronger than my caution long enough for me to take a risk and do something dumb. I crept back to the edge of the Sky Palace and peeked down at the lower courtyard.

No Name, Alex Smith, and Jonas Ical were standing near the foot of the stairs. With them were three people in camo fatigues, equipped with some serious armaments. All of my gun knowledge comes from video games, so it's pretty damn spotty. Suffice to say, these looked like the kind of thing you'd loot off enemies about three to four levels. These things weren't starter equipment. No one at the foot of the pyramid looked very happy.

"We found the bus, as promised. Now we merely have to find the Reliquarian and his team," Alex Smith said. He was defying the sweltering humidity with a button down shirt and white linen pants.

Bare ankles were sticking out of his loafers. The warlock looked like he had dressed for a trip to the mall in the 80s rather than traipsing around the jungle. "I told you Tinito would come through."

*I knew Tinito was a bastard.* Even so, I silently cursed at the betrayal. Elena and Sylvia really needed to find a new employer.

"He hasn't come through yet," No Name hissed. The distance did nothing to lessen the welling up of terror I experienced at the sound of the demigod's voice. If anything, I'd forgotten how scary he was since our last encounter. I wanted to jump off the back of the pyramid and take off running. Never mind that I probably wouldn't survive the fall. "A bus isn't the same as giving us our quarry. I *need* that witch. She's pivotal. I can taste it in her magic... The knife already knows her."

"How is that possible?" Jonas Ical said.

I didn't hear the response. Yuri yanked me away from the edge and dragged me back toward the rear of the Sky Palace. Wherever Sylvia and Elena had decided to hide, I didn't see them in the dark doorway they'd hidden in before.

Yuri's grip on my arm was rough. His face was set in hard, angry lines. Much worse than when he'd suspected that I was a rival agent of some sort. I knew stealing a peek at the people that had scared our guides wasn't my brightest move, but I'd overheard some really useful information. Tinito had sold us out. The three from the beach were still working together. They were as interested in finding me as they were in finding Yuri. I had no way of conveying any of that as he dragged me across the grass, not without giving away our position at the top of this pyramid. I didn't know how well the sound carried down the steps, but it had travelled up just fine.

He didn't release me until we were at the back corner of the Sky Palace, in one of the smaller structures. It looked more like ancient housing than temples. We were blocked from line of sight should anyone get to the top of the stairs. I leaned against the wall and tried to catch my breath. The water bottles in my bag made protest-crunching sounds as they dug into my back. Yuri stalked back and forth like a caged tiger.

At that point, I think the silence was too much for both of us.

"What did you think you were doing?" Yuri asked. His hiss almost matched No Name's for ferocity. "They could've looked up and seen you at any point during that little stunt, and then all four of us would've been looking into the barrel end of those M-4s."

"I was trying to figure out who was down there," I said. My voice was soft. I wanted to be angry with him, but he made too much sense. I could still feel the place on my arm that his fingers had pressed into my skin, though. Even in his anger and handling me as roughly as he ever had, there weren't going to be bruises. I had to appreciate that level of control. I knew I was being reckless... I hadn't considered that I was being reckless with everyone's fate, not mine alone. "I'm sorry. I wasn't thinking."

He stopped pacing directly in front of me. With a hand placed on either side of me he leaned in, staring hard into my eyes. I thought No Name and his goon squad could've heard my heart beat as it turned to thunder in my chest. I opened my mouth to say something, but no words came out. Yuri's lips were on mine between one breath and the next. His kiss was wild and deep, like he was trying to drink me in. We should've been focused on the danger and finding a way out of this mess, but with Yuri's body pressed against me and his tongue parting my lips it was hard to focus on much of anything. While the shroud of deific attention wasn't purged from my being, it and the knife were blasted back from the limelight. Time was sucked away into a dimension where it lost all meaning. I had no way of knowing whether we were locked together at the lips for twenty seconds or twenty hours.

I'd wanted him this way since we'd met, and my body was eager to explore him. Well before I was ready, he broke away. "I'm... I'm sorry. This is not the time…" he sounded breathless as he lifted off of me. "I shouldn't have done that."

"I thought you weren't interested in me as anything but a partner," I managed to say after my head stopped swimming. I remembered to keep my voice down, but it was a struggle. There were parts of me that had awakened during that kiss that were refusing to go back to sleep.

Yuri's features went through a lot of different emotions. Before he could find whatever words he was searching for, we were interrupted by the sound of a foot crunching rock against rock. We both froze. The don't-notice-us spell would've taken too long to anchor and my concentration was thoroughly shot. Hell, I'm pretty sure that I'd forgotten I was a witch during that kiss. Not to mention, I would probably give us away during the casting. Magic's most noticeable when it's in motion. Spells that have already been cast, like my bracelets, tended to fade into the ambient magical white noise of a region. If I went slowly enough, I could weave super tiny spell threads, but hiding us that quickly would've been like slamming a door in a game of hide-and-seek.

As I felt the panic bubble up in my chest, a more rational piece of my mind pointed out that my paracord bracelets weren't burning. Either I wasn't in immediate danger, or my aunt's spells had burned out.

Yuri pulled something out of one of his many pockets, but I wasn't in a good position to see what it was. I'd never actually seen Yuri fight anything. He didn't have his own magic, so I'd always kind of assumed he had no protection against it. But that didn't make much sense, if he was a Reliquarian… A title that seemed to be something between a Bond-like secret agent and Indiana Jones without the whip. Unless he'd pulled a whip out of his pocket.

"It's us," I heard Elena whisper.

Even though we'd already separated, Yuri took two big steps away from me like we were kids making out at a school dance and he'd noticed the approach of a chaperone. I'd never been one of those kids. Watching Yuri back away from me now, I wondered if those teenagers were as embarrassed as I felt. A part of me wondered if Yuri would've put that much distance between us if it had been No Name or one of the warlocks.

Sylvia and Elena crept into our hiding spot. With all four of us in one chamber, it was much more cramped than before. Once they'd shifted in, Elena motioned for us to duck down into a squatting position. I lowered myself to the ground and waited for some sort of explanation. Our tour guides obviously wanted to talk.

"Two of those guys down there are the ones that torched the cab," Sylvia said. She spoke in a normal tone, but her voice seemed to die the moment it reached my ears. Her eyes were oddly dilated for the amount of sun that was bearing down on us.

"Um...?" I started.

"I've inherited some of the same abilities as Eddie," Sylvia said. "Shamanistic powers require mind alterations. Eddie drinks. I require something with a stronger punch. I'm not nearly as strong, but Eddie's been building up his reserves for years. My uncle could probably sneak us out of here without that group noticing. Best I can do is mute us from listeners for a brief conversation. We've got..." Sylvia's eyes seemed to roll back until nothing but the whites showed. "... until the flower swallows the sun."

Elena held up a bit of cellophane-wrapped brownie as explanation before she stashed it back in her fanny pack. She seemed miffed, but there was a warmness to her expression. "I always thought it was weird that my gyal carried edibles but wasn't much for the party scene. Every time she got high, we were in a dangerous situation and I thought I was doing my best to protect her. Turns out she was getting high to protect me."

"Mates, I'm not sure when the flower is supposed to swallow the sun... but our voices being muted won't help us if we don't figure out how to get out of here," Yuri said.

Slowly, the sensation of being watched by something much bigger than any of us was crawling back into place. The temporary reprieve Yuri's kiss had garnered me had been revoked and the muting buffer Sylvia was holding over us didn't offer any protection against the eyes of the divine. Whomever it was, I got the impression that they didn't want me to go. My presence was amusing for them.

I didn't like it. I wasn't sure if the gods watching might try to raise the stakes if I wasn't entertaining enough, or if their entertainment was derived from some sort of insight that would get us out of this in a hurry if we could just *see* it. There were more options. Things I couldn't even guess at.

"Sylvia," I said, a thought occurring to me as I mulled over my divine problem. "You can see things that we can't right now, yes?"

"I can see between the cracks of mortar and space," Sylvia said, giggling a bit. "The molecules of tomorrow shift too much."

"Can you see the best way for us to leave?" I asked. It was almost too much to hope for, but the most straightforward solution sometimes gets skipped because people don't ask about it. Too easy becomes impossible. Aunt Shay once solved a dispute between one of our cashiers and a customer that wanted more creamer in a cup that was already full by offering the customer a larger cup. The cashier had been new to our store and it simply hadn't occurred to him.

Sylvia's dilated eyes fixed on my face then seemed to look past me. I fought the urge to look over my shoulder. I knew that whatever she was seeing wasn't in the physical world.

"Wow... Your family's *old*," she said.

"Thanks...?" I mean, really. What was I supposed to say to that?

"This," Sylvia's hand snaked out and grabbed my wrist. The wrist with my paracord bracelets. "This is our way out. One for now. The second will come. In time."

I retracted my hand from her grasp and swallowed. Like I said, people don't ask about the most straightforward solution. It didn't occur to me that I'd have to give up one of my last links to my aunt's protection.

## 21

UNTYING THE CLASP ON my paracord bracelet took a bit of work. My hands were shaking and I didn't have any tools to help me. Yuri offered me use of a pocket knife, but I couldn't risk damaging the spells that Aunt Shay had woven into the rope. I wasn't sure how this was going to work. We were at the top of a very large pyramid, one that was well over one hundred feet high. I didn't have that much cord around my wrist. I'd worn the two bracelets every day since I'd arrived in Belize and they'd never hidden me from the crew who were currently looking for us before. They'd helped protect me and had maybe provided additional shielding the one time that Eddie had sent me a spell. But that wasn't the same thing.

It took me almost three minutes of unlacing plus however much time was eaten by the initial clasp untangle. I had no idea how close we were to Sylvia's flower-eating-the-sun cut off.

We had roughly twenty feet of cord when I was done, plus the two bits of clasp that no longer seemed very useful. I stashed them in my pocket and then turned to Sylvia. "What now?"

"With four climbers, we each have three anchors. There is only the climb."

*Fuck.* I wasn't the best rock climber. I'd only attempted a rock wall once as part of a high school graduation night. That evening had led to a sprained ankle and two weeks of crutches. Aunt Shay swore up and down she wasn't letting me out of the house without a protection spell ever again.

*Holy shit*, I thought as that memory passed through my mind. *She knew.*

Since the moment that Debra Downs and I had found the bracelets in that tattered box, I'd wondered if my aunt had known that I was leaving Kansas. Up until this moment, everything could've been written off as coincidence. Some of it would've been rather unlikely coincidences, but it still worked. Very strong protection spells were nearly always useful. But a bracelet with enough cord to tie me to three other people and protection spells? I was convinced that Aunt Shay knew something about my future. Maybe not *this* specific, but something like it.

I didn't waste time pondering over my personal epiphany. Passing the cord over to Yuri, I let him tie the cord around a belt loop. He cinched onto one of my belt loops next and then turned toward Elena and Sylvia. "Which of you is the better climber?" he asked. "I'm putting the weaker ones in the middle."

"I'm weaker, huh?" I asked. It was probable that I was, but I didn't like that he'd assumed it.

"I was watching your face when Sylvia said what the plan was," Yuri said. Sylvia had pointed at her own belt loop in response to his query, so he moved to her next and tied her onto the string.

"Ah." No point in arguing with that. "Fair enough."

"How are belt loops supposed to anchor us if one of us slips?" Elena glowered at Yuri as he approached her. "This is barely enough rope to anchor one person to a harness, let alone bind all of us together."

Yuri waited for her to finish complaining before he simply asked, "May I?"

With a roll of her eyes and tsking sound, Elena crossed her arms but nodded. "I can't let these two try to navigate their way down without a second anchor, can I?" Her expression softened as she looked at Sylvia, "Never mind taking into the jungle with this one seeing stars that aren't out."

Sylvia smiled and reached a hand toward Elena. "You are the brightest star in my galaxy," she said.

Elena locked Sylvia's reaching fingers with her own and kissed them with a tenderness that made my heart melt. I may have experienced a slight pang of envy right then. The unbridled desire in the kiss Yuri and I had shared earlier was fun and all, but that situation was still complex and unresolved. It was nothing like seeing two people completely and utterly devoted to each other share a moment. I hoped I was lucky enough to have something like that someday.

Despite Elena's complaint about belt loops, there was a rightness about this that I didn't need Sylvia to verify. The former bracelet was being used for its intended task. It wouldn't let us fall due to a faulty seam or slipped knot. It was almost as though I could feel Aunt Shay's energy belting invisible harnesses to us and replacing the knots Yuri tied with heavy duty carabiners.

A clacking, like the loudest typewriter I'd ever heard, rolled its way up the side of the pyramid. Yuri froze as the sound rippled through the surrounding jungle before he looked at Sylvia. "How long would you say we've got before the flower swallows the sun?"

In response, Sylvia looked toward the sky. We all followed her gaze. Above us, a cloud roughly the shape of an orchid was edging its way over the bright white orb. It looked like our brief window for speech was nearing its end.

The sound happened again, but this time I equated it more with a jackhammer. I'd never heard a semi-automatic rifle in person before, so it took me longer than the others to recognize that the people at the base of the pyramid were shooting at something. I heard the raised voice of one of the warlocks shouting at them to stop. It may have been Jonas. Whichever warlock it was, he sounded annoyed but far from frantic.

"Alright, ladies. Let's move," Yuri said. He had gone back to using much softer tones in hopes that we wouldn't be heard. "Quietly as we can."

Trying to creep to the edge of a pyramid while tied to three other people while hearing gunshots going off isn't an activity I would recommend as part of someone's Belize experience. If I'd been a normal tourist, and there weren't armed warlocks and a demigod after us, it would've been a cool day trip. Still, I'd leave out rock climbing while attached to three other people, especially if one of those people is high as shit.

We made it to the lip of the pyramid after quite a bit of bumping into each other. Every scrape of our feet against the stone, every time one of us bounced off a wall, and every muffled curse made my heart pound a little harder. We had no way of knowing if all of the people hunting for us were still at the base of the pyramid, or if they'd split up to cover more ground. I worried that the shooting was a distraction, covering the sounds of others searching. I tried to push the fear away and trust in the comforting presence of my aunt's energy. Even Aunt Shay's protection only comforted me so much when we went over the ledge.

Climbing a rock wall is much different than free climbing the side of an ancient monument. Rock walls have easy-to-spot, brightly colored stones, which stick out visibly from the even, grey surface that they've been bolted on. The side of the Mayan pyramid was rough and uneven. If I'd thought that the stairs on the front of the thing were designed to be difficult, trying to find a path that hadn't been built was quickly changing my mind. On one side of me, Yuri was pacing me. He'd guide my hands where he could and coax me with soft reassurances that we were making progress and everything would be fine. Sylvia, on the other hand, would occasionally let go with both hands and attempt to catch butterflies that none of the rest of us could see. Even Elena was fighting to keep her temper in check before we'd managed to put our feet on the rim that marked the halfway point.

"Keep me from falling, please," I requested. Yuri obliged, placing one hand firmly at my waist as I took advantage of the larger ledge to swing my backpack around and grab one of the water bottles. I took a deep gulp and swished it a few times to make sure my entire mouth felt wet. It felt like I hadn't drunk anything in hours. Judging by the darkness seeping into the surrounding trees, that wasn't hyperbole.

I offered the bottle to Yuri. He cocked an eyebrow at me and wiggled one of his fingers against my waist. *Oh... Yeah. This isn't awkward*, I thought sarcastically as I held the bottle to his lips so he could drink.

After Yuri had slaked his thirst, I offered the bottle to Elena and Sylvia. Sylvia had calmed down a lot since she'd caught one of her invisible butterflies and absorbed it. I wasn't sure how that helped but, since it meant we didn't have to deal with her crashing on top of everything else, I was happy that she'd achieved her goal. Our guides politely declined my offered water. Elena still had her own bottle strapped to her fanny pack. We stayed on the ledge for a bit longer, none of us looking forward to the next part. The bottom portion of the pyramid was longer, and the darkening sky was going to make what was already difficult infinitely more tedious. I was surprised no one had noticed four people latched to the backside of the Sky Palace, but perhaps my aunt's gift was at work.

With one more glug of water a piece, we began the last leg of our climb. My fingernails were ragged and ripped. Mosquitoes feasted on my exposed legs. My hands burned with scrapes and scratches. I slipped once, fell the full length of our slack and let out a tiny yelp. As Yuri helped me regain my footing and Sylvia clung to her hand holds, Elena's head whipped around wildly. I knew she was listening for any footsteps approaching our location. It was the same thing I'd be doing if I hadn't been reattaching myself to the rock. Once I had my footing back, we all stayed frozen in the dark stillness, anxiously awaiting discovery.

This was when I noticed the overwhelming sense of divine attention hadn't followed me down the side of the temple. I wanted to be relieved, but I wasn't. There was too much tension in the air to catch even a minor breath of solace.

The darkness grew denser. If the four of us had been given a chance to stop there, I think we might have packed it in for the night. Unfortunately, there's no such thing as changing course when you're strapped together forty feet off the ground no matter how dark it gets. We continued our climb. Time slipped away in heartbeats and exhausted breaths. I would've gladly eaten ten johnnycake sandwiches by the time we made it to the bottom of the man-made mountain.

"I *never* want to do that again," I murmured softly as Yuri began untying the cord. He gripped my shoulder, silently agreeing with me, before handing me the spent, unwound bracelet. Aunt Shay's stored magic, one of my last connections with her, was gone. I wasn't sure if her spells had turned attention away from us or if it was my fall that had drained the energy, but I was ready to cry as I tucked the completely mundane cord into my backpack.

We passed the water around again as we recovered from the hellish climb. As tempting as it was to collapse now that we'd made it down, sleep wasn't an option. If one of No Name's people rounded the corner, there was no cover. The dark wouldn't protect us from bullets. Trying to cast something might give us away. I considered attempting to sense No Name, Alex Smith, or Jonas Ical. If I sent a soft enough magical ping, they might not notice. I still had one bracelet of Aunt Shay's protection. But I wasn't really in a hurry to give it up. Having the bracelets was like having my aunt back. A little. It wasn't the same, but it was comforting. Using up Aunt Shay's last spell on something like a ping, that might backfire anyway, was reckless. I'd already done a couple of stupid, reckless things since arriving at Caracol—since arriving in Belize, really. I didn't need to add to the list again quite so soon.

"We need to go back to the bus," Elena said. "If we get there, we can get out of here and come back when those men are gone."

"They're watching the bus," I shook my head. "If they haven't claimed it entirely. I heard them talking before we all hid."

All three of my companions were looking at me like I'd sprouted horns. "What? What did I say?"

"There's no way you should've been able to hear anything spoken at the pyramid's base at the top of that staircase. Not unless they were using megaphones or you had some sort of super hearing ability. We've done enough tours to Altun Ha to know that you can't hear things said at the bottom of the Sun God temple from the top—and that pyramid is only a third the size of this one," Elena said.

"Have you always been able to hear things from that far away?" Yuri asked. "Is this one of your normal enhanced abilities? Can you always hear someone as long as you can see them?"

I was as baffled as the rest of them. "No. My ears are generally only as sharp as the average human's. I thought it was something to do with the acoustics of the stairs." Had the deity watching me carried the conversation to me? That was the only explanation that made any sense, but I was loath to bring it up now that the entity had finally drawn its gaze away.

Sylvia seemed to sense my desire to move on with the subject, because she drew the conversation away from *how* I'd heard anything to *what* I'd heard. "Anything else of note?"

"Tinito told them we'd be out here."

Cursing sharply under her breath, Elena's expression morphed into one of pure, unadulterated hatred. "That fucking bally better be praying tonight, because his soul is mine come morning."

Sylvia didn't look much happier, but she refrained from whispering threats into the bug song of the night. Foreign squeaks and undulating chittering sounds bounced through the canopy. I missed the crickets of Kansas. I shivered a little, but not because I was cold.

Wandering around the jungle at night wouldn't be the smartest thing in the world. There were snakes, jaguars, guerillas, pits, cliffs, poisonous plants, spiders, and somewhere close, a knife-wielding maniac. Somewhere very close. The distance between the knife and myself was shorter than before.

"The three of you need to get somewhere safe," Yuri said. "But I still have a mission."

"We have a mission," I corrected him. I wasn't sure if he was including me with the others because he'd decided that I wouldn't make a good partner or if he'd become more protective after he'd kissed me. Either way, I wasn't about to get left behind. Not when we were so close. "I'm not leaving this half done."

Taking my hand in his, Yuri looked into my eyes. It was dark enough that our foreheads were nearly touching and his irises faded into his pupils, looking like ebony wells that I might fall into if I wasn't careful. "You're sure you still want to do this? That climb... You said you never wanted to do that again. I can't promise anything like that. If you sign on, we might be doing something like that every Tuesday."

Heat pulsed through me with his touch. I shifted back on my heels, very aware that Sylvia and Elena were watching this unfold. I'd sidestepped the last time he'd asked if I was sure by telling him I'd see this mission out. He wanted a firmer answer, but I still wasn't ready to commit to the IACI like that.

"I told you that I would see the rest of this mission out before I made up my mind," I reminded him. Again, I skirted the actual question. I wasn't certain though. Yuri made me feel like I could tackle whatever came, but I had to look past him and witness the IACI at work. I had a feeling that I wouldn't really know until we'd resolved the knife issue, one way or the other.

That was when it hit me. *No Name can't sense the knife.* So if we made a beeline for the knife and dealt with it before No Name and the others found us, we could leave before they figured out everything was already over. "More importantly, right now, we've all got to get out of here. Our goal is nearby. That might be our best bet."

An electronic bleep that had no place in our primal surroundings perforated the night's symphony. In between static bursts, a metallic, echo-chamber voice asked, "ssh zhzh...Any zzk sign of kklzz them... yet?"

Someone with a walkie talkie and a flashlight rounded the corner of the pyramid. As much as I didn't want to get shot, I wasn't much happier at the idea of dueling a warlock. I recognized the light-colored, long pants that practically glowed despite the darkness. Alex Smith looked away from us as the brush rattled on the other side of him. His flashlight swept the trees and he ducked his head toward a receiver that was invisible to me in the darkness. "Not yet. Nor will there be if you keep giving away my location."

"kzzzptt... Wouldn't...half to zzsh keep checking... if... zzzzhh someone kept to... kshk protocol."

Sylvia and Elena took Yuri and me by the hands and dragged us toward the closest copse of trees. I recognized the need to move, but my limbs seemed to be made of lead. My steps were plodding and clumsy as we approached cover. I was certain Alex would turn his light on me any moment.

"What's that? Couldn't hear you... Someone must have forgotten to charge..." Alex said, mimicking the way the other voice had faded in and out. I felt something immediately following. It was similar to that pinching sensation when jeans snag onto a single hair. Uncomfortable. Painful.

*He drained the battery*, I realized.

That was when something else clicked. The reason that I hadn't noticed when he'd hexed the bottle was because I actually *had* felt it. Warlock magic translated into pain when it happened near me. At the time, I simply hadn't recognized it as casting magic. If they weren't born with power, it had to come from somewhere. He'd syphoned away a layer of my magic. That's why my body had ached so much after our last encounter.

"I know you're out here, little witch," Alex said, still scanning the trees. "I'm fairly certain you are still carting around a former associate of mine... When we find you, you'll wish you'd come quietly."

None of us had managed to get very far into the tree line. The underbrush was thick. Sylvia sank to her knees with Elena right beside her. Yuri ducked behind one of the larger trees. I still felt like I was moving through taffy. My legs didn't want to cooperate. What was going on? I turned to see how far away the sweeping light was from our position.

My right leg took a step forward. I hadn't told it to do that. And then my left leg followed suit. A foreign pain throbbed through my ankles. Two more steps. *Shit!*

This shouldn't have been possible... Unless they'd found something of mine. Something like a lock of hair, a fingernail, or a personal possession that I treasured. I couldn't think of anything they could have to use on me. Most of my personal belongings were in my condo. They wouldn't have been able to catch us that quickly from San Pedro, unless they had a much faster means of transportation. Besides, the stuff in the condo had been pretty secure. My salt wards had been intact when I left this morning.

*Well, actually, there's one thing...* I thought. My hands moved through space like they were set in slow motion. They inched toward my pockets, where I remembered tucking away the clasp of my sacrificed bracelet. Empty. The clasp must have fallen out on the top of the pyramid when I was wiggling my way over the rim. I'd diligently worn both bracelets, clipping them onto my wrist every morning and placing them within easy reach every night. I hadn't had them long, but it had been long enough for attunement.

My companions were hissing at me, telling me to get down. Urging me to stop. Even though I couldn't turn my head toward him, I could feel Yuri's fear and anger growing like a fire at my back.

Right leg.

Left leg.

Right.

Left.

If I didn't think of something soon, I'd find myself out of the forest's cover in about four more steps. Out of desperation, I reached for the two connections that had drawn me to Belize. The connection with Yuri reached back, but before I could grasp on, the *other* connection enveloped me.

*MINE.*

The knife's hostility made its voice practically audible outside of my skull. I'd felt it drawing closer, but I'd failed to notice just how fast it was rushing toward us. My grasping for salvation had triggered something in it though. All sense of the world fell away as I was swallowed by a burning cold. The last thing I saw before the knife's essence drew me out of the world was a crazed figure in torn shorts and a soiled rag of a shirt jumping out of the trees as the flashlight grazed over the underbrush. Colliding with Alex, the figure brought down the same knife that had just taken me hostage.

Everything else was lost to the void.

# 22

"INTERESTING," ALEX Smith's voice said from somewhere much too close. I opened my eyes and jumped away from the lanky warlock.

I checked myself—I was back in the red triskele shirt, burgundy jacket and brown-tinted jeans. Billowing fog obscured the black stone of the floor, and while there wasn't a light source, everything was weirdly visible. We were in the misty plane that I'd found myself in before.

Only, unlike any of the others I'd seen inside of this place, Alex was not greyed out or unmoving. He was as alive and functional as I was. Though, he hardly looked like the same Alex Smith. Long sun-bleached hair was pulled back into a pony-tail, and he was wearing a pair of carpenter jeans, a chain wallet and an old concert t-shirt for the Magical Space Skeleton Army.

"What the hell are you doing here?" I asked. I wanted to sound imposing, but I couldn't keep the quaver out of my voice. While I'd been looking for a way out of my predicament, I'd never wanted to find myself here again. Let alone here in the company of one of my pursuers.

"I could ask you the same question," Alex said. The look on his face wasn't *quite* a sneer, but it could've been mistaken for a close relative. "I was stabbed. A glancing blow. Not enough to actually draw my soul out should I have chosen to stay. But I felt your spirit slip past me on the way in, so I came to have a little chat."

There wasn't anywhere I could run. There wasn't anywhere I could hide. Inside the knife, there were the lifeless souls that stood in the endless mist and little else. I knew my magic worked here, so I assumed that meant Alex Smith could access his as well. But the knife itself seemed to be on my side. Maybe I was safe? "A chat about what?"

"About who you choose to befriend."

I scowled. I had no interest in chatting with a man that sided with No Name, nor in joining up with a guy that used stolen magic. There was a reason every spell he'd cast when I was nearby had caused me pain. His magic drained whatever sources were handy for power.

Alex spread his hands in a soothing gesture. "I can see that you're not about to team up with me, and that's fine. I'm merely suggesting that we talk before you do something like sign on with Yuri Knowles and the IACI."

"What do you get out of this?" If he wasn't trying to give me the Dark Side pitch, I wasn't sure what his angle was. Also, I have to admit, I was a little disappointed. Not that I meant to join him, but it's nice to feel wanted.

"*Magic*," Alex said. His open hands gripped the air as though he could pull the power floating around us into him. "I'm only as powerful as the existing magic in the world allows me to be. What the IACI does is destroying the remaining pool. And they will only see you as an asset until they decide you're the enemy. I've seen it happen before. Why do you think you've never met another of your own kind?"

"I was raised by my own kind," I argued.

"You were raised by your aunt—a domestic witch that ran a coffee shop and tried to teach you spells out of a family book. And for reasons you've never fully understood, they rarely worked," Alex corrected.

My jaw suddenly lost the will to fight gravity. I wanted to say something, to contradict him, but all I could think of was the number of things that I'd never been able to do right. I was a witch, but

I wasn't the same kind of witch. We'd called me a Tacomancer, and I'd embraced it, because it kept me from dwelling on questions I'd feared the answers to: What was I really? Was something wrong with me? Why couldn't I cast spells correctly?

"Judging by your expression, I hit the nail on the head."

Fighting down the bubble of panic surging its way up my throat, I got my jaw back under control. "How did you know about my aunt?"

The warlock raised his eyebrows at me. He knew I was stalling for time. "You can treat this as seriously as you wish. When my limp body is found, they'll know you and your companions are close by. Jonas is far less patient than I am. Our employer is worse."

"Okay. Why would my joining the IACI be a big enough problem for you to risk talking to me instead of capturing me?"

This time, Alex nodded. Apparently I'd found an acceptable question. "I don't much care how we get you out of the way, only that you get out of the way. But, as I said before, my biggest desire is to keep more magic in the world. A relic like you is worth preserving."

"A relic like me?"

Alex Smith's mouth twitched. I could tell he was struggling not to grin. I'd finally fumbled my way into the conversation he'd been wanting to have. "Do you have any inkling how far back your bloodline goes?"

I shook my head. I knew I shouldn't listen to him. Alex Smith was the enemy. He'd been party to the burning of Elena's cab. His group had done something horrible to the beach when Yuri and I had gotten away from them. Nothing on Earth should have convinced me to trust anything he had to say. Except that he hadn't lied to me yet. Not once. Yuri had lied to me, even after learning that I was a witch.

"The House of Egibi dates back to ancient Babylonia. Your archaeologist boyfriend knows all about it," Alex said.

Something cold rolled into my stomach. I dimly recalled Yuri listing off the regions that his expertise covered. I'd been all but lost, staring at a sketch of the very knife I was currently standing in, but it was there. He'd mentioned Mesopotamia. "What does that mean exactly? Why does it matter how far back my lineage goes?"

A moment stretched into a while, a while stretched into minutes, minutes stretched into eons. Alex and I blinked at each other, neither of us twitching a muscle. I couldn't read his body language and his expression was as neutral as a professional poker player. Just as I was about to break and tell him to forget it, he started laughing. Not a maniacal, menacing laugh—this was a whole-hearted guffaw. "Aren't you precious?"

I crossed my arms and waited. No one likes being laughed at, but I've had my share of practice.

After Alex laughed himself out, his hand on his stomach like he'd actually caused his gut pain, he turned back to me with a much more serious expression. "Look, I'm sure he's given you the spiel about how these relics acquire their power over time. The more people believe that the thing is special..."

"The more power the artifact, relic, etcetera accrues," I said. His meaning sank in seconds after the last word left my lips. "That... That happens with blood lines, too."

"There's a lot more to the theory, but yes, that's the jist. The longer a magical line is aware of its magic, the more powerful that line becomes."

"But I can't do anything!" I protested. "How can that be even remotely true? If I were as powerful as you seem to think, why would I be running from you and your cohorts? Couldn't I zap you with lightning bolts or something?"

"Have you tried?" There was a glint in Alex Smith's eyes at that. Whether it was a glint of challenge or amusement, I couldn't say, but there was a new tension in the air as he waited for my response.

"...No."

Triumph flashed across Alex's features. "There's a lot about the world you don't know yet, little witch. Try asking Yuri Knowles about your family. Ask him if he knows anything about the kind of magic you wield. Before you get tied to a harness and muzzled by the IACI."

Without warning, Alex Smith was gone. The mist that had clung to his feet swirled into the sudden vacuum Alex's departure left behind. I wasn't sure how he'd gotten out, but I needed to follow him. As far as I could tell, the spell he'd been using to draw me out of the jungle didn't work while I was inside the knife. That didn't mean he couldn't find my body and take it somewhere while I was unconscious. I assumed I was unconscious. This wasn't my physical body, after all.

*I wonder what the others must be thinking.* Yuri, Elena and Sylvia seeing me drop suddenly after walking toward Alex Smith like I'd been possessed... I wasn't sure what I would've done in their position.

I didn't want to think about the things Alex had told me. He hadn't been lying, but that also didn't mean he was telling the *whole* truth. Still, the idea that Yuri knew something about my lineage and hadn't shared was upsetting. He'd warned me that the International Anti-Cataclysm Initiative had trouble retaining magic users. We'd both avoided talking about the implications. I'd been satisfied to think I was saving the world. I'd continually pushed the complications away, to be dealt with later.

We were going to deal with the knife, a knife that thirsted for human blood. A knife that was currently sheltering me because I'd magically cried for help. "Knife?"

There was no response.

"Should I call you something else?" I asked.

**I am nameless. Call me as you wish.**

A shudder ran through me as the voice of the knife answered. I'd forgotten how off-putting and inhuman the multi-resonance chorus sounded. Echoes of the dead vibrated through my soul with each word. "I don't want to kill people! Why would you want me as a wielder?"

*You* **must** *wield. YOU* **MUST** *WIELD!*

Covering my ears didn't help, but I curled into the fetal position as I held my arms against my head anyway. I was crying. Desperate, wracking sobs were making it impossible to gulp down enough air. A somewhat removed piece of my mind was watching the rest of me fall apart. I suddenly recognized that not all of the emotions crashing against me were my own. "Why me?"

**Mine. Chosen. Protector. Protected.**

None of it made any sense. I needed to get out. The emptiness was threatening to overwhelm me. "Let me out. Please."

I felt a flicker of indecision. The knife didn't like letting people out once it had them, and one person had already escaped its grasp. While I could have pointed out that I couldn't wield it from the inside, I refrained from saying anything that might be construed as a promise. Sobs continued to jolt through my chest. Then the gloom surrounding me changed. Instead of the black stone beneath the sea of mist, I was on the fragrant, mulchy soil of the jungle floor.

Hands grabbed my arms on both sides, pulling me up to my unsteady feet. I looked over toward the spot that I'd last seen Alex Smith. He was still on the ground, breathing slowly. He looked more like he was sleeping than he'd been stabbed by an ancient sacrificial dagger. At least, he did until I saw his eyelids flutter open. We made eye contact. My breath caught as I waited for him to sound the alarm.

Instead, Alex Smith twisted his lips into something resembling a smile as my friends dragged me further into the jungle's waiting branches. That scared me as much as the knife's claim on my spirit.

His gaze didn't falter until the distance between us hid me from his sight.

WE RAN FROM THE CLEARING around the Sky Palace as quickly as the surrounding jungle would let us. It was like jogging across an active dodgeball game with a strobe light going. Move a few feet, tree trunk, a few more steps, tree trunk, a little farther, duck a branch. After we'd put a fair amount of distance between ourselves and our pursuers, we came to second clearing. A stonework dais rose out of the ground by about six inches on all sides. It wasn't entirely solid, the jungle having done much to break up the floor and reclaim what structure was left, but it was long enough that it hadn't been swallowed entirely. Maybe thirty feet from one end to the other. There was one short, overgrown wall near the center of the raised platform and some scattered stones that may have been adjoining pieces to the earlier structure.

"Was this originally a house?" I asked, my voice hushed. I was still hesitant to speak at a normal volume.

Yuri took a look around, his glasses glinting in the moonlight. The two tour guides were also inspecting the clearing with more technical knowledge than I possessed. "I'd hazard a guess that this was a highway of sorts. This wall might have been an arch. I wish I'd gotten a chance to talk with Professor Gentle," Yuri lamented. "This area may have even held a small shrine or altar."

"That's possible," Sylvia said. "I haven't gotten my graduate degree yet, but I can tell this area looks a lot like some other sections of the Sacbe. Some of those roads were more elevated and more paved than others. If this one led to the Sky Palace, it was probably pretty important."

Picking up a rock, Elena tossed it at high velocity into the vines that clung to the wall. Expecting the sharp clack of stone against stone, I was surprised to hear a meaty smack. A long, lithe body fell out of the leaves and slammed against the floor stones. It didn't move for several breaths. When Elena finally took a step toward it, it slithered down into the tall grasses of the clearing. "Whatever it used to be, it's not much of a shelter now."

I shuddered at the idea of sharing our respite with snakes or ants. I'd never camped without a tent before. Most people have this idea that witches are all about the outdoors and the natural order. We get confused with druids. Maybe it's just that nature is associated with the mystical because of the belief that magic and science don't mix? Biology is a form of science, though. I don't know. I don't have the answers. Maybe I'm just a weird witch that likes having conveniences like walls. And rooves. And plumbing. And beds.

*Looks like I'm out of luck for coffee in the morning, too,* I thought with a suppressed sigh.

"Better than nothing," Yuri said. "We can take shifts to watch for danger. Briar, would you mind doing your ignore-me spell? I know you said it wouldn't stand up to too much scrutiny, but anything that buys us a few seconds might make a difference."

Alex's accusations about Yuri, how he knew more about my brand of witch and all about my bloodline, taunted me as I darted a quick look at my would-be partner. I wanted to ask him. But I didn't want to let Alex manipulate me. "Yeah, I can cast it," I answered after too long a pause. "You want me to anchor it to the stones, or should I draw a circle?"

"Whatever you feel is best," Yuri said. Even in the dim moonlight, he was trying to read my shift in mood. I was being more closed off with him than normal. As much as I didn't want to ask the questions Alex Smith had handed me, we weren't going to get past this without broaching the subject.

It could wait until we were safely hidden, though. I sat down on the stones and began pushing the magic out of my body and into the spellforms that would cause us to be less significant to the outside world.

# 23

WHEN I CAME OUT OF my spell trance, I was greeted by the sight of Elena and Sylvia in the middle of a passionate, full-tongue, face-swallowing kiss. I averted my eyes, the blush in my cheeks rising. I'd never gotten used to public displays of affection. Light kisses, hand holding, hugs, maybe even the occasional butt-grab between consenting adults were one thing, but this kiss was only a few steps away from clothes flying off. "Don't... Don't mind me," I said, letting them know I wasn't entirely blind. "I'm just going to go... check on Yuri."

I got an acknowledging wave, or maybe a signal to go away. It was hard to tell which. I wasn't inclined to hang around to ask for clarification.

Yuri wasn't hard to find. He was still on our chunk of ancient road, after all. It would hardly have made sense to walk away from where I was laying the spell he'd requested to hide us.

"Hey," I said. "Did I miss something while I was out of it?"

With a glance over his shoulder at the couple, Yuri grunted a quick confirmation. They were still keeping things in the PG to PG-13 region, but it was clear they needed some space. "While you were working, Elena proposed. I think it's pretty obvious what Sylvia said."

Nodding, I tried to think about how to broach the next subject.

"I went into the knife again."

His face muscles didn't twitch, but I could feel the tension flowing through our connection. "When you collapsed, I figured it was probably something like that. The wild man that ambushed Alex

Smith didn't stick around afterward. He kind of looked in our direction and then ran back into the trees."

"Alex was in there with me," I said.

With a deep sigh, Yuri scuffed his feet against the edge of the elevated road. The urge to pace was fighting with the need to give our tour guides some privacy. "I have a feeling I know where this is going..."

"Really? Because I gotta say... I don't." I broke at that point. Emotions I'd barely been keeping in check boiled to the surface and thrust themselves out. "Yuri, I'm lost! So lost! You want me to be your partner! We can't date! You kiss me! I tell you that I'm not a great witch and ask you not to lie to me, only to find out that you know more about my heritage than I do! You have the whole time! This is a thing I found out from one of our enemies! I don't know what to do anymore! Who are you? Who am I? What exactly does the IACI plan for me in the long run? Will they use me until they get tired of me and then dispose of me? Like I'm a dangerous trinket? You said you trusted me... Was that even true?"

My swell of rage spent, it left deposits of guilt in its wake. I didn't quite regret blowing up at Yuri, but I didn't feel good about it. Acid knots were playing bumper cars in my stomach while I waited for Yuri to say something.

"Everything I have or haven't said in the last couple of days, it was all in an effort to protect you."

*Truth.*

"Okay," I said. It was more an acknowledgment than an acceptance. "I can see where this job makes you play things close to the chest. But I need more than that, Yuri. Why don't you start with what you know about my family? And why my Aunt Shay couldn't teach me traditional spellwork?"

I *really* wanted to start at the part where he'd kissed me despite having told me that we couldn't date, but trying to broach that with the newly engaged couple exploring each other's tonsils in the background seemed a bit loaded. Best to get the less romantically charged issues out of the way first.

Beckoning me to sit down, Yuri slid from his feet to the pave stones in one fluid motion. Again, I was reminded that I'd never actually seen him in a fight. He didn't have the same unearthly grace Alex Smith exhibited while walking, but Yuri was a lot more poised than the average guy on the street. Swinging my backpack down beside him, I tried to find a somewhat comfortable position on the rock next to him.

*Reminds me a bit of storytime in kindergarten.*

"Your family name, Egibi, dates all the way back to ancient Babylon," Yuri said. This much, Alex had told me, but I didn't dare interrupt now that Yuri was actually talking. "It's one of the oldest family names ever discovered. Your family was always magically inclined, though most of the public records label them as merchants. It's possible that your family was founded by one of the first demigods or wove a few of them into the line along the way. Whatever the original source of your line's power, it's increased over the centuries. Your aunt's spells persisting two years after her death is proof of your family's increased powers. Witches with younger lineages, their spells are gone the moment their spirit departs our plane."

Removing his glasses, Yuri started to polish them with the rag he kept somewhere on his person. It was too dark to really make a difference in his ability to see, but it kept his hands occupied while he spoke. His voice adopted that cadence professors get mid-lecture, when they know their audience needs this information for the next test.

"Here's where it gets tricky. Once every couple of generations, your line seems to be... visited? Remembered? I'm not sure there is a correct word for this, but someone gets tapped by one of the Mesopotamian pantheons. Given that your family started in Babylonia, it's often Marduk. But it's not limited to him, by any means. Some of these deities don't affect the natural flow of your witchly powers at all. Some of them do. In your case, it's seemingly shifted all of your abilities toward your divine patron's strengths."

"And you know which deity I've been tapped by?"

"I'd be more comfortable calling it an educated guess," Yuri said. His assured tones faltered. "Please bear in mind that I could be mistaken and these gods do *not* like to be called on lightly. They come from an age in which humanity was considered only a step or two above dirt. So, even if I am correct, don't assume that this is going to be someone that you can count on in a crisis."

My throat was dry as I nodded my understanding. "I promise—no calling out to strange deities on a whim."

"Not unless the situation is truly dire," Yuri pressed. "Calling on a deity from Mesopotamia is as likely to backfire as it is to help."

"No calling my patron without harrowing circumstances," I said. I half-expected Yuri to make me promise a third time to ensure that I couldn't break my word. Instead, he stuck me with one of the most piercing stares I'd ever received. As though if he tried hard enough, he could use my ability to suss out the truth. For several moments, we sat there, staring in the dark. Him, waiting to see if I'd retract my promise, and me, waiting for him to continue.

"Gibil," Yuri said. "I think you were chosen by Gibil, the Sumarian god of fire and weapons. It all seems to fit, anyway. Your medium of hot sauce, your connection with the knife, and he was also supposed to be gifted with metallurgy. With your beach trick, I'd say that falls into the realm of purification. Not that anything to do with magic and deities is an exact science—how could it be?"

Something inside me clicked into place as soon as the name slid off Yuri's tongue. *Gibil.* It wasn't a name I'd ever heard before. It wasn't a name I'd ever forget. My patron. My deity. *My source.* Even with my family's lineage pumping magic into my veins, I recognized a second energy intertwined with my own. Our magics were fused. That was why I'd never been able to tap into the same spells that Aunt Shay used on a daily basis. Cleaning magic, protection charms, spells that kept the milk fresh a few extra days. Domestic magics. Very human needs. Not worth an ancient Sumarian god's time.

I wasn't a failure as a witch. I was a fucking Tacomancer!

Okay, so I doubt that they actually had tacos in Mesopotamia. But I didn't live in ancient Sumaria or Babylonia like my ancestors. Just to be sure I wasn't stepping on any toes, I decided to ask, "Was there a name for witches like myself in the ancient times?"

"Actually, the term witch itself is pretty recent. A lot of magical things weren't named in ancient documents. They were around, but it didn't seem as though ancient civilizations felt they were different enough to give their own names and labels. Demi-gods and kings were practically synonymous, so if you were powerful enough not to be a commoner or worse still, a slave, your family was probably connected to something or someone magical or militant. Strength was key."

"Sounds like I'm sticking with Tacomancer," I said.

Letting out a rough chuckle, a lot of Yuri's tension ebbed away with my comment. I wasn't sure why this part of the conversation had him so wound up. "How was not telling me about this protecting me?"

My would-be partner slid his glasses back on before leaning back on his hands. Despite the casual pose, I could feel his hesitation. He was still trying to juggle how much he told me and I didn't like it.

"Yuri," I said, the warning clear in my voice.

"Telling you the name of your patron deity awakens your power in a way that other magic users can perceive. Alex Smith, Jonas Ical, and the one you call No Name... they'll recognize the change. If they're familiar enough with your deity, that may even tell them what you're weakest against. As long as I kept you in the dark, you might not have achieved your full potential, but neither were you anywhere near as exposed," Yuri explained. "I wanted to spare you from that until you'd at least decided one way or the other about joining the IACI."

*Shit...* There was no way that Alex Smith hadn't known about the awakening powers thing. I'd played right into it. He'd tugged on my insecurities about Yuri with all the right words. Even though he hadn't lied once, Alex had tricked me. "Fuck..."

Even though he didn't say anything, I could read Yuri's agreement in the silence. Well, the quiet that wasn't taken up with muffled sweet nothings coming from Sylvia and Elena on the far side of the Sacbe fragment. The elation I'd felt at finally recognizing my power was quickly sinking beneath a wave of concern.

"What about the rest of it?" I asked, hugging my knees to my chest.

While I was waiting for Yuri's response, my attention drifted. The kissing sounds had shifted into soft murmurs. I couldn't tell what Elena and Sylvia were talking about, but I didn't want to strain our newly mended friendship by eavesdropping.

Soon it would be chilly enough to change back into my sweatpants. I wasn't looking forward to changing in front of an audience, but it wasn't like I'd be stripping down entirely. A change of pants was barely worse than showing off a swimsuit. Still, these weren't the circumstances I'd have picked to show Yuri my undies.

Monkey song and the odd clicking and whirring of insects seemed quieter than it had earlier. I wondered if it was my imagination, if the world was holding its breath with me in anticipation of Yuri's next words.

My thoughts froze as I realized *why* the jungle had gone silent; the four of us weren't alone anymore.

# 24

I TRIED TO CATCH SIGHT of Elena and Sylvia on the far end of our make-shift campsite. They were still there, but they'd also gone quiet. I wasn't sure if they'd stopped talking or if Sylvia'd taken another bite of her brownie. Either way, I was grateful they were silent. My don't-notice-me spell worked best when people weren't doing anything that would otherwise draw attention—which made a lot more sense to me now. Traditional spells weren't completely off the menu, but I was only able to cast them at half power. Gibil's energy couldn't be tapped for things outside of his domain

Yuri's gaze was locked on our visitor. I wasn't sure how well he could see in the gloom, but his focus never wavered.

As I peered through the darkness, moonlight broke out from behind the clouds, illuminating the figure at the edge of the forest.

No Name.

He was every bit as terrifying as I'd remembered him from our encounters on the beach. Actually, with the shadows dripping off of his ill-defined features, I found him even scarier than I had when he'd cornered me after I'd mended the beach. Anger rolled off of him like a fog, rippling across the landscape.

"Spread out and search this place," he said, throwing the orders over his shoulder.

Four more figures emerged from the trees. One of them was the large figure of Jonas Ical and the other three were carrying those large automatic rifles. They spread out, scanning the brush with every step.

There was no way that my spell was going to survive this kind of scrutiny.

"Briar," Yuri said, speaking softly enough that I almost missed it. "Briar, I need you to do something."

I shifted my focus back to Yuri, even though every instinct I had clamored at me not to take my eyes off of the sunspot after-image that was No Name. Looking at No Name was painful, but looking away felt deadly. But even with my questions and doubts, Yuri and I were a team. At this moment, I had to trust him or all four of us could be in mortal danger.

"Get to the other side of the Sacbe," Yuri said. "Or behind the wall, if you can. Whatever you do, hold your spell in place as long as possible."

"Yuri," my voice cracked, even at a near whisper.

"Hold the spell," he said again. "Now, go, please."

I didn't like this plan. I wanted to argue with him. I wanted to scream at him that we could figure something else out. Even though I wasn't sure what he was going to do, I *knew* this wasn't going to end well. Still, I couldn't think of anything better than following his instructions. He was a Reliquarian. He had the training. I was still in my probationary period.

Without giving myself a chance to second guess the impulse, I unsnapped my last bracelet from Aunt Shay and clicked it around Yuri's wrist. "Don't die on me."

Briefly, our fingers intertwined and he gave a light squeeze of agreement.

Then I was on my feet, my backpack hanging in one hand. It seemed too dangerous to risk swinging the straps over my shoulders. No Name's attention was like a spotlight scouring the clearing. Eventually, our protective veil would crack and peel under the pressure. Or one of his underlings would trip over the wrong stone and the Sacbe would become visible. I was uncomfortably aware of Aunt Shay's protection being absent from my wrist—it was like one of those nightmares where you show up to a test without pants.

One slow step at a time, placing my feet carefully so I could avoid scuffing sounds or crunching rocks, I made my way over to the far side of the ancient road. Sylvia and Elena were definitely aware of our guests. They were laying side by side, both of their faces pointed toward the approaching minions. As I approached, Sylvia beckoned me to sink down beside them.

"We're muted, again. Don't worry. This is our path," she said with a tiny giggle.

"What about Yuri?" I asked.

Sylvia didn't answer me. I was pretty sure that was a bad sign.

As nervous as I was about the approaching gunners, I turned my head to watch what Yuri was going to do now that I was as safe as I was going to get.

Yuri was standing. I wasn't sure when he'd gotten to his feet, but it had happened at some point during my trek across the stones. I watched as he made his way to the edge of the Sacbe. His movements looked as careful and deliberate as mine had—until he took a step down into the clearing.

It was like a flipped switch. All of the searching figures went from cautious sentry mode to fully alert battle robots. The three wielding guns turned and ran toward Yuri, flanking him and telling him to get on the ground. Yuri's hands were raised in a gesture of surrender and he didn't argue as they poked and prodded him with their gun barrels. Flashlights came out and illuminated his face.

The desire to feed more power into my spell was nearly overwhelming. I wanted to spread it out, swallow Yuri back within the safety of the ignore-me borders, but I knew that would be counterproductive. There was no way that No Name wouldn't see the power flowing when he was this close to us. Trusting Yuri was harder than ever, but I made myself keep watching.

Jonas Ical loomed out of the shadows. Even though they had automatic weapons, the humans shrunk back from the large warlock.

"Where are your friends?" Jonas asked.

"They doubled back toward the bus. They didn't want to risk staying out here overnight," Yuri said. I hissed through my teeth, hoping I was the only one in the clearing that had the ability to sense lies.

"You'd best hope we find them before they manage to get back, then," No Name said. "There's no telling what might happen if they try to start that engine."

Blood crystalized in my veins as I realized I couldn't read when No Name was lying. It was disconcerting to me not to *know*. He was nameless, his voice didn't trigger my truth detection, and his appearance was more shadow than form. If I hadn't been told he was the child of a god, I'm not sure I would've believed he actually existed. No Name was more like a walking nightmare than a person. And yet... Aside from his appearance, this was how normal people interacted with *everyone*. If I were ever stripped of my abilities, I wasn't sure I could handle it.

Yuri managed to look concerned, as though he really believed we were heading into a trap. "What did you do? What did you do!"

"We left a little surprise. That's all. Just a token of our esteem," No Name said. His voice slid into my ears like oil. I *hated* No Name. He was currently approaching Yuri like a predator stalking toward a sleeping fawn.

I tried to push myself up, but found I was being held down by Sylvia's hand. I hadn't noticed when she'd placed her hand on my back, but it was a reminder that I would put us all at risk if I attempted to help right now. Alex Smith's taunt about whether I'd ever tried to throw lightning was playing through my head on repeat.

*He wasn't being your friend*, I reminded myself. *His goal was to get you to expose your true nature.*

Still, if there was ever a moment I'd wanted to throw lightning, this was it.

"Whether your companions are out here or back at the bus, it doesn't really matter. We'll find your little girlfriend eventually, but she's not our main objective. We want the artifact," No Name said. The creature slid a finger down Yuri's cheek and up under his chin.

Aunt Shay's energy flared briefly. I felt it in my wrist, despite no longer wearing any of her bracelets. One of the other spells she'd woven in must have enhanced my attunement with her gift. That was why Alex Smith had been able to use a piece of the unwound one to control me. Now I could feel the protection spells keeping Yuri's skin intact.

No Name retracted his finger with a hiss. It seemed he'd felt the flare of protection as well.

"I don't have the artifact," Yuri told his abductors. "We came out here to find clues."

"Doesn't matter," Jonas Ical said. The massive man pulled a sash out of one of his back pockets and began to bind Yuri's hands behind his back. "We know it's been used recently. Alex was able to identify the object when it pierced his flesh. Unless a new sacrifice is found soon, the knife will consume its current host. All we have to do is leave you out on one of the pyramids and the knife will find you."

As soon as Yuri's hands were bound, Jonas hauled Yuri to his feet. Pushing Yuri in front of him, the giant and all of the gunners faded back into the jungle. No Name lingered, scanning the clearing one last time. I could feel my veiling spell buckle under the intensity of his gaze, but it managed to hold.

Finally, No Name also disappeared into the trees.

I WASN'T SURE WHAT my next step was supposed to be. Yuri had let himself get captured. I knew I needed to rescue him, but figuring out *how* to rescue him was causing some headaches. With the adrenaline flowing through my system, I barely felt the chill of night anymore.

"You can't just waltz in there and take him back," Elena said. Her arms were crossed over her neon tour shirt. Even with the moonlight fading into a distant whisper, she and Sylvia were pretty visible against the jungle backdrop. "Those men have guns. Big guns! Whatever you are, I don't think you're bulletproof!"

"I'm not," I agreed. "But I can't hang around here all night while we let them use Yuri as bait."

As the creatures of the night resumed their warbling, Sylvia danced over the Sacbe, trying to absorb her butterflies again. After this was all over, I really wanted to have a sit down with her to find out more about her powerset.

"You remember a few days ago, you crawled into my cab and were talking about exploring Belize and maybe house-hunting?" Elena asked. She was watching Sylvia with a softness that spoke volumes about the amount of love they shared. As dire as our situation, I was glad they'd carved out a piece of happiness together.

*Yuri...*

"Simpler times," I nodded. "I hope Chicken's doing okay, and I'm really sorry about your cab. I'll help you put a downpayment on a new one. It's the least I can do for dragging you guys into all of this."

"Chicken will be fine. He had fresh paper when we left and plenty of water. One of our friends has a key, so we'll call in the morning to get him fed. We may take you up on that offer for the cab payment," Elena said, before steering back to the bigger matter at hand. "Now, what we gonna do about your bally?"

Before I could think of a response, Sylvia pranced her way over the road and did a twirl in front of us. "The order of operations demands that you multiply before you subtract," she grinned. Her pupils were still impossibly wide from her earlier brownie so I knew that as random as that bit of advice seemed, there had to be a path she was guiding us toward.

Exchanging a look with Elena, I raised an eyebrow. "Is she suggesting what I think she's suggesting?"

"It's not like we've had any better ideas," Elena said.

Sylvia raised both of her arms to the sky in a pose that I recognized from a video game as *praise the sun*. I really hoped this advice was actually lent through her powers and not a half-baked thought induced by the brownie. If it was the latter, we were all in big trouble.

# 25

MULTIPLICATION, IN this context, I translated as enhancing our position. Subtraction, I was guessing, meant taking Yuri away from the bad guys. Eddie was still in San Pedro. Any park rangers or military close enough to walk to were too far away to help in time—not to mention, unlikely to stand up to a demigod, a couple of warlocks and a couple of semi-automatic guns. The only thing I could plug into this equation that made any sense was the knife.

The knife wanted me. It beckoned to me. I could feel its pull in the depths of my being.

This was such a horrible idea.

"What if I can't control it?" I asked. "It's driven at least two people mad that I know of. Probably many, many more through the ages. What if the first thing I do when I get a hold of it is attack one of you?"

The longer we discussed this plan, the less I liked it.

More than anything, I wanted to have a shower and a cup of coffee. I was covered in dirt, blood and residual sweat grime. If I could get clean, center myself, maybe grab a nap, I was sure that something else would occur to me.

Well, maybe not *sure*. More like thirty percent certain?

Okay, fine. I had nothing. Zero ideas.

But I really didn't want to do this.

Sylvia and Elena were every bit as bedraggled as I was. Having absorbed sufficient butterflies, Sylvia was laying down on the ground, slowly sipping from one of our water bottles. We were lucky Elena had piled water bottles into my arms when we'd started exploring

Caracol earlier in the day. The pinch of hunger that comes when someone goes without food or sleep for too long was squeezing all three of us. Those johnnycake sandwiches I'd nibbled on over twelve hours ago were well out of my system.

"We'll have to split up to make sure that doesn't happen," Sylvia said. "It is ultimately your choice on whether to call the knife or not. Just remember, it is looking for a sacrifice either way. If you don't do this…"

"It will aim for the easiest target," I sighed. I had no doubt in my mind Yuri was being tied to an altar as I baulked. The knife wanted blood. There was no way that No Name and his crew didn't have a trap in place for the knife-possessed madman. "Damn it. Alright. I'll do it. You two just keep your distance and try to stay out of trouble okay? I don't think I could live with myself if I ended up hurting either of you."

"We're going to have to do our own thing to help with this," Elena said. "You're still not bulletproof, yeah? Having the knife might be your way in, but we're gonna find you a way out."

The set of Elena's jaw didn't invite arguments. She wasn't going to continue discussing this ad nauseum. The moment I'd agreed to my part in things, she'd decided to do something too. Despite our rather recent acquaintance, there were times it seemed like Elena and I had known each other for years. She could be every bit as stubborn as Aunt Shay.

"Here," I said, handing Elena my backpack. "It's got the paracord we used on the climb down the temple, another water bottle or two, and some of my clothes. I'm not sure what you're planning, but I hope this helps."

Accepting the bag, Elena hefted it over one shoulder. Regarding me in the spotty, dim light of the moon, she suddenly grabbed me by the arms and pulled me into a hug that rivaled Debra Downs for intensity. "We are friends, gyal. Don't let me down."

I hugged her back for all I was worth. Yuri's hugs had always been in response to my tears. Debra's hug had been an embrace of goodbyes and sorrow. This hug was different. There was a sense of urgency, a bit of departure, but the overwhelming emotion swimming through my body was acceptance. We were friends. Nothing would change that now.

Sylvia got to her feet and wrapped her arms around both of us. "You'd better survive. We need a wedding guest that can handle being around my Uncle Eddie for a couple of hours."

In spite of everything, I managed to laugh. "I'll do everything in my power to be there," I promised.

When we all let go, Elena and Sylvia exited into the jungle. They were careful not to go down the exact same path as our enemies. For a moment, I worried that they would get lost in the dark. I saw Elena slip a shiny bit of cellophane into Sylvia's hands right before they vanished into the trees. They would be alright.

It was me I needed to worry about.

CALLING THE KNIFE HAD been much easier when I'd been in a full-blown panic, unable to control my own limbs. Sitting alone on a broken stretch of ancient road, striving to summon a death bringer was much different. Every twig snap, every falling branch, every rogue shadow caused me to lose focus. I wanted Elena and Sylvia to come back and keep watch. At the same time, I didn't want them out here at all.

In frustration, I pulled my hair band out and shook my braid loose. It was always harder to do this without a brush, but it gave my hands something to do. I began pushing the plaits of hair back into place, tightening the weave as much as I could. Rewrapping the hair tie, I returned to my task.

I'd thought that my first night in a strange country, sleeping in a strange bed, was lonely. This was lightyears worse. My don't-notice-me spell was still in place, so I didn't need to be this jumpy. But there was a big difference between being stranded in the jungle with my friends and watching a jaguar pass by my hiding place with not even a fence between us.

The big cat paced its way back into the forest without glancing my direction. I let out a deep sigh of relief and returned to my attempted meditations.

As much as I loathed it, I decided that it would be easier if I closed my eyes.

It wasn't hard to find my connections with Yuri and the knife. They were there, pulsing with energy. As I brushed against them, a wave of Aunt Shay's protection drifted through the tether I had with Yuri. It wasn't much, a mere twinge of heat. Not like someone was actively trying to kill him. Hopefully that meant I still had time.

Touching the bond I had with the knife, I knew why this was so hard. It wasn't that I didn't want to do this. I was fighting the part of me that *craved* this.

I recognized it now. My yearning to wield the blood knife came from my patron's energy, the part of my magic I'd only recently come to recognize. The part of my energy I'd not yet learned to control. There was no way of knowing if I could come back to myself after this. I didn't know what that half of me was capable of.

*I can't do this.*

Another nudge from Aunt Shay's spells.

*I have to do this.*

I tugged on my connection with the knife, calling it toward me. There was nothing left to do but wait.

IT TOOK A WHILE TO notice the figure at the edge of the clearing. The eyes burrowing through the gloom and all the way into my skin caught me off guard.

I recognized his name immediately. There wasn't much chance I would forget it.

*Professor Phoenix Gentle.*

When I'd seen the symbol for death and heard his whisper, I'd assumed someone had killed him for talking to Yuri. Then, when I'd encountered him inside the knife, I'd assumed that it was because the wielder of the obsidian blade had sacrificed him. Somehow, it hadn't occurred to me that none of us searching had found the artifact yet. A professor of archaeology and Mayan history encountering an ancient knife only to become ensnared made a lot of sense.

Where No Name's gaze burned, Professor Gentle's dug in as though it would core me if it could. I probably wouldn't have noticed him if it hadn't been for the presence of the knife. The knife's energy was practically shaking with eagerness.

"Hello?" I said.

My veiling spell was still intact, but it was obvious that Professor Gentle, or what was left of him, could see me. His eyes didn't waver at all as I stood up and brushed the worst of the dirt off my rear.

"I'm Briar Egibi."

Not even a blink. I'd seen him inside the knife. This shell wasn't really the professor anymore.

He stepped out of the deep shadows of the night. Moonlight carved harsh borders over the lines of his face. Step by plodding step, the-man-that-had-been-Gentle walked toward me like the killer in a horror movie. Because I'd called the knife here, I didn't see the danger until it was nearly on top of me.

A savage scream erupted out of the former professor's throat as he lunged at me, hefting the knife over his shoulder.

Letting out a sound that was part yelp and part shriek, I dodged out of the knife's path. Blood dripped on the stones as Professor Gentle whipped his hand through the air. His grip on the blade was causing even more blood to ooze through his fingers.

Pelting over the paving stones, I didn't worry about being quiet as I jumped off the opposite edge of the Sacbe. I ducked behind the only standing wall. Desperation colored my thoughts as I ransacked my brain for any of the protection spells Aunt Shay had taught me.

*What the hell is going on? I thought the knife wanted me to wield it. I can't do that very well if I'm dead!*

I risked a peek around the wall that was my current refuge.

Professor Gentle's empty stare was only inches from my face. He let out another guttural snarl and attempted to thrust his hand into my hair.

If I kept my hair loose, he would've gotten me right then and there. But the tightly woven plaits against my scalp didn't offer the same sort of grip and I slid away from his fingers with one jerk of my head. If he'd grabbed the actual braid instead of the top of my head, it would've been a handle. I thanked my lucky stars that I'd rebraided my hair recently, and he'd missed his hold. He may have torn out a few hairs, but better a small pain than a big one. Like, oh, say... A hole in my chest?

Running to the far side of the wall, I climbed back up on the Sacbe. I wasn't really sure where to go. It wasn't like I could leave here without that knife, but I wasn't about to let myself get stabbed.

Mumbling a quick cantrip, meant for cutting onions rather than preventing murder, I felt the spell fizzle. I tried another, more generalized, spell but that one also evaporated as it parted my lips. In frustration, I tried to conjure a salt ward without salt. That one, admittedly, was a long shot.

"Knife? You want me to wield you, right? How am I supposed to do that if I'm a sacrifice?"

I'm not sure what good I thought would come of talking to the knife. But I was out of ideas. I wasn't having any luck with the protection spells and Professor Gentle seemed beyond the power of reason.

***"Sacrifice is called for."***

Professor Gentle's mouth was moving, but the voice was that horrible chorus of souls, the voice of the blade. I'd never heard it with my ears before. The few times I'd been trapped within the misty plane of the knife's interior, I'd thought it couldn't get any worse than having that voice reverberate through my soul.

I was wrong.

Hearing that cacophony come out of person sent ripples of terror through my entire body, tweaking every nerve ending I possessed. Something about the duality of seeing a human and hearing something so *inhuman* was enough to make me queasy with fear.

***"A price must be paid,"*** the voice said.

I was glad Elena and Sylvia were long gone. I'd suspected the knife would call for a sacrifice of some sort. But I hadn't even considered it might call for *my* blood. Given that the Mayans were a bloodletting culture, it was one hell of an oversight. I didn't major in history, but I did know some stuff. Not enough, though.

Keeping my eyes on Professor Gentle's body was harder than it should've been. He didn't appear to have moved but, at the same time, he seemed closer than he'd been before. I took a few steps back, not caring that he watched me do it. I didn't want him getting within knife range.

"What kind of price?" I asked. My voice shook with the effort of keeping my sanity together.

I was starting to understand why everyone I'd seen use the knife was completely nuts. If the knife was constantly barking instructions in their heads, it would be difficult to endure. The average person, with little to no knowledge of magic, would hear that voice as confirmation the world was lost.

*"Blood!"*

Somehow, he was right next to me. A wild slash that would've caught me in the throat parted the air over my head as I dropped to the ground. I fell backward and smacked my elbows against the rocks. There was barely time for me to register the pain as the professor's shell loomed over me.

He brought both hands together and raised the knife over his head. There was no way I was going to dodge this one.

I felt an odd sort of calm wash over me as I saw the knife coming toward my chest. Almost as though everything had gone into slow-motion. It wasn't that the danger had passed; it was more like it didn't matter. The knife demanded payment, but that didn't mean *I* had to bleed. Professor Gentle was already dead. I'd seen him within the knife. But he was still bleeding, so his body should still count.

Watching my hand lift itself up toward the professor's chest, I felt like I was watching someone else dance. A delicate purpose and grace defined the movement, wholly unlike my previous scrambling.

This wasn't me. At least, not the me I'd previously been. Not the version of me that had grown up awkward and friendless in Kansas. This was the half of me that was tied to my patron. And this half didn't hold back.

Flames burst forth like a spear, plunging through Professor Gentle's chest. The part of me that was still a quivering mess insisted that flames didn't work like that.

*Hush, girl. This is magic.*

The thought was both mine and not.

Slowly, as though it were just occurring to him that something had gone amiss, Professor Gentle lowered his arms and slumped on top of my body. The knife clattered across the stones and lay inert only a few inches from my hand.

As quickly as it had come, the calm that had overtaken my senses rushed out. Shoving the still form of Professor Gentle off with shaking hands, I started crying. I'd already cried for this peaceful man once, when I'd heard his last whispered thought. Now I was crying for him again. I tried to come to terms with what I'd done. It was a matter of survival, self-defense, him or me. Not one of those things did anything to settle my stomach.

I fumbled my way over to the edge of the Sacbe and dry-heaved. All that came out was what little water was still in my gut. Another dry-heave. A third. I wasn't sure even a shower would help wash away my new layer of guilt.

Finally, when my stomach stopped trying to wretch, I got to my feet and ambled over to the knife. I didn't want to think about the way it seemed to fit in my hand—like it belonged there.

It was time to save Yuri.

# 26

AS I TRUDGED MY WAY out of the jungle, the grey shades of twilight cast themselves over the ancient city. My "You better Belize it!" shirt was no longer blue. It was a testament to everything I'd been through in one night. Blood, mine and Professor Gentle's, had seeped into the fabric. Grime and dirt had worked their way into the weave. It was riddled with small tears I hadn't noticed acquiring.

If the rest of me looked as badly off as my shirt did, it wouldn't be hard to convince No Name and the others that I was every bit as insane as the late Professor Gentle.

I couldn't waste time looking for them, though. They'd laid a trap for the knife wielder. My bond with Yuri was beckoning me to the top of the Sky Palace.

Sending a silent prayer to any deity that might be listening, I pleaded that Yuri and I wouldn't have to climb down the back of the thing again. Despite it being a new day, I still hadn't slept since the last time we'd scaled the pyramid. I wasn't even sure I'd be able to make the climb back up the stairs. Bone-tired, that was the phrase.

The moment I crossed into the courtyard, the feeling of being watched sharpened. They'd noticed me: No Name, Jonas Ical, and Alex Smith. I could almost tell where they were hiding, their focus was so intense. Almost, but not quite. Whoever was handling the wards was handling them well.

In order to convince them I was unable to handle the knife, I had to act like the only thing in the world that mattered to me was finding the next sacrifice. The act wasn't much of an act, which scared the shit out of me. As soon as I'd picked up the blade, it began clamoring for its next target.

*Wield me. Quench my thirst. Satiate me.*

*This isn't why you chose me,* I argued with it mentally. *Why did you want me?*

*A price must be paid. To wield, you must accept.*

That didn't bode well. I'd honestly thought that Professor Gentle's final death would be enough for this thing, but it seemed that the death of someone it had already consumed didn't count.

*I'm not a killer.*

*Wield me.*

Shit. Fuck. Damn. This wasn't good. This. Was not. Good.

I fought the urge to scowl and whimper as I reached the stone steps. When I felt the heavy gaze of a god's attention join the other eyes watching me, I almost welcomed it. Whatever else was going on, at least I was still entertaining! Visit the concessions stand and get your heavenly equivalent of popcorn! A giggle started to bubble up in my chest.

I was cracking under the pressure.

The strange sense of calm that had interceded when Professor Gentle was about to skewer me was MIA.

Climbing the stone steps required use of my hands but the knife refused to leave my grip. My hip drop bag was still belted around my waist but, the moment I reached for it, the knife jerked in my grip. It wanted to stay put.

Naturally, that meant the obsidian bit into my fingers every time I used the hand gripping it to steady myself. I bit my tongue to keep from cursing. That strategy only worked a few more times before my tongue protested the additional abuse.

*Yuri better fucking appreciate this*, I thought. *He's buying my new house when this is all over. One with a pool. And a butler. And a yacht. And two dogs named Steve and Stevie.*

My imagined list got more and more extravagant, not to mention bizarre, the farther I climbed. I think I was trying to distract myself from the pain in my hand and my awareness of my audience. Suffice to say, by the time I reached the upper courtyard of the Sky Palace, Yuri was effectively funding a magical fantasy castle with a beach view and roller coasters. It was the least he could do.

I spotted him at the top of the middle pyramid. They'd strapped him in place on his knees between two stone plinths, his arms raised as though in supplication. I hated seeing him like that.

The knife loved it.

*A price must be paid.*

Oh, no. No, no, no, no, no. No! This was not happening.

*You* **must** *wield me.*

I'd summoned the knife to help Yuri. I had no intention of using it to hurt him. I was there to save him!

*You* **WILL** *wield me.*

For the third time in less than twenty-four hours, my limbs started to move without any conscious input from me. As scared as I was, there was a tiny piece of me fuming about how ridiculous this was getting. With my powers, there had to be something I could do.

Something.

Anything.

Tears were flowing down my cheeks as I wrestled for control, mustering what forces I could to shove the knife out of my mind. Its grip on me tightened as my blood flowed over it. Mist rose from the ground around me. The knife was drawing me into it as it had its previous wielders. I remembered Professor Phoenix Gentle's last thought:

*"Please... Let me go..."*

I understood now. He'd seen the mists too. He'd known he was falling away from himself. I hadn't seen any of his victims, but I'd only explored in one direction while I'd been inside of the knife. What if there had been more souls to the right or left? Or maybe he'd managed not to attack anyone and the knife had taken him instead? Was that what it was doing to me?

The knife and I were cresting the top of the stairs as twilight became dawn. Shades of pink and orange light made the scene that much more surreal. Yuri met my eyes and for a moment there was a flash of hope, but it was quickly followed by total and utter dejection.

"Yuri..."

I tried to put as much feeling as I could into that one word. His name. I wanted him to know how much he'd come to mean to me, how much I'd hoped to mean to him. I wanted him to know how sorry I was, that this wasn't me. I wanted him to forgive me, even though I had done a dumb, *dumb* thing. And we were both about to pay for it.

My arm arced above my head, much as Professor Gentle's had right before I'd blown a hole in his chest. Darkness was clouding my vision, even though the light on the pyramid was getting brighter. I beat against the mental barriers closing between me and the rest of my body.

It was over.

I'd lost.

All I could do was watch as the knife came down.

And stopped.

The tip of the blade was resting against his flesh, but the skin was barely dimpled under the impact. The knife's confusion rang through my thoughts as clearly as my own. *What?*

White light flared out from the point of the obsidian and swept up my arm and through my being. Aunt Shay's energy coursed through me. Her presence was so strong, I could practically smell her. She'd always carried the scent of the coffee shop and cinnamon buns with her. That, plus a whiff of fabric softener. Her light knocked

down the barriers erected by the knife and chased the invading energy out of my head.

It wasn't enough to sear my bond with the object of power entirely, but it was enough to give me full control of my own body
again.

I didn't waste time second-guessing my newly found freedom.
Bringing the knife away from Yuri's chest, I used it to cut through
the sashes binding him to the rocks. As soon as he was free, he began
massaging his wrists. My bracelet was still snapped in place, from
when I'd told him goodbye on the Sacbe.

Of course.

It was filled with my aunt's protection spells. Spells she'd designed specifically for me. I'd been in real trouble and I'd come within range.

But it was the last time Aunt Shay was going to be able to help
me. I didn't even have to touch the bracelet to know that it was
tapped out. I'd lost the last trace of Aunt Shay's power, my last magical link to my family.

Soft sobs that had originally started for Yuri switched to soft sobs
for my aunt's final gift. I sank to the ground, hugging my knees while
Yuri pulled me in for a hug. He rocked me gently as I accepted what
comfort I could against his soiled shirt. She was well and truly gone
this time. No more mysterious boxes. No sensing her down the hall
in our old house. No whiffs of fabric softener coming through Sit-
a-Spell Coffee. I'd sold the house. I'd sold the business. I'd spent the
magic. Aunt Shay was nothing but a memory.

*A price has been paid.*

I nearly jumped when I heard the knife's voice.

At the time, I didn't quite process the significance of what it had
said.

"I can't believe you came for me," Yuri whispered into my hair.

Despite everything, a rough chuckle tumbled out of my throat. "Dude, I tried to stab you! I'm not sure you should be grateful for that."

He tilted me back and looked into my eyes. His glasses were missing. Probably taken or broken by his abductors. Abductors that had watched me come up here. We didn't have long before they sprung whatever trap they'd laid for the person carrying their prize. All the same, I didn't want to look away.

"Briar, I'm still breathing because you gave up your protection. I can't even imagine what you had to do to get your hands on the knife. I'm supposed to be the Reliquarian here. Finding things like that is my job. You are going to ace your field test."

Now, I wanted to look away. I didn't want to think about the IACI and its damn field test. Tonight had been hellacious. I was tired, I was hungry, I was dirty, and I wanted this to be over. All of it. The knife. No Name. Alex Smith. Jonas Ical. The guys with the guns. Booby trapped busses. Magical spy stuff. I needed a gallon of coffee and a year's vacation. I'd thought Yuri was building toward kissing me again. Instead he was back to business.

With a sigh, I slumped forward and butted my head gently against his chest. "I couldn't just leave you hanging. Also, you owe me a castle."

Yuri laughed a little, though his throat sounded almost as rough as mine. The two of us weren't in the greatest shape. The sky was brightening into a brilliant azure as we helped each other to our feet. It took a lot of grunting and pulling on both sides, as banged up as we were.

Reluctantly, we climbed down the stairs toward the upper courtyard where three figures waited for us. There weren't really any other options. We could either climb down the front of the pyramid and face them, or scale the back without the benefit of Aunt Shay's protective spells. We still had the cord from the final bracelet, but that wasn't going to help much if they shot at us with bullets or spells.

"Well, well, well..." No Name gloated. "Looks like all of the flies flew into my web, doesn't it?"

Alex Smith and Jonas Ical exchanged expressions behind No Name's back. They seemed surprised about something. Surprised and concerned. Something had shifted in their dynamic with No Name. As I watched, Alex shifted his shoulders. The once-pristine button-down shirt he'd been wearing the day before was cut so his shoulder was exposed from the neck to the armpit. His sleeve had been fashioned into a make-shift sling and his stab wound was heavily gauzed. Maybe the shift had something to do with his injury? Maybe not. I couldn't put my finger on what had changed.

"I'm sorry. Have we met?" I asked. I knew we'd met. Our encounters on the beach, getting chased into the jungle, basically my entire trip to Belize had consisted of this demigod making life hard on my friends and me. I wanted to trip him up. I wanted him to feel insignificant.

His head shifted ever so slightly and those burning eyes narrowed.

"You wish for an introduction? Truly?"

"No!" Yuri said, rushing a few steps forward, placing himself between me and the demigod. "We have no need for your name!"

The two warlocks were tenser now than they'd been before. Another misstep on my part, caused by a lack of education. Why hadn't I learned about the rest of the paranormal world when Aunt Shay was teaching me about warding spells or tea leaves? I could've used a cheat sheet for all of the various pantheons that were apparently still procreating. Or a heads up that witches weren't alone. My first trip abroad, and I'd already encountered demigods, shamans and warlocks. If I went elsewhere, would I find out vampires and werewolves were real? Ghosts? Angels and demons? Selkies and banshees? Baba Yaga?

No Name was still staring at me, waiting for a response. Yuri's stepping between us hadn't changed the charged atmosphere at all. This was my decision. The smart thing would be to agree with Yuri and deny the request.

***Ask his name.***

# 27

MY JAW WORKED AS I vacillated between Yuri and the knife.

There was no logical reason that I should trust the blade. I'd come so close to doing something incomprehensibly awful while under the knife's power—it would make more sense never to trust the thing again. I wasn't entirely sure why I was still holding it, aside from keeping it away from No Name and his lackeys.

Yuri had lied to me a few times and kept things from me, but I knew he wasn't trying to mislead me here. Something about asking No Name to say his name was dangerous. I didn't understand how or why, but I believed it.

This should've been a crystal clear decision.

"Yes. Who are you?"

Turning toward me with a look of betrayal and horror, worse than the expression he'd had when I'd nearly killed him, Yuri hissed, "What do you think you're doing?"

"Honestly," I said, "winging it..."

I wasn't sure the whites of Yuri's eyes could get any bigger. They were bulging out almost as much as a cartoon character encountering a ghost. For the first time since I met him, Yuri was scared. Not hesitant or intimidated, but truly horrified.

Alex Smith took off running down the steps of the pyramid as fast as his lanky legs could carry him. His supernatural grace kept him from tumbling head over heels and soon he was a speck pelting across the lower courtyard.

All of the color drained from Jonas Ical's face, but he maintained his position. I could tell he wanted to run. As far away as I was standing, I still saw the sweat beading across Jonas's sallow brow.

No Name laughed. Not a maniacal villain laugh, either. It was a genuine sound of mirth. Almost a laugh of relief. I wondered how long it had been since he'd last found something funny. With everyone else's reactions, like I'd set the timer on a bomb, laughter wasn't what I'd expected.

"Let's be formal about this. It's only fair to give me your name first," No Name said. He was rubbing at his eyes, like he'd laughed hard enough to tear up.

Something in me recognized this as the second question. Did I have to affirm this decision three times? Was an introduction with a demigod some sort of binding?

*Do it.*

The phrasing the knife chose made my skin crawl. I felt like I was being pushed closer and closer to the Dark Side. Still, I didn't have a better plan, so I plunged forward.

"My name is Briar Egibi," I said. "Your turn."

"Last chance to change your mind," No Name grinned.

*It is a binding!* That was why I couldn't read his name like I could with normal people. It was like trying to read a book without opening the cover. Possible if you expend way more magic than it's worth and potentially dangerous to the fabric of reality. Which meant, revealing his name would unbind him.

*Uh oh.* I wanted to stop. There was no telling how powerful No Name would be once I released him.

*Awaken him.*

*Knife... What are you doing?*

*Awakening reveals all.*

Yuri had kept the knowledge of my patron deity from me because, despite the increased abilities that came from being an awakened witch, he'd worried that our enemies would recognize my weaknesses. The knife was trying for the same play on No Name. There was one big problem that I could see with this strategy.

*And if he doesn't have a weakness?*

**Everything has a weakness.**

Taking a deep breath of the fragrant morning air, I took a moment to appreciate how heavy the humidity felt in my lungs. Sun kissed the landscape around us and monkey calls mixed with the songs of a thousand jungle birds. I gave Yuri as reassuring a smile as I could muster. If this was a huge mistake, I hoped he'd be able to get himself out of here. Maybe he'd be able to find Elena and Sylvia and the three of them would be able to call in reinforcements.

Moment of peace over. Time to get this party started.

"Tell me," I said.

A line of deathly ashen clouds formed on the horizon. They came charging across the sky, blotting the sun from sight. Gusting winds threatened to blow the four of us right off of the Sky Palace. Well, three of us.

No Name seemed to be growing as the weather worsened. It was hard to tell at first, but once he surpassed Jonas Ical in height and breadth, it was painfully obvious. His eyes no longer hinted at burning. They became like two suns in a face that gained more definition the larger it got. A strong, beak-like nose, skin the color of clay, and hair that matched the on-coming storm.

"I am Babajide! Son of Huracan!"

One seam popped. Then a second. The rest of them all went in a burst. Babajide's clothes shredded off of him like sunburned skin, leaving absolutely nothing to the imagination. Only his shoes were still intact. Weird. Perhaps they were enchanted.

Yuri grabbed me by the arms. The wind was whipping past us so hard that we had to yell into each other's ears just to be heard. "You just unleashed the son of a Mayan god that's said to be the Destroyer of Humanity!"

"Does that mean you're revoking my job offer?" I screamed back. He was not amused.

Living in Kansas for my entire childhood, I know what it looks like when a tornado is forming. A tornado took my parents from me. It's not something I'm inclined to forget. I'm much less familiar with what it looks like when you're smack dab in the center of a hurricane, but the way the clouds were opening to the blue sky overhead and the winds sweeping out to bend the trees around us in a counter-clock-wise ring seemed to be a hint. Funnel clouds dipped and twirled, threatening to meet the ground and tear holes into the surrounding forest.

"Aren't hurricanes supposed to form over water?" I asked.

"This isn't a real hurricane," Yuri said. We still had to shout, but not quite as loud now. "He's calling on his father!"

I swallowed my next question. I was going to ask how we were supposed to stop him, but I realized that Yuri wasn't the person that had that answer. *Knife? How do I stop this?*

**You cannot.**

"What?!" I was so startled that the question came out louder than my previous shouts at Yuri.

**You cannot stop Huracan. Only a god can stop a god.**

*Fucking Deus Ex Machina...* The thought was equal parts frustration and resignation. I'd come this far, though. There was no quitting now.

I only had one god that I knew would probably answer my call.

"Yuri... I have another idea," I said. "I don't think you're gonna like it."

Before I could tell Yuri the latest insanity I was planning, we were interrupted by Jonas Ical thundering toward us like a loose bull at a rodeo. I'd almost forgotten he was still up here.

"You pendeja! What did you think you were doing?" he snarled at me. "I've been trying to keep that one happy for weeks! You think you're so smart that you can call up the very gods and they will thank you for it?!"

His questions were purely rhetorical.

The moment he'd stopped talking, an aching sensation rippled through me as the warlock began syphoning magic out of my body. If it hadn't been for my previous experiences with Alex Smith, I wouldn't have been ready for Jonas Ical to hurl something constructed of my own energy at me. Fire flowed through his fingertips. It wasn't as strong as the jet of flame I'd used on Professor Gentle, but the heat of it was enough to singe my arm hairs as I scrambled backward up the steps.

"Leave her alone!" Yuri barked. He was almost as upset with me as Jonas was but, somehow, that didn't stop Yuri from jumping to my aid. Putting himself between the large warlock and me, Yuri tugged something out of one of his pockets. "You were trying to appease that monster? To what end? Demigods want power! That's all they want! They feed and they feed and they feed until they think they can take on their parents!"

Jonas seemed alright with the shift in target. Squaring off against Yuri, it looked like it would be a short match, especially since Jonas was still leeching magic out of my system. I attempted to call up a shield or barrier to cut him off. Unfortunately, all of my techniques were still spells my aunt taught me, and I wasn't strong enough with those. Assuming we made it out of this, I needed to find someone that could tudor me in tapping into Gibil's energy.

Whatever Yuri had pulled out of his pocket was small enough that I couldn't see it. At least, not until he dropped one end. It was a whip! Yuri had a freaking whip! It wasn't a long one, just a little get-back whip made of woven leather, meant for self defense. But he was an archaeologist with a whip. Despite the circumstances, a spike of utter glee filled me for all of five seconds.

The large warlock didn't wait for Yuri to make the first move. A spurt of flame shot toward Yuri while he was still settling his grip on his whip. Yuri ducked the attack casually, like this was an everyday occurrence for him. For all I knew, fighting warlocks was pretty standard.

Having his would-be partner unbind a demigod, less so.

Snapping the small whip at Jonas's face, Yuri moved into close range with the larger man and popped an elbow into the warlock's ribs. Jonas Ical gave a minor grunt of pain or frustration. I couldn't tell which. Before he could retaliate, Yuri had jumped back up two steps.

Instead of a lance of fire, Jonas unleashed an entire ring, spreading out from his body in all directions. Dropping to the ground to avoid being caught in the attack myself, I missed seeing how Yuri dealt with it.

Within moments of the fire wave, Yuri was right back in Jonas's face. Whip, elbow, knee, fist. The Reliquarian was relentless, but it also seemed like he wasn't really getting anywhere. Everything Yuri threw, the warlock seemed to absorb.

Jonas Ical was a big man. He could take a lot of punishment.

"FATHER!"

Babajide's voice sent a shockwave through the air, causing all three of us to turn and look at the burgeoning son of Huracan. No one wanted to deal with that issue quite yet.

Yuri used the momentary distraction to jump up and kick Jonas Ical in the face. It was like watching a real-life bullet-time sequence: Yuri's knee lifted into the air, his hips twisted, and he planted the ball of his foot into the bottom of Jonas's jaw.

The massive warlock's head jerked back hard. It took a few seconds for the rest of his body to follow. Yuri and I winced together as the big man's head smacked against the stone stairs and the rest of him continued to skid down the remaining steps. I didn't like the angle his neck was at. Blood was already running down the left half of his face when he finally came to a stop.

Babajide was still growing and not paying the slightest attention to his underling's predicament. "FATHER! I KNOW YOU CAN HEAR ME!"

Yuri and I rushed down the pyramid. I wanted to make sure Jonas was still breathing. I think Yuri was trying to make sure I stayed alive.

Lacking anything like medical training, I got to Jonas's prone form and froze. My first thought was to put my head on his chest and listen for a heartbeat, but he was still the enemy. If he was actually alive, that would end really badly for me.

The knife wanted him. It wasn't demanding that I wield it or trying to coax me into killing someone, but I could feel it yearning to drink in the blood from Jonas's head wound. "I think he might still be alive," I told Yuri.

Scowling at me, Yuri shook his head. "Shouldn't we be more concerned about Babajide!"

I looked up at the demigod. He'd stopped growing. One of his legs looked weirdly slender. And green. As I watched, the leg undulated and hissed as an enormous snake head worked itself free of a sizable shoe.

"Ummm, yeah... maybe a bit," I said. Holding my hands up, I took two big steps back from Jonas Ical's body.

The snake head lunged forward and enveloped the former warlock's torso with its jaws. It barely needed to unhinge its jaw for the massive man's shoulders. If I hadn't completely emptied myself out the night before, I would've vomited again. Watching the lump that was our enemy work its way up the serpent's body and through the unnatural joint where the snake body met hip.

"He's taking on his father's aspect," Yuri said. "This isn't going well, for the record."

"Right, right... I had an idea," I said.

I gripped the knife for comfort, despite the way it cut into my fingers. The pain wasn't what I was after. It was the reassurance of holding a weapon. I needed something to ease my panic as the snake lifted itself from the ground once more and looked in my direction.

"What if I called on my patron?" I asked, not daring to look away from the unearthly serpent.

"FATHER! COME AND FIGHT ME! I SHALL DO WHAT YOU FAILED AND WIPE THESE MORTALS FROM THE LANDS YOU CALLED OUT OF THE SEA! LET ME CLAIM MY PLACE IN THE HEAVENS!"

Babajide rose his hands toward the eye formed by a wall of twisting, churning clouds. His human face was paying us mere mortals no mind. But his snake leg was weaving its way through the air, slithering toward us as we edged our way back up the pyramid.

"Even if he were to come, we're in the middle of Mayan territory, facing a god that shares the aspect of fire with your god. There's no way Gibil would be able to overpower Huracan in his own lands," Yuri said. "It's not a bad thought, but we'd need someone that would be friendly to us and able to reign all of this in."

Someone that had been watching me since we got to Caracol, perhaps. "Have any thoughts on who that might be?"

Flailing arms right next to me nearly caused me to break eye contact with the snake. I risked a peek at Yuri with my peripheral vision. He'd fished his little leather journal out of his shorts and was flipping frantically through the pages. "I listed a bunch of Mayan deities in here somewhere... Give me a second."

*Any thoughts, knife?*

**Aim for the eyes.**

The serpent shot forward, its fangs like daggers thrusting toward me. I dodged on pure instinct. Following the knife's advice was harder. I wanted to keep moving away from the snake, not rush at it. I swiped at the snake's head as it retracted, managing to miss entirely.

"Tohil! Call on Tohil!" Yuri called out.

"Why me?" I demanded, dodging another strike from the serpent. This time I managed to bring the knife down on the snake's side.

The sharpened piece of obsidian didn't even pierce the skin. My entire hand bounced to the side and my fingers flew open from the shock of the impact.

Yet, the knife remained in my hand. Questions tried to form in my mind, but I shoved them away for another time. "I'm a little preoccupied at the moment!"

"Calling down another deity was your idea!"

"It was the knife's idea if you want to get technical!"

Another lung, another miss. I never played baseball outside of gym class. I sincerely hoped that the universe didn't adhere to strikes.

"You followed the advice of a tool of death?!"

After this was all over, I had the feeling that Yuri and I were in for a very long discussion on the way I made decisions. If we made it to that point, I would happily sit back and let him yell at me. It would mean that we'd come out of this in one piece. "Fine! I'll call him down! How exactly am I supposed to do that?"

"I didn't write down instructions! We weren't supposed to awaken any demigods in the first place!"

Dodge, stab, hiss. Repeat. This was the worst dance rehearsal I'd ever been a part of. Not that I'd ever been to a dance rehearsal. I guess that also made it the best I'd attended? My focus was slipping.

A familiar wave of calm swept through my muscles. My tension eased and the world around me slowed. The snake's head swam past me like it was moving through syrup. I shifted my feet and jabbed the knife into one of the shiny black orbs.

Time resumed its normal pace as the snake jerked back, writhing all the way up to the hip. Babajide cried out with a sound of anguish as he withdrew his serpent's head. He cradled it in his gargantuan arms. As he nursed his wound, my calm vanished in a breath.

*Now's your chance,* the Gibil half of me coaxed.

I didn't need to be told twice. Grabbing Yuri's arm, I dashed up to the top of the pyramid and fell to my knees. "Tohil! Tohil! I beseech thee! ***Tohil, God of Sun and Sacrifice! This one seeks your aid!***"

Words that weren't mine poured out of my mouth. Hundreds of voices, speaking in many languages. This was the voice of the knife, only far more harmonious than it had ever been before.

A roar of rage came from behind us. The demigod was moving toward us with murder in his eyes. His snake head functioned as a foot, though he was limping with it. I'd barely given him the divine equivalent of a stubbed toe.

"YOU TWO WILL BE THE EXAMPLE I MAKE TO THE REST!"

Then the wind died.

# 28

THE WINDS DIDN'T TAPER off or decrease gradually. They just stopped. Thunder roared through the darkened clouds and thousands of lightning strikes struck across the tree tops. What had been the eye of an unnatural hurricane didn't close. It framed the sun like eyelids around an eye.

Through the pocket of empty sky, seemingly out of the sun itself, a brilliantly colored feathered serpent came spiraling down. Its feathers were like jewels embodying the elements, each one holding the essence of fire, the soul of a storm, or the rage of the sea. A human face was clenched in its jaws.

*Q'uq'umatz*, my gift told me. *Carrying Hunahpu.*

My gift could recognize unbound deities. Good to know.

But why these two? I'd lit the beacon to call on Tohil, a name that was mysteriously absent from the scene.

Watching with a mixture of rage and horror, Babajihe shook his head. "NO! NO! I WANTED TO FIGHT HURACAN! LEAVE THIS PLACE! YOU HAVE NO PART IN THIS!"

Q'uq'umatz didn't land so much as evaporate from view. I could feel that the larger serpent was still present, but the only visible evidence was a shower of feathers drifting away in a gentle breeze like flower petals. In the spot where Q'uq'umatz's snout had pressed against the ground stood a man that embodied perfection. *Tohil.*

Ah. I still didn't understand but, given that we were dealing with gods, I wasn't sure that mattered.

He was Mayan. He was Warrior. He was Intelligence. He was Grace. Though Tohil was no taller than Alex Smith, he seemed to look down at the gargantuan Babajide as they stood side by side on the Sky Palace's upper courtyard.

"I was summoned," Tohil said. "Your father sent me to defeat Seven Macaw when I was younger than you are now. Do you really think to keep me out of a fight on my own threshold? You are not a warrior, Babajide. You are a child throwing a tantrum. I have no time for you."

As Tohil spoke, Babajide shrank. The serpent leg morphed back into a mortal's leg and his eyes went from burning suns to the pupils of an average human. He continued to regress. Babajide was shedding years the same way he'd shed his clothes. When he'd been a giant, I hadn't thought about his age—watching the years spin in reverse, I thought he may have been in his fifties. He spun through his forties and thirties in a wink. During his twenties, his jaw and cheeks regained a bit of youthful fullness. Watching his teens was an uncomfortable mess of puberty in reverse. Still more years swept away from him and he finally stopped as a child around the age of four.

Slumping down on the ground, heedless of his nakedness, Babajide started crying and pulling up clumps of grass. "It's not fair! Not fair! Not fair! Not fair!"

The child that had been a demigod continued to bawl as Tohil turned his attention to Yuri and me. We were kneeling in between the plinths Yuri had been tied to earlier. I wasn't sure what to expect. I didn't know whether to come down the steps to meet Tohil or to press my head against the stone edifice and pretend that I hadn't been staring.

Looking away hurt me on a physical level. It's hard to explain, but the presence of something divine is a heat that fills your soul. My sight never felt so whole before and removing Tohil from my vision felt like I'd lost something. Blinking was like reliving my first heartbreak.

College was the first time that I'd had the opportunity to meet people as someone other than the weird kid. A guy in my biology lab made eyes at me. His name was Evan West and I fell head over heels, despite knowing that he was already involved with another girl in class—Naomi Ramos. Things had gotten complicated. Evan lied to me. When I confronted him, he accused me of spying on him. Naomi found out about my high school reputation and it all went south from there. I showed up on Aunt Shay's doorstep one night during a storm. My hands were shaking, tears were mixing with the winter rain streaming down my face, and I couldn't get my key into the lock. Aunt Shay opened the door and swept me into the house. I received one of the biggest hugs of my life. She had hot chocolate ready on the stove and a pair of my flannel pajamas freshly pulled from the dryer. Wrapped in a fuzzy fleece blanket, sipping hot cocoa, my aunt had made me feel loved. Unconditionally. Like she knew my soul. But that warmth had an undercurrent of remembered heartache.

Tohil was that loving warmth, but he was also that heartache. He could read everything I was. He could see through everything I was.

Ascending the steps, Tohil didn't crawl or bow. I wasn't sure if the Sky Palace actually had been built for Tohil or one of the other Mayan deities, but it was his while he was climbing it. Much like a cat sitting in a box, the fit determined ownership. I couldn't even bring myself to look at Yuri as the god approached.

"So... here we have the mortal that called my name. What did you seek to ask of me? My blessing? A boon? Are the gods yours to beckon?"

As much as it pained me to look away from the divinity, I glanced down at the screaming child. "I... I didn't know what else to do. He was going to kill us."

Raising one perfect eyebrow, Tohil's expression conveyed no malice. Merely curiosity. His words, however, scared the bejeezus out of me. "And I won't?"

All the moisture evaporated from my throat at once. I tried to swallow but my mouth refused to produce any saliva. A thousand protests fizzled before they could cross my lips. Tohil's eyes never left mine. Not even to blink.

"You aren't one of my people. You're not even a citizen of one of my countries. Even if I do find you entertaining—which is the only reason I'm drawing this out—it wouldn't do to let you go, feeling as though you'd bested the heavens. Best to end you now. Unless you have anything that could compel me to spare you?"

*Me.*

I brought my hand forward at the knife's urging, not daring to speak. Careful not to make any movements that could be interpreted as aggressive, I presented the knife to Tohil.

***Take me. I am a creation of sacrifice and blood. I bear many souls. My wielder sacrificed much to hold me. I aided her call.***

Tohil's features softened as he took the knife from my hands. "I see. You aren't one of mine, but this is. Obsidian is my stone and I am a being of sacrifice. I will see to this. As the chosen wielder of a lost blade, I will grant you your life, and that of your friend. I do not advise you to call on me again, scion of Egibi. I'm not often forgiving."

Tohil's parting words weighed heavily on my mind as he leapt into the air and hung there, suspended above the Sky Palace. A whirlwind of feathers swirled up from the courtyard and the surrounding buildings, coalescing into the long body of Q'uq'umatz. Tohil vanished and Hunahpu's aspect was once more clenched in the winged serpent's jaws. Lightning crackled down from the sky like a curtain. The feathered dragon took to the sky, spiraling out of sight. Thunder rolled across the landscape, taking the clouds with it as it faded into the morning.

The knife, and my connection to it, were gone.

I wanted to check on Yuri, find Sylvia and Elena, take care of whatever had been done to the bus and head back toward civilization. I wanted to take a nice, hot shower. I wanted to brush my teeth. I wanted to eat five burgers and a mountain of ceviche.

Instead, I sank down onto the rock like it was the world's most comfortable bed and fell into a deep sleep.

"OH, GOOD. WE WERE STARTING to worry about you, gyal."

Squinting against the afternoon sun, I found myself waking up in roughly the same spot I'd fallen asleep. My "You better Belize it!" sweatpants were folded into a make-shift pillow under my head and one of the remaining, half-drunk water bottles was set next to my head. Elena was sitting nearby, her back propped against a wall.

"Sorry," I said with a yawn. Sunburned face muscles protested their sudden use. "I wasn't expecting to conk out like that."

"That's why we let you sleep. Figured you could use the rest."

A wave of grief crashed over me. My bracelets, Aunt Shay, her last gift, my last connection to my family... I felt the loss like my aunt had died all over again. I curled into a ball and shook with sobs. Elena let me cry. She didn't try to rub my shoulders or hold me. I knew Yuri would've wrapped me in one of his massive supportive hugs, which made me cry harder. No one held me through the long, dark nights of grief the last time I'd lost Aunt Shay, and I felt weak for wanting comfort now. Slowly, the darkness in my heart eased enough for me to function, though a shadow remained. It was a shadow I was familiar with. We'd been acquainted for two years.

I pulled the cap off the water bottle and took a long, slow sip. As much as I wanted to gulp it down, I didn't think my system could handle it. Between dry-heaving, bleeding, sweating, sleeping in the sun, and crying, I was probably dangerously dehydrated. I didn't need to risk vomiting up what water we had.

"Where are Yuri and Sylvia?"

"Talking to authorities. They wanted to arrest the four of us. Tinito reported his bus stolen when we didn't come back last night. Unfortunately for him, your boyfriend actually has the credentials to prove that he's with your super secret agency. Sylvia is giving her own statement. They will likely want to talk to you, too, now that you're awake. Assuming your bally lets them near you."

Working my shoulders, I did a mental assessment of every stiff joint, every laceration, every bruise. And then added a sunburn to the total. I was battered, but nothing was broken. That was a plus. I took another sip out of the bottle. The water wasn't even remotely cold. It had that too-long-in-the-car flavor.

"So what happened on your side of things, after we split up?"

Elena took a deep breath and let it out, shifting her position on the rocks. "Well, our plan was for Sylvia to lead me to the best position to jump one of the men carrying guns. I spent a few years with the Belize Defense Force before I came out. I'm out of practice, but if I could get my hands on one of their guns, I have enough training to even the odds. We were going to wait until the other three went up to the Sky Palace to deal with you, then we'd take the gunners out one by one and tie them up with your rope. Then Sylvia ate her brownie and plans changed."

I didn't want to interrupt, but I needed to get up. My hips were complaining about the rough surface and my head was aching from a lack of caffeine. Among other things. "Can we walk and talk?" I requested.

Nodding, Elena pulled herself to her feet. She held out a hand and lifted me off the ground. "So, like I said, Sylvia took a bite of her brownie. Normally, one is all she needs. But then she takes two more. She's eaten almost half a brownie when she starts leading me to where I think I'm going to hide in a tree and jump at one of the mercenaries. Only, she's leading me away from Caracol. I stopped in my tracks to ask her what happened to the plan. You were counting on us to thin the numbers. She tells me she's taking the best path."

Facing the steps to the upper courtyard, I experienced a moment of vertigo as we passed through the area I'd faced off against Babajide's snake leg. Despite knowing the fight was over, the animal part of my brain wanted to stay hidden. Elena had to help me down the stairs, letting me hold her arm for support.

"Where did she take you?" I asked.

"To a cenote. It wasn't one that we'd been to before, and I don't know that I could find it again. But she leads me to it and tells me that we have to hide there until the ants come," Elena said. "Well, I don't understand what she means, but I'm learning to trust that she's got these powers, so we hide. After a while, here comes this bally in fatigues with his rifle. Looks like he's gotten turned around in the jungle. I don't even have to jump him—he falls in the cenote. Sylvia leads me over to the lip of the cave and we find him hanging by his gun strap. We tell him we'll help him up if he leaves the gun down there."

Relief danced through my body as we stepped onto the grass of the upper courtyard. The patches that Babajide had ripped out during his tantrum were visible against the rest of the greenery, but there didn't seem to be any giant footprints or scraps of clothing. No trace of the epic battle that had cost Jonas Ical his life and nearly killed Yuri and me.

"Did he agree?" I asked.

Elena shook her head. "No. He thought he was the big man and could yell at two women until we decided that maybe he was right. Like we were gonna help him out of the hole and then hold still and let him shoot us! We went back to our hiding spot and waited. Sure enough, another one comes along and hears the first bally yelling."

I was walking as quickly as my drained body would carry me, but it still felt like a sloth could overtake us any second. Another sip from the over-warm water bottle and several more yards. Next time I was in a life or death situation, I'd try to make sure I wasn't stuck at the top of a Mayan pyramid. If I never saw another Mayan temple again, I doubted I'd be heart broken. Not after the last two days.

Now came the big stairs.

"The second bally is being extra careful around the lip of the cenote. Gets down on his stomach in order to look over the edge and talk to the first man. I'm sitting there, feeling like this is it. This is my moment to jump one of them and take two of the guns out of the picture. But Sylvia catches my arm and shakes her head. So we continue to wait."

Offering me her arm again, Elena paused her story. She was rock steady, but I was afraid to put too much weight on her. We were a long way up and Jonas's fall was still fresh in my mind. I was tempted to sit down and scoot my butt down one stair at a time. I hadn't gone down stairs that way since preschool, but it seemed like the safest solution. But damn, would it be to stand up again once I got to the bottom!

"This place could use an elevator," I said, only half joking.

"You aren't the first to suggest it," Elena said. "Though, you may be the first to mention it while on the way down."

Another moment's hesitation, then I took her arm. If Elena felt like she could keep us both upright all the way to the ground, I owed her a bit of trust.

Elena resumed her tale as soon as we started climbing again. "As the second man pushes himself up, the wall of the cenote crumbles away and he falls into the cave, too. Sylvia lets me go look, and I'm being even more careful now. Both men are hanging off the same gun. I shout down that I'll help them up if they leave the guns down there. The first man says no again, but the second man starts arguing with him. Before they decide, Sylvia says it's almost time to go. If they don't want our help, they'll have to climb out on their own.

The second man tells us to go ahead and send the rope down. Then he punches the first bally in the nose. They both agree to leave their guns after that."

My foot slipped on a rock. I teetered for a moment, watching the pyramid steps loom toward me, until Elena steadied me. Oddly, the slip reassured me. I was a lot more confident the rest of the way down.

"We helped them out of the cenote, and then tied them to a tree. Later on, when the authorities came in after everything was over, they'd already found and arrested those two. The two men had left the guns in the cave like we'd asked, so Sylvia and I were still unarmed as she guided me back to Caracol."

Midway, at the pyramid's flight division, we stopped for a breather. My water bottle was nearly empty. I took a swig and offered Elena what was left. That was when I realized I'd left my sweat pants at the very top of the pyramid.

"Fuck..."

"What is it?" Elena asked. When I told her what had just occurred to me, she waved me off. "Don't worry about it. We'll get your bally to send someone up. Actually, I'll be surprised if they don't send someone to check on us soon."

Sure enough, almost before Elena finished her sentence, Mateo Carrillo, a tall young man with a tawny complexion and an athletic build came jogging onto the lower courtyard. He was wearing the uniform of the Belizean police: a khaki colored button up shirt with a rank patch sewn onto the sleeve and matching pants. He didn't glide up the steps with the same grace as Alex Smith and he definitely didn't own them like Tohil, but Mateo Carrillo did make the effort of climbing a Mayan temple look easy. I tried not to hate him for it.

"Are you two okay? I was sent to see if I could help with anything," Mateo said.

"We left a pair of sweatpants at the very top of the middle pyramid. Do you think you could go grab them for her?" Elena said.

"Sure thing," Mateo said, giving me a wink and a smile, showing nearly all of his teeth.

It was all I could do not to laugh. Some people just can't help but flirt with the world. I had no illusions about how attractive I looked right now. Although, with the brown shorts and the jungle grim, maybe I was throwing out a bit of a Laura Croft vibe. That could be it.

"So what happened with that last mercenary?" I asked as soon as Mateo was out of earshot.

"He escaped with that tall man. The one that got stabbed," Elena said. "Sylvia led me back to Caracol just in time for us to seek shelter from the hurricane winds in one of the wings off the smaller pyramid. They ran right past us without noticing. But we saw everything. The giant demigod, the lightning, the feathered serpent... If I had any lingering doubts about any of it, they're well dead."

When Mateo returned with my pants, the three of us continued down the pyramid. I was more than ready to say goodbye to the Sky Palace.

# 29

AFTER ELENA AND MATEO had ushered me into the arms of the waiting authorities, I answered several dozen questions. None of their questions involved gods or demigods. They only asked for clarifications on relationships, what parts of the park we'd visited, and how long we'd been on the scene.

They gave me fresh water and one of the worst sandwiches I'd ever tasted, though I could've eaten ten more just like it. Freaking terrible. Soggy bread, plastic cheese slice, mayo, lettuce, and something that may have been meat once.

I didn't see Yuri during the questioning.

With Sylvia's help, I guided Mateo and his supervisor to Professor Gentle's body. I had to remove the veil in order for them to retrieve it. I told them he'd been dead when I found him. It wasn't exactly the truth, but it wasn't a lie either. His body was the knife's puppet when we fought. They seemed willing to believe me, especially since I wasn't in possession of anything remotely resembling a high-powered plasma torch.

I wanted to tell them more, but most of my experiences were already classified. They shushed me any time I veered away from their questions.

Babajide's powers were gone. They were registering him with the Belizean foster care system as an abandoned child. I hoped, for his sake, he didn't retain all of his adult memories. It was unlikely he remembered any of it. He didn't seem to know what he was upset about. When asked who his parents were, he shrugged and cried some more. I almost felt bad for the kid, but I couldn't forget seeing his serpent leg swallow Jonas Ical.

Most of the trip back was a blur. I rode back to Belize City in the back of an official Jeep. Sylvia and Elena were already gone, along with the bus. I don't really remember riding the water taxi back to San Pedro. I came back to myself when the air-conditioning hit me. The condo seemed weirdly empty now. After polishing off what pizza was left in the fridge, I took one of the longest showers of my life. My body wash stung like hell when I scrubbed my many, many cuts. Once I was clean, I slept for fourteen hours straight. By the time I woke up, my sunburn had vanished, leaving a light tan in its place.

Eddie swung by with Elena and Sylvia in tow. The three of them convinced me to go out to celebrate Elena and Sylvia's engagement. We went to Eddie's favorite beach bar. He swore it had the best tacos in San Pedro. I didn't have much basis for comparison. The only tacos I'd had in Belize were in Belize City, when Yuri and I had been hiding from Alex Smith, but the San Pedro tacos were delicious. The bar marinated their meats overnight in some sort of signature sauce, and then slow-roasted and served them with pickled red onions and cilantro on fresh pressed tortillas. It was a wonderful night.

I missed Yuri. Somehow, with everything we'd been through, I'd never gotten his phone number.

At the same time, I appreciated the space. I still hadn't reached a decision regarding the International Anti-Cataclysm Initiative position as his partner. Hell, I wasn't even sure that offer was still on the table. I'd probably broken every rule in the book. Not that I'd seen the book. Or been briefed on its contents. Given that it was some sort of government agency, they probably wouldn't care what I did or didn't know about their rules.

Professor Gentle's university held a memorial service for the students, faculty, and friends. The university had been the late professor's home and his job was the closest thing he had to family. Eddie tried to explain the practice of a nine night wake that was a time for the community to come together. Food, drink, singing, and memories were all shared. Belizeans believed in celebrating the life of the departed.

"It's pretty beautiful, chica. You should go. People need people," Eddie said.

We were sharing a beer on the front porch of my condo. I hadn't seen Yuri in nearly a week.

"I'm not sure it's appropriate," I said, taking a swig from my beer. I'd bought limes since Eddie insisted on checking in on me. He didn't know all of the details, but he knew that somehow I'd been connected to the late Phoenix Gentle. "We didn't really know each other."

"But he was a part of your journey," Eddie said. "Elena and Sylvia are going. He was one of Sylvia's teachers, you know?"

"It never came up." Ouch. I already felt bad for my part in things. Knowing he'd taught Sylvia, I felt even worse.

Eddie shrugged, sensing that he'd probed a sore spot. "Your choice, amiga. I just want to see you get back out there. When you showed up, you were ready to set the world on fire and it showed. Now you're the turtle that got scared of the sun."

"Well, it was awfully bright," I sighed. "But I get what you're saying. Thanks for the talk, Eddie."

He got to his feet and waved over one shoulder as he continued to chug his beer.

I appreciated the encouragement, but I didn't go to the wake. I stayed in the condo, hoping that Yuri would show up so we could plan my next step. My only real decision since our adventure was that I wasn't house hunting in Belize. As much as I would miss Elena, Sylvia, and Eddie, Belize wasn't my home. The mainland's calling had vanished with the knife, and there was so much more out there to see.

A SHARP KNOCKING RATTLED the front door, waking me out of a sound sleep. I fumbled for my phone on the nightstand and then winced at how the bright screen cut through the dark.

2:37 a.m. Who on earth could be pounding on my door at 2:37 a.m.?

Of course.

Yuri.

He'd finally come back!

I tossed the blankets off and dashed for the door, not even bothering to check the peephole.

One of these days, I would learn the meaning of the word *discretion*. Unfortunately, this was not that day. It was the middle of the night and I'd woken up before my common sense had.

As I flung the door open, ready to jump out and hug the person on the other side, I realized my mistake. When my connection to the knife had evaporated, my connection with Yuri had remained. He was still somewhere distant. And I was face to face with Alex Smith.

"Hello, there," he said, giving me a tight-lipped grin. As thin as his lips were, his current expression made them vanish altogether.

I tried to slam the door in his face, but it stayed open no matter how hard I strained. It was frozen. Dormant. Immobile. I wasn't sure how he was doing it but he was holding it firmly in place.

"What do you want?" I asked, not bothering to hide my antipathy. "How did you find me?"

"Please," Alex said, rolling his eyes. "Let's not pretend you've been trying to hide for the last week. You assumed you were safe and all the pieces were off the board, so you let your guard down. I didn't even have to work at it."

He wasn't wrong. I'd barely looked over my shoulder since leaving Caracol. Alex Smith hadn't been the one I was looking for the few times I'd cared to glance. Somehow, I'd imagined when Alex Smith ran away from the big fight, he'd left the country. Silly me.

"Congratulations. You found me. Now what?"

I'm not sure what I expected Alex to say or do. Part of me was ready for him to pull a gun out and part of me was waiting for him to lunge through the door. I almost wanted him to try the second thing. Even if he was able to hold the door open, my salt wards were as strong as the day I'd put them down. Maybe stronger. I'd fed them more power after my fourteen hour sleep. Before I'd gotten complacent.

Alex Smith ignored the question as he examined me through narrowed eyes. I tried the door again, but it still wouldn't budge. I didn't know what to do. If I walked away, I wasn't sure he could stop me. But then I'd basically be leaving my door open with an enemy standing at the threshold. It wasn't like I could go back to bed with him looming there.

"You took my advice and talked to Agent Knowles about your patron. Well done," he said at last.

"Like you didn't already know," I scoffed. "You and Jonas Ical both noticed when we were at the top of the Sky Palace."

For the first time since I'd opened the door, I saw something like respect flash through Alex's gaze.

"Are you done wasting my time yet? If you just dropped in for a creepy chat, you could've done so at a more appropriate hour." I folded my arms over my chest; partially because I was annoyed, partially because the salty air coming off the ocean was chilly, and partially to keep myself from continuing to fiddle with the door. It was fine if Alex knew I was annoyed, but I didn't want him to know I was afraid.

"You could at least invite me in, maybe offer me a coffee," he said. "It would only be polite."

I was at a loss.

"I'm sorry. What?"

"It's hardly polite to leave me standing out here in the cold."

The warlock's face was impassive. I was reading nothing but *truth* off of him, but that didn't help much when he was refusing to tell me anything important.

"You hexxed my hot sauce," I reminded him.

"I did hex your hot sauce, yes. But you seem to have survived it, so all's well, right?"

He seemed to think that was the truth, too. As he saw things, my survival equated us being squarsies? The more I tried to wrap my brain around this conversation, the more confused I got.

"Aren't we enemies?" I asked.

Alex threw back his head and let out a single, "Ha!"

Then he realized I was serious.

"Look, I know it might be confusing, given that you're new to the game, but no. We aren't enemies. We are rivals. Actually, technically, Agent Knowles and I are rivals. You, my dear, were a pawn. At some point during this match, you became another player. Right now, you're an unaffiliated player. I've come to make an offer," Alex explained.

Comprehension finally clicked in. This entire experience, for me, had been a life or death roller coaster with clearly marked sides. For Alex Smith, this adventure had been another day at the office. He really didn't see us as enemies. In his mind, it was more like I was the new hire at the rival coffee shop across the road and he wanted to poach me because I'd been offered a jump up to shift leader after my first week.

"I have no interest in working with people like Babajide," I said. "Or those that would side with him."

"I don't work for Babajide," Alex responded immediately. "That was a temporary alliance at best. I was never supposed to actually let him get his hands on the artifact."

Intriguing. I was actually a little curious, now that it was clear to me Alex Smith didn't intend me any harm. Any *further* harm. Until we found ourselves at odds, again. I didn't see myself signing on with his organization, but maybe talking to someone other than Yuri would give me more perspective when it came to the IACI.

"If I let you in, do you swear that no harm will come to me or anyone I know for the duration of my visit to Belize?" I asked.

"I can't promise that natural accidents won't occur. But I swear I have no intention of harming you or yours, and I will not harass you further if you find my employer's offer unacceptable. Unless we are rivals on intersecting missions again, naturally." Alex Smith said. He ran his finger over his heart in a tiny x motion and held up his other hand like he was taking an oath.

*Truth*.

With a deep sigh, I beckoned Alex into my condo. Once he was inside, the door swung closed. I appreciated that he didn't attempt to lock us in. Vow or no, I wasn't comfortable enough with the rival agent to be stuck in a locked room with him.

If we were going to talk at three in the morning, I was going to put on some coffee. I had a feeling I was going to need it.

# 30

AS SOON AS I INVITED him in, Alex Smith settled himself on Yuri's stool. I grimaced as I turned my back to concentrate on the coffee pot. Despite his vow and reassurances, I had trouble not thinking of the warlock as my enemy.

"I only have coconut milk," I said as I added grounds into the filter. Back in Kansas, I would've ground my own beans. But back in Kansas, I'd had access to a roaster. I missed Sit-a-Spell Coffee. More than I thought I would. Not that I wanted to go back to Wichita. The ink was dry on all of the contracts. Going back wasn't even an option. "I hope that's okay."

"That's fine," Alex said. "I take it black."

Awkward silence followed as I finished up with the coffee maker and set out two mugs. I didn't know what to ask first. Hell, I didn't know if Alex would answer the questions I had. I wondered why he was hesitating. Surely if it was important enough to drag me out of bed in the middle of the night, he had some idea of where to start.

"What kind of salary has the IACI offered you?" Alex asked.

I turned around and raised an eyebrow. "So, I know Yuri's background in archaeology. You were a Reliquarian too, right? How did you get started?"

Alex folded his long fingers together and fixed me with a look of his own, like he thought I was trying to trick him. "Not that I see how this is relevant, but I had a degree in Classical Studies. Before I was certified as a warlock, I was one of IACI's Mythologists."

I really wanted to come back to that warlock certification thing, but I didn't want to provoke Alex too much. My only protection

240

with him on the inside of my salt wards was his vow. Well, and my on-again-off-again flame powers. Until I could tap into those on purpose, it was best not to count on them. "I ask because I have a business degree. You don't come on a recruitment run and ask what the other side offered right away. You tell me what you're offering and then I can counter with the other side's offer."

"Then how do I know I'm offering more than the other side? That seems inefficient."

"How do you know there is another offer?" I asked. "Maybe I'm completely freelance and have my own rates." That thought hadn't occurred to me until I spat it out there but, as I flipped it over in my head, the idea had some merit. I didn't know what would be involved in setting up my own shop for this sort of work, but I could certainly look into it.

"Okay, fine. I can see your point," Alex sighed. "Quite frankly, Reliquarians are not normally recruitment officers. It's rare that a talent for this sort of work is found in the field."

"It's probably also rare for a witch to get a business degree," I said.

"Fair point," Alex agreed.

The coffee pot signalled its readiness and I turned my back on the flustered warlock once more. Pouring him a full mug, I slid it over the counter. I began doctoring my own coffee. Oh, heavenly smell, soon to bless my veins with awakeness!

First sip is best sip.

"So, who do you work for? And what are they offering? What position would I be in? Expected duties? Paid training?"

Shooting back his coffee like an espresso, Alex Smith set his mug back down with an expectant expression. He was treating my coffee as though it were cheap diner coffee-water.

"Do that again and I'll throw you out," I told him. I'd made a full pot because I didn't know how much to anticipate Alex drinking, but that didn't mean I had to watch him abuse his coffee privileges.

Refilling his mug, I watched with narrowed eyes. He decided to sip like a civilized person this time.

Better.

"Has Agent Knowles mentioned the name Kailey Callahan to you?"

I nodded. Like I could forget Yuri telling me about his former paramore. "The name's come up."

Alex's lips quirked at that. I got the feeling I hadn't managed to be nearly as casual with my response as I'd hoped. "Well, Ms. Callahan is now the head of Reliquarians at the Progressive American League of Magic. She was very excited when I mentioned you were born in Kansas."

"Why's that?" I asked. I sensed my guest was leading up to something, but I had no idea what it might be.

"Because most American witches are from the New England states, or California. The fact that you were born and raised in the middle of the U.S. means that magic is regaining its footing in the world."

"Does it? My dad was born in Britain and Aunt Shay was born in Belize. They moved to the States as kids. I mean, my mom's family was from Missouri, but I'm first generation on my magic side," I said.

"They may have been born elsewhere, but they stayed," Alex insisted.

*They stayed. I left.* I could've said it outloud, but I was tired of the focus being on my place of birth rather than the potential job. A potential job I wasn't sure I wanted. Though, the concept of magical preservation was intriguing.

"What sets the Magical Progress League of America—"

"Progressive American League of Magic," Alex corrected. "PALM for short."

"Okay," I tried again. "What sets PALM apart from the IACI?"

"The IACI is mostly concerned with keeping the world safe from magic, no matter the cost. Even when it means keeping the world's potential repressed. PALM is dedicated to bringing about the return of magic. We want to see a future in which the paranormal people of the world can come out of hiding. We want the relics we find to be properly labelled and on display to the world, not disguised as mundane artifacts. We want the gods to return. You saw the might on display on top of that temple, right? Can you imagine a world where that happened in Times Square, not on an old pyramid?"

I could imagine that. I could imagine that all too easily. For a pitch that was supposed to inspire me, I was more terrified. Unleashing Babajide in New York or Los Angeles sounded... Cataclysmic. I recalled the injured warlock bolting down the side of the Sky Temple before the real battle began. "You weren't in a hurry to stay and witness that."

"Maybe what happened in Caracol is a bad example," Alex shrugged. "Babajide wanted to return to the old world, not create a new one. The point is, we want the world of science and the world of magic to mesh. Currently, we're gathering traction. But the IACI has too much influence for us to go public yet."

"Uh huh," I said. I took a long sip from my mug. The longer Alex Smith talked about PALM, the less interested I was in signing on.

"That's one of the areas we think you could help us with. You said you wanted to know some of the job duties for this position, right? Well, we'd want you to take the IACI job for starters. And we'd want you to hand over the knife. It wouldn't do for the IACI to realize you still had it, later on," Alex said. Despite my earlier warning, he gulped down half of his second mug in one swallow.

"The knife?"

The request that I voluntarily become a double agent didn't escape my attention. If I'd been leaning away from PALM before, I was dead set against working for them now. That didn't mean I couldn't let Alex Smith dig his own hole as deep as he was willing to go.

"I'll admit, when you showed up with your awakened powers and they were confined to fire, weapons, and purification, I assumed Jonas and I had overestimated you. That's why I ran. I thought that there was no way a witch, Babylonian or not, could stand up to a demigod with a lesser patron. Anu, Enlil, or Marduk, maybe. I'd been counting on Marduk. I am curious how you managed to keep the knife away from Agent Knowles after the fight, though."

Alex had left the fight before I'd called down Tohil. Which meant that he didn't see what had happened to the knife. I hadn't even been able to explain to Yuri that the knife had volunteered itself. "What makes you think I still have the knife?"

"We know that your Reliquarian friend didn't turn it in with his report. Babajide wouldn't be a powerless child if he'd managed to get it away from you. I'm still trying to work that one out. Transmogrification on that level, you must have practically drained the knife to do it." Alex finished off his second cup of coffee and raised both eyebrows at me expectantly. "So... are you interested? We'll supplement your pay from the IACI—we can hide it by increasing your existing stocks or something. Don't worry about being traced through that avenue. You'll get all of the benefits they're able to provide. Training, medical, dental, all that. Then, when we finally get to the point where we've got nations backing us, we'll extract you and you can help reshape the world. Just hand over the knife and we can get started."

I didn't reach for the coffee pot again. Alex Smith had gotten all the coffee I was willing to give him. He'd woken me up in the middle of the night and barged into my condo because he thought he could bully and bribe me into betraying Yuri. I almost admired his brazenness. Almost.

"I don't have it."

"What do you mean: you don't have it?" the warlock's tone
turned dangerous. It wasn't exactly friendly before—condescending
and flippant, but there had been a veneer of civility. He didn't move
his teeth at all as he stood and leaned in over the counter toward me,
his words coming more from the chest than his throat. "I was inside
of it with you. I know you're *bound* to it. Where. Is. The knife?"

"I. Don't. Know," I said. I couldn't match Alex's intensity, but I
did match his cadence. Perhaps I should've refrained from mocking
the big, bad Reliquarian from PALM. One of these days, I will have
to work on that whole impulse control thing. But really, after everything I'd been through, it took a lot more than bluster to ruffle my
feathers. I'd come face to face with an actual god. Tohil was so much
scarier than Alex Smith that it was barely worth the comparison.

"Tell me what you *do* know."

"No."

We both stood there, eyes boring into each other, waiting for the
other person to break. It was more like a game of Chicken than a staring contest.

After several minutes of intense glaring, Alex Smith slid his coffee cup back across the counter and my front door opened with
enough force that it rattled the dishes in the cabinets.

"Should you change your mind about working with us, here's
Ms. Callahan's information," Alex said. He was practically spitting
the words at this point. Tossing a business card at me from the door,
he didn't look at me as he walked out. "She'll be waiting for your
call."

The front door slammed behind him and the dryer popped
open. Whether I decided to call Kailey Callahan or not, Alex Smith
and I weren't going to be friends.

Clearing the counter of the coffee things and giving Alex's mug
a thorough scrub—including a salt water rinse, just to be safe—I debated what to do with Kailey Callahan's business card. My first in-

clination was to throw it out on principle, but one of the first things they taught me while getting my degree was not to needlessly burn bridges. It was too late with Alex Smith. I threw a handful of salt on the card and waited to see if it started smoking before I picked it up and tucked it into my wallet.

I had zero interest in working with PALM based on today's interview. But that could change. I could find out that they fired Alex Smith for being too reckless and militant. His pitch could wildly differ from actual policies. Or I could find out that the IACI routinely killed puppies.

It wasn't like I could look either institution up on the internet. I'd tried searching for the IACI while I was waiting for Yuri to reappear. While I hadn't looked for PALM, it seemed unlikely they'd be any more accessible until the government backing Alex mentioned actually happened.

The next time I saw Yuri, I was going to have a lot to ask him about.

Locking the door, I turned and headed straight back to bed. I hoped I could fall asleep after a cup of coffee and my encounter with the warlock. So many things were going through my head, but the issue I was trying hardest to ignore was the same thing making me nervous.

I'd made a genuine enemy out of Alex Smith.

# 31

I SPENT THE NEXT DAY in Belize City with Elena and Sylvia. We went to the beach to play ball with Chicken. We kicked the ball back and forth across the sand. Chicken pumped his stubby little legs as fast as he could, barking at the rolling sphere as though he could intimidate it into stopping. Taking a break to make sure the puppy wasn't thirsty, we plopped on our butts in the sand.

"So, you remember offering to help me buy a new cab?" Elena asked.

"Yes," I said. "Did you find one?"

Elena shook her head and her russet skin went rosier than normal. It took me a few seconds to realize she was blushing. "No, I was just wondering... Could we maybe ask you to help with the wedding instead?"

"Of course! I mean, I'd be glad to chip in. Assuming the wedding isn't going to be too much more than a cab," I said, plucking Chicken off the ground and holding him in my lap. "It's not going to be more than a cab, right?"

"Probably not," Sylvia said. "But we're wanting a destination wedding."

"And after the ceremony, we're thinking about not coming back to Belize," Elena said. She was still blushing, but her expression was also a little sad now. "I think it's time for us to go."

"I don't understand," I said. Chicken decided our conversation wasn't focused enough on his cuteness and started trying to lick my face while I was looking from Elena to Sylvia for clarification. "I thought you two loved Belize?"

"We do," Sylvia said. "Maybe someday we'll come back. But I graduated last winter, and neither of us are tied to jobs here anymore. It's not like we're ever going to work for Tinito again."

"And I can't continue to give tours of ruins after the things we saw," Elena added.

I gave up trying to wrangle Chicken, which is when he lost interest in my face. He romped his way over to Sylvia and barked for her attention. Sylvia scooped the rambunctious pup onto his back and cradled him like a baby until he calmed down. She set the dog on her lap where he promptly curled up and fell asleep.

"Where are you planning to go?" I asked.

Elena and Sylvia exchanged a look before answering me. "We were thinking of Puerto Rico. Our marriage would be legal there, and Sylvia could legally identify as a gyal," Elena said after a long pause.

"I also have a brother there," Sylvia said. "He's still working on being okay with who I am, but he's agreed to hire us at his car rental shop until we find other work on the island. He didn't agree with my parents kicking me out. He's like our Uncle Eddie. Family first, no matter who they happen to be. At the very least, he's not Tinito."

Elena didn't look entirely happy about the idea of working with this soon to be brother-in-law, but I didn't think she'd appreciate any interference. "Okay, so you guys are going to move to Puerto Rico and get married there? How much are you going to need from me?"

"Plane tickets for us, and dresses?" Elena asked. "Would that be asking too much?"

I shook my head. The IACI had already paid me for working with Yuri on his knife-finding mission. I could easily get them both Vera Wang dresses and fly in a few more guests. "I can pay for Eddie's ticket too, if you'd like."

"Thank you! You are an angel," Elena said. She stood up and gave me a hug.

Scooping a protesting Chicken out of her own lap, Sylvia wrapped her arms around the both of us. Chicken ran around all our legs, wanting to be part of the action. The three of us broke off and formed a new ball kicking circle, which made Chicken an ecstatic little pupper.

Wherever I was headed after Belize, it looked like I was going to make a stop in Puerto Rico. Before I headed back to the water taxi, we made plans to meet up at Elena and Sylvia's apartment the next day so I could either buy tickets or transfer funds. Giving Chicken a few extra goodbye scritches, I set off toward San Pedro island.

It was weird to think that in a few weeks, Eddie would be the only person among us still living in Belize.

YURI WAS SITTING ON my porch as I walked over the sand. The sun was setting and my stomach was full of conch ceviche. I'd felt our connection shortening, but I still hadn't been expecting to see the errant Reliquarian. He stood up as I approached.

"Hey," I said. "I was starting to think you'd left for good."

"My debriefing took longer than expected," Yuri said.

It had only been a week and a half, but I'd forgotten how gorgeous he was. Now that he was in front of me, my heart thundered in my chest, demanding that I say or do something to make him stay.

"I... you didn't even ask my side of things," I said. It wasn't how I'd imagined starting this conversation. All of the things I'd stored up for this moment seemed to jumble inside of my head until I wasn't sure where to begin.

Taking off his glasses, Yuri pulled out his polishing cloth. I wondered if he wore Hawaiian shirts and cargo shorts outside of tropical locations or if this was a disguise he'd adopted to fit in with the local culture. We'd spent so much time together during our adventure, but I still knew so little about him.

"I had to tell my supervisors what I'd seen before I forgot anything. Mortal minds aren't meant to witness the divine, so we tend to start forgetting things faster where the gods are involved."

*Truth.*

"Does that mean I'm going to forget what happened, too?"

With a sigh, Yuri pushed his glasses back on and looked at me. "I don't know, Briar. I'm not an expert on witches."

Something was wrong. I wasn't sure what it was, but Yuri was acting like he was disappointed in me. Maybe I'd screwed something up between him and his agency, or maybe he knew that PALM had tried to recruit me and thought I'd actually agreed to sign on. "Yuri, why are you being so stand-offish? Did I do something wrong?"

"I'm not sure. Did you?" he asked.

Okay. He *definitely* knew PALM had contacted me. The next question was *how* he knew. But I could deal with that after I dealt with his trust issues.

"While you were gone, Alex Smith paid me a visit," I told him. "I can tell you about it, if you'd like to come in."

I walked past him and unlocked the door, letting it swing open into my living space. It wasn't going to be my space for much longer. In another week and a half, I'd be returning the key to the lockbox and taking my single suitcase to the airport. I'd spend a few weeks in Puerto Rico and then... My plans after that were still a big question mark.

Yuri was torn. I could see it in his body language. Anger stiffened his spine while a flicker of hope blazed in those amber eyes. He was watching me through the open doorway without actually stepping inside. I filled the coffee maker with a mug of water and turned it on, holding the mug in place so it wouldn't crack while sitting on the hot plate at the bottom.

"I'm making you tea."

I don't know if it was the English in him or the gentleman, but my ploy worked. After I'd already started brewing, Yuri couldn't refuse the invitation. Closing the door behind him, he walked over to the counter and switched stools when he thought I wasn't paying attention. Hmm.

"Alex Smith came by, you say?"

"Something you already seem to be aware of," I said.

I wanted to look Yuri in the face for this. Unfortunately, the hot water picked that moment to start streaming. Risking a quick glance, my hand shifted under the spout and I felt the sting of boiling water singe a finger. *Ow.*

Yuri didn't say anything. The mug filled and I tore open a tea bag, setting it aside to steep. For once, I didn't feel like coffee. I pulled myself a soda out of the fridge and leaned against the counter, careful not to put my rear anywhere near the hot coffeemaker. "So how did you know?" I asked.

Studying me through his lenses, Yuri came to a decision. He pulled off his glasses and took out his polishing cloth. Before I could protest that he'd just wiped them, he handed me both objects.

As soon as I closed my hand around them, I felt the energy of a stranger's magic coursing through my skin. I held the glasses up to my face and looked through to see the world awash in strange colors. That's not to say they were painted over everything, but I could see my own trail from the door to the kitchen as a line of orange fire. The trail was currently the most vibrant but the same orange ran up the walls—my salt wards—like highlighter ink built up on a page. Dozens of duller trails wound all over the condo. I spent a lot of time in this kitchen, apparently. There was a fading band of deep violet around my wrist where I'd worn my paracord bracelets. And around the front door and on the stool that Yuri had moved, there was a sickly yellow that resembled my orange if it had faded out in the wash several times.

"If you can see magic with these, how come you didn't know I was a witch when we first met?"

"It doesn't see the magic inside a person, just residual trails and enchantments. They aren't perfect at doing that much. If there's too much residual magic or magic in use, they stop working entirely. The cloth will recharge them for a brief period. This is a brand new pair. My old pair broke before we climbed off the Sky Palace. I tried to recharge them while we were resting on the Sacbe and it didn't take at all."

I looked at the glowing trails for a moment longer. As I watched, the colors seemed to dim. "Why bother with the enchantment if it fades that fast?"

"Because every so often, it reveals a trap or a traitor," Yuri said. His voice hardened on the word *traitor*. For a magical spy, he was anything but subtle.

"I didn't make any deals with Alex Smith," I said. It was an effort to keep my tone reasonable. I had never been anything but honest with Yuri. He was the one that kept lying to me. Hell, after everything we'd been through, he was just now letting me know he had glasses that could see enchantments! Faulty or not, that would've been useful to know!

"He came by to try to recruit me and I told him no. He stormed out because I refused to play double agent. Tried to offer me benefits through the IACI. I was given a business card for the head of their Reliquarian department. I can turn it over to someone if that will make you feel better, but I don't think the IACI would like it if I gave it to you directly."

"And why is that?" Yuri asked. He was standing now, ready to storm out on a moment's notice.

"Because it's Kailey Callahan's number."

I let that sink in as I slid Yuri's tea in front of him, along with his glasses and the recharging cloth. He sank down onto the stool, the anger and rigidness falling away from him as he rested his head in his hands. "I'm sorry. I'm so sorry. I saw his trail and I assumed it was happening again. I was right back in Mongolia, tied up and losing... Losing someone important to me."

*Truth.*

"So how'd the debriefing go?" I asked, wanting to change the subject.

*Why did you kiss me at the top of the Sky Palace?* The question was so tantalizing, waiting at the tip of my tongue to be launched into the world. But we'd barely made it through the awkward reminder of his ex.

"About as well as I'd expected. They want to schedule a proper field test for you. One in a controlled environment after you've had a little time to look over the field manual," Yuri said. "Assuming you're even still interested."

I'd had time to recover from our Mayan adventure. Now that I wasn't dying of exhaustion and hungrier than I'd ever remembered being, I recognized the longing that had taken root in me after the adventure was over. For days, I'd moped around without a sense of purpose. Working for the IACI, being Yuri's partner, would give me back my drive.

"They still need a field test after what we just did?"

"Briar, they need to know you can follow directions. You are incredibly headstrong and unpredictable. They want to see how you handle a situation without me acting as your buffer."

Considering the last time I didn't have Yuri as an influence I'd bound myself to a blade of ritual sacrifice, I had to admit that the IACI's concerns might have some merit.

I would take their test. I would become Yuri's partner. And then we could get this whole maybe-romantic thing between us sorted. Having made a decision, I felt better than I had since first arriving in Belize.

"I'm in. Where are we headed?"

"We'll have to visit IACI headquarters, to fill out some paper-work and let you familiarize yourself with the handbook. You'll also get introduced to some of our trainers there. Then they'll send you to one of the test sites with a supervisor."

"Great. But first, I have to go to Puerto Rico," I smiled. "Want to be my plus one?"

# Epilogue

ELENA GLOWED AS SHE walked down an aisle lined with candles. The sun hadn't quite set. It reflected through her diaphanous white gown adding layers of lemon, coral and honey that hadn't been present when she'd tried it on under the fluorescent store lights. Her hair was a cascade of thin braids. Ribbons of blue and pink glimpsed their way out of the tightly woven locks, along with the occasional seashell or bead of glass. Elena's bouquet of blue and fuschia plumerias accented the sunset's colors beautifully.

Sylvia walked down her own aisle. Her dress was technically pink, though the color was soft enough to pass for cream. It looked like an antique, something from the pages of Gatsby. Sylvia radiated as much happiness and enthusiasm as her fiancee as she clutched her own bouquet of plumerias. A few extra flowers were clipped into her raven hair, along with pearl beads and rhinestones.

Both aisles met in a pavilion draped with filmy white chiffon and fairy lights, set on a sandy beach. The pavilion was surrounded by a half circle of white lawn chairs. Neither Elena nor Sylvia had desired attendants or someone to give them away. In the middle of the pavilion, opposite the officiant (Oliver Heaton), an altar was set with two crystalline vases so they could deposit the bouquets. The rings were waiting on a royal blue cushion between the vases.

I sat in between Yuri and Eddie on chairs that looked out toward the waves. Sylvia's brother, Alejandro Velasquez, sat across the aisles from us with his girlfriend, Sandra de la Torre, and her family. Sandra's family were warm and welcoming to the new additions to their clan, even though Sandra and Alejandro weren't technically engaged yet. Sandra had embraced Sylvia and Elena as her sisters-in-law immediately, and had attempted to wrap Yuri and me into the adoptions as well.

No one could resist Chicken. He was an immediate favorite with the de la Torre family.

Elena's mom had wanted to come, but Elena's father was in the hospital from a recent fall. Despite their absence, Elena had been touched at how many times her mom had called to apologize. I didn't know the full history but, Sylvia told me during the rehearsal dinner, it was a big step for the woman.

It was good to see my friends so happy. I couldn't bring myself to listen to the wedding officiant's speech about love and partnership. Words weren't necessary. Sylvia and Elena were beaming, shining brighter together than they ever could apart.

A single tear rammed the gates, clearing a path for the rest to escape as Elena and Sylvia were asked to exchange vows.

Unfolding a worn scrap of paper, Elena cleared her throat and clutched both of Sylvia's hands in her free one. "Sylvia Velasquez, gyal, my gyal... You know I'm not that good with these kinds of speeches. Before we met, I was lost. Things would get sorted, or they wouldn't. It didn't matter. When we first met, I didn't think we'd last a week. But you didn't let go. You held on when I tried to stay lost and you became my guiding star. You helped me find my feet when life flooded our way. Now we stand here, in Vieques, Puerto Rico, and I get to spend the rest of my life's journey with you. If I had a million choices in a million life times, I'd always find my way back to you. Your light guides my path. My one and only love. My star. I bind my heart to yours with this ring, a band to signify our forever."

Elena handed the paper over the officiant and took one of the rings from the cushion and slid it onto Sylvia's waiting finger.

I couldn't stop my hand from seeking Yuri's. He squeezed my fingers, pulled a bag of tissues out of a pocket and offered them to me.

Yuri was wearing an actual suit, but I didn't doubt that the jacket was custom made with about a thousand pockets. I'd never been into men in suits, but the Reliquarian wore it well. I might have to rethink that whole never-ever dressing up thing I'd been doing my entire life. Maybe just for weddings. It was a mark of just how much I liked Elena and Sylvia that I'd willingly bought a skirt for today—albeit one that was long enough to hide my jogging pants underneath.

It took Sylvia a moment to compose herself. She was trying not to cry, and it was taking a lot of restraint for her not to jump ahead to the kiss. After a few seconds of deep breathing, Sylvia pulled out her own crisp sheet.

"Elena Tillett—" Sylvia started.

Almost immediately she welled up and had to start again.

"Elena Tillet, I never thought that I'd meet someone that would be able to accept me for who I am. I definitely never thought I'd meet a woman that not only accepted me, but made me feel more like myself. Every day I'm with you, I am more the person I was meant to be. Your encouragement, your compassion and your love have enhanced my core self. I wouldn't be me without you and I can't imagine a world without you in it. You are my everything, the other half of my soul, and with this ring, I pledge my eternity."

Apparently, I'd only thought I was crying before. Now, water was finding new paths out of my face. I had to retrieve my hand from Yuri to try and pile up tissues like sandbags to staunch the flood.

"I am pleased to announce that you are now wife and wife! You may now both kiss your bride!" Oliver Heaton said with a big smile.

Sealing the covenant with a gentle, fervent kiss, Elena and Sylvia intertwined their hands and rested their heads together in a moment of pure bliss. Then the sound of steel drums started up and my friends rushed down the aisle to beat everyone to the buffet table. It was going to be a full night of celebration.

In the morning, Yuri and I were catching a flight to London.

I needed to let Debra Downs know I was country hopping again.

# Acknowledgements

THESE SECTIONS ARE often a long list of thank yous and gratitude and while we will get to those, I'd like to spare a moment and reflect on everyone I lost during the journey of this particular book coming together. Those readers that follow my website are aware that my husband and I lost Amulet, Mad Cat, and Scythe over the course of the summer. I was less vocal about my Papouli's passing, but he left us on the same day as Mad Cat. His funeral was the day after we lost Scythe. This book provided me a lot of comfort during a very hard summer. My first thank you goes out to those we've lost but are still very much loved.

As always, a thank you to my parents. Thank you, Dad. Thank you, Mom. Thank you, Stephen. I know you're always behind me and you've always got my back. I love you all very much.

Thank you to Sean, for being an awesome brother, to Michelle, for being a badass SiL, and to Kayla, McKenzie, Sean Paul, and Kendra, for being outstanding niblings. Beach time and family dinners were a big help this year. With all you guys have done for us, this shout-out is long overdue. Much love and many hugs to all of you.

I'd like to thank Leah with OA Design for my cover art. This was my first experience with a new designer and your work on this blew me away! I can't imagine a more perfect cover for Briar's first book. Truly extraordinary! Thank you so much!

As always, mega thanks to all of my betas, the Writing Room, and all the docks! (You know who you are!) Seriously, every one of you helps my writing, and me, improve and I appreciate the hell out of it. Special thanks to Becca, Trish, Wendy, Merritt, Katja, Errol, and Ama. You guys were rocks in the storm this summer. So much love to each of you.

And thank you to my husband, Terence. You are beyond my dreams.

# About the Author

When she was younger, Christina lived in Michigan, where she earned a black belt and took archery classes. She loved running through the forest, climbing through sand dunes, and swimming in Lake Michigan. She started writing in the fourth grade, with a story about her big, orange tabby cat wanting to be a rock star.

Now that she's older, Christina lives in Texas with her husband and their cats, Dagger and Glyph.

She's worked all kinds of jobs—from retail to waiting tables to warehouse to massage therapy to management. She has earned her Associate Degree with focuses on Creative Writing and History. Through all of it, her dream was to see her work in print on someone's shelf.

Christina's hobbies include playing board games, role-play games, video games... basically games... reading, and traveling. She's always up for a ren faire, exploring an ancient ruin, or taking a cruise.

Read more at https://christinadickinsonwrites.com.